Third and Long

CHRIS FISHER

Third and Long

CHRIS FISHER

COTEAU BOOKS
WWW.COTEAUBOOKS.COM

Edited by Fred Stenson.
Book and cover design by Duncan Campbell.
Cover image, "Bench Marks," 1981, acrylic on masonite, by Margaret Vanderhaeghe. From the collection of Lorna Crozier and Patrick Lane.

Printed and bound in Canada at Gauvin Press.

National Library of Canada Cataloguing in Publication Data

Fisher, Chris, 1957–
Third and long / Chris Fisher.

Short stories.
ISBN 1-55050-290-5

I. Title.

PS8561.I7595T44 2004   C813'.54   C2004-901624-5

1   2   3   4   5   6   7   8   9   10

401-2206 Dewdney Ave.
Regina, Saskatchewan
Canada   S4R 1H3

Available in the US and Canada from
Fitzhenry & Whiteside
195 Allstate Parkway
Markham, Ontario
Canada   L3R 4T8

The publisher gratefully acknowledges the financial assistance of the Saskatchewan Arts Board, the Canada Council for the Arts, the Government of Canada through the Book Publishing Industry Development Program (BPIDP), and the City of Regina Arts Commission, for its publishing program.

To Danny and Denny,
for the life lessons through Sport.
One taught me passion;
the other, perspective.

CONTENTS

LILACS

We were standing on the deck, leaning with our backs against the railing. I sipped my iced tea and Dad took a slug of his rum and Coke. The aroma of lilacs floated in from the bushes around the side of the house. Dad took off his suit jacket and laid it over the back of a lawn chair. I loosened my tie and took a deep breath.

"Lilacs," I said. "Whenever I smell them I think of home, of here."

Dad did the same, but I could tell from the whistling and gurgling noises coming from his boxer's nose that he couldn't smell anything.

"Ahhh, you betcha," he said. "Nothing better than fresh country air."

It was a dig about where I now live. I ignored it. "Lots of people in the church today," I said.

Dad nodded. "Fullest that place has been in years. Too bad it's always a funeral, and never a wedding."

He took another slurp and held his glass up to eye level. "Could use one more ice cube."

"Maybe a bit more Coke, too," I said.

He looked at me sharply so I added, "It's two-thirty in the afternoon. Could be a long day."

"Don't you worry about me," he said. "If you're here to harp about how I mix my beverages, then you should have kept on down the highway."

I was starting to wonder myself if stopping had been a mistake. I was only here because I had called him on Tuesday to say I would be passing through to visit Mom in Moose Jaw, and he had told me about the funeral. Last night had not been a problem because I arrived after midnight, and he was already in bed. This morning we both slept in and then he made pancakes while I told him about my job in Calgary. He explained in return how his business, Caldwell's Garage, was still able to survive.

"Personalized service," he said. "Customers appreciate someone remembering their name, their vehicle's history, the time you take doing a good job, and the little extras you can do for them. It keeps them coming back."

I expected that the forty of rum in the office didn't hurt, either. As a customer, I would prefer that the mechanic worked on my vehicle sober.

Dad often said that he owed everything he was to the Canadian Navy. They had taught him his engine mechanics trade right out of grade ten, working on the Halifax frigates. Once he started to box in his unit, he never again had to buy a drink while he was in the Service. He could walk into any bar up and down the East Coast, and someone would shout *Set one up for*

Bruisin' Bob Caldwell. Mom's answer was that they should put his picture on a bottle of Navy rum, because that was what Boozin' Bob Caldwell was going to be best remembered for.

The funeral had been at one o'clock. I thought I could get on the road by mid-afternoon, but then he invited everyone back here.

"Come on over," he had repeated about twenty times. "We'll hoist one for Norm, and Bobby Junior's home."

The first thing he did when we got back was organize a bar on the deck, a sturdy wooden table that was now full of bottles, mix, and ice.

"I gave up worrying about you years ago," I said. "I'm just glad I was able to make it for the funeral."

"Good timing for you," said Dad. "Not so good for Norm."

"Norm was a popular guy," I said. "And that crowd today shows that dying young still brings out the curious."

Dad shook his head. "Maybe that's true in the city," he said. "Everyone there today came to show their respect for Ruth and the family. Surely you remember that much." He drained his drink, smacked his lips and continued, "Forty-eight isn't that young, anyway. I was reading in Readers Digest about life expectancy. A couple of hundred years ago fifty was considered a ripe old age."

"Sixty-two makes you ancient, then," I said.

The doorbell rang. "Jeez," Dad said, "I told everybody to come around back." He walked over to the deck's screen door and slid it open.

As Dad disappeared inside, three men walked around the side of the house. They were wearing their old ball jackets but I didn't need to look at the names on the sleeves to remember Scoop, Hummer, and Gerry. Norm's buddies were carrying two twelve-packs of beer and a bottle of whiskey still in the bag, along with a litre of Coke.

"Hey, Rookie," Scoop said, scanning the empty deck. "Are we early or late?"

"Just on time," I said. "Come on up."

"Had to stop for supplies," Hummer said, holding up a twelve-pack of Boh. "Drinking Norm's brand today."

I shook their hands as they came up the steps.

"Long time no see," said Gerry, switching the bottle to his other hand so he could pump mine properly.

I directed them to the table in the corner, where bottles of rye, rum, and vodka were set out along with orange juice, Coke, Sprite, Clamato juice, water, plastic glasses, and ice.

"Help yourselves," I said.

"We always do," Hummer said, and the others laughed.

Dad was shepherding an elderly couple through from the kitchen, so I opened the screen door for them. "I'll put a note on the front door," Dad said. "Could you get the Murrays a drink?"

The next fifteen minutes were spent finding more chairs, getting more glasses, pouring drinks, and greeting new arrivals as the deck gradually filled up. I overheard for the fifth time how the coffin had to be custom-made, and required eight pallbearers instead of the usual six. At six-foot-four, Norm had towered over most men of his generation.

"Handy being across from the church," I said to Dad, when we were in the shed looking for more lawn chairs.

"This getting together is the part Norm enjoyed," Dad said. "Never was much of a church-goer."

"Not that you'd know," I said.

"I see whose vehicles are parked there every week," he said. "Norm's brown half-ton made it every Easter and sometimes once right after harvest."

"Did he start going more often once he knew...?"

"About the cancer?" Dad snorted. "Nope. Wasn't his style." He said it with that tone of pride everyone used when talking about Norm.

The crowd on the deck had spilled down the steps and spread out under the trees in the backyard. Dad had opened some bags of potato chips and there was a container of frozen chocolate chip cookies sitting on top of the barbeque. The guys from the old baseball team were standing in a half-circle at the edge of the house, in the shade of the lilac bushes. I wandered down to listen in.

"Hey again, Rookie," Scooter said.

I smiled. "I haven't been called that in a while."

Gerry said, "You need to show up more often. How are things in Calgary?"

"Pretty good," I said.

"Still with Pan Canadian?"

I nodded.

"How long you staying?"

"I'm heading on to Moose Jaw tonight. Mom's birthday on Sunday."

There was an awkward silence.

"Lilly's a nice lady," Hummer eventually said. "Say hello from us."

I nodded. "Will do. How's the farming life, guys?"

"Not that great," Gerry said. "Two auction sales last month, one of them at Thompson's. If they can't make a go of it, I don't know who can. Prices keep going up. There's talk of closing the elevators."

Scooter said, "No more talk of that today. Rookie, how are your two sisters?"

"Bonnie's married, living in Regina, and Barb, she's in grade eleven."

"Grade eleven," Hummer said. "I remember when she used to toddle around on that deck. She'd bring us a beer and take the bottle cap back to her dad."

"She doesn't remember much about here," I said. "Not like me and Bonnie."

There was another brief silence, and then Hummer said, "Speaking of remembering, we were just talking about Norm and that most famous Badger Bowl. Were you around for that?"

The lilac perfume filled my nostrils again. It's funny how a smell can dredge up a memory. This was one I wished I could forget.

Our town used to be a perennial powerhouse in the southwest's Whitemud Baseball League. Norm was the big left-hander on the mound, while Dad was the manager. By the time I was finishing grade eleven and old enough to play with the men, the senior league had dried up along with most of the small towns along the Whitemud River. Some towns had switched over to fastball, and our baseball team only survived to play weekend tournaments. Still, it was better than nothing and I got to wear the uniform. I even played in some games, due to a lack of warm bodies. Though my dad was the manager, he never decided who played when or where. He knew more about jabs and hooks than balls and strikes. He was a good organizer, lining up the games and handling the money, but left the on-field coaching to Norm.

The Badger Bowl was the largest baseball tournament the seniors played each year. It took place in Shaunavon and, besides teams from the surrounding area, always included city teams from Medicine Hat and Swift Current. Games started on Friday afternoon and the 'A' final was late Sunday afternoon. It was good ball, with all Shaunavon Badger games and the A and B finals played on the main diamond, in front of the big roofed grandstand. At other times during the summer, the grandstand was filled with people watching horse racing and the rodeo. This tourney was the big time for our team, more accustomed to three rows of bleachers behind the backstop and cars parked down the first and third baselines. The only event that approached it in size was our home tournament, when the cars might circle the entire field.

Our first game in the Badger Bowl that Hummer was asking me to remember was played at 5 p.m. on Friday afternoon against the Gull Lake Greyhounds. I got a ride in early and walked around the grounds in my uniform. I had my spikes thrown over my shoulder and was standing by the big concession stand, close to the poster on the wall that listed the tournament draw. A fresh brushcut meant I needed to resize my ball cap and I had started working on the brim as well, getting the curve just right. That's when I first saw them – or rather, when I first heard them.

It sounded like a flock of crows getting louder and louder. Suddenly a half-dozen real ballplayers burst around the corner of the building, pushing and jostling. They had on light grey uniforms with red stripes, red socks, and red hats. They all wore black jackets with their numbers on one sleeve, their nicknames on the other: *Juice, Heater, Torque.* The back of each jacket said, in big red fancy letters, *Jr. 'AA' Red Sox.* Their sports bags had the team name on the side, along with their individual uniform numbers. I expected that handy bag held their ball glove, spikes, and maybe even a batting glove. They probably carried spare hardballs and that black stuff to put under their eyes.

I shrugged my spikes off my shoulder and set them on the ground. My ball glove, hanging at my waist where I had it looped through my leather belt, felt heavy and awkward.

This was Swift Current's handpicked twenty-one-and-under junior men's baseball team. I had been reading about them in the *Southwest Booster.* They played in the top senior league around, and were gearing up for Provincial playoffs against other junior teams from Weyburn, North Battleford, Moose Jaw, Regina, and Saskatoon. The winner of that moved on to Nationals in

Ontario. Playing in tournaments like the Badger Bowl was a way for them to get in some extra games. There was no stipulation on who was eligible to play at this tournament. The entry rules were simple – the first sixteen teams whose cheques cleared the bank.

"Hey, Juice," said a heavy guy with *Slim* written on his sleeve, "check out the draw. See who we crush first."

I didn't think it was our team, but I double-checked to be sure.

"It says Frontier," said Juice. "I thought Shaunavon was the frontier. Is it possible there's some place farther out?"

They all laughed and Heater said, "You're farther out, man. You're waaaay out there."

They all stood a head taller than me, except for Slim. But he was as wide as he was tall. I imagined him swatting the little white ball over the fence with one massive arm. They had long hair flowing out the back of their ballcaps, reaching to the bottom of their necks.

One of them noticed me standing in their midst and nodded. "Howdy, Buckwheat," he said.

I lowered my eyes.

"Is your team playing today?"

I nodded and pointed us out on the draw.

"Whew! Lucky us, boys. Buckwheat's team's on the other side of the draw. Won't have to meet them until the final."

To me, that didn't appear likely.

The fellow, whose jacket spelled *Crusher,* sized me up. "Batboy?"

I shook my head. "Right field," I said.

"Beg your pardon. Hey, Torque," Crusher hollered, "we're scouting out a new right fielder today, so you'd better be ready."

"I was born ready," Torque answered.

They all hooted and someone gave Torque a shove.

"Hey," said Heater, "let's grab some munchies and head back to the van."

They swarmed over to the counter and started placing orders. I was numb. I had run into one or two cocky people before, but a team full of them was something new.

It wasn't long before the first games started. One of my dad's favourite sayings from his boxing days was "It ain't considered cocky if you can back it up." This applied to the Jr. Red Sox. Their game with Frontier was called after four innings because the Red Sox were up by more than ten runs. We also won our first game, with Norm pitching a three-hitter and driving in two of our four runs. I didn't play, except to pinch-run for a guy who took a fastball off the kneecap.

Our next game was Saturday at noon against the Shaunavon Jets. The Jets were made up of players who either weren't good enough to play with the Badgers or held some grudge against the manager. We beat them by five and I played two innings, catching a one-hopper in the field and throwing it in to second base. I grounded out to the first baseman on my only at bat. After I had run out my grounder and trotted back to the dugout, Norm said, "Good hustle, Rookie. You got some wood on it." Then he explained that I needed to anticipate quicker, get the bat around to meet the ball a fraction of a second earlier. If I did, I'd soon be driving the cowhide down the third baseline.

In between games, our team hung out together. I looked forward to that as much as playing, sitting on a tailgate or around a picnic table, listening to the stories and jokes, and wolfing down Norm's wife Ruth's famous egg salad buns. It was like being let into the inner circle. On weekdays they were farmers and bank managers and ranchers and teachers, but on the weekend their uniforms transported them into another world, one filled with Scooter and Hummer, and beer and girls.

Norm didn't like anyone drinking between games, but wouldn't say anything if the guys kept it to one. More than that and they were benched for the next game. I wasn't allowed to drink at all in public, because of my age. There were lots of jokes about slipping me a brewski when Dad wasn't looking.

"Come on," he'd say, lifting his fists, taking up his boxer's stance. "Do whatever you think best. Just remember that you'll be answering to my pals Joe 'n Rocky here." Then he would kiss the knuckles of each hand, do a couple of quick jabs, and everyone would laugh.

Our next game that Saturday was scheduled for four o'clock against the Medicine Hat Rattlers. It was hot and windy and while we waited, sitting in the shade of the vehicles, some of the guys sipped on bottles of Pilsner. Norm reminded them to keep their mitts off his stash of Boh cooling in the blue metal picnic basket. Three of the Jr. Red Sox players strutted by with sunglasses perched on the brims of their ballcaps. Two girls were giggling between them.

"They win again, Rookie?" Scooter asked.

"Eight-zip," I said. "One guy hit it so far it landed in the next diamond."

"Norm's done that before," someone said.

"Not for a few years I haven't," Norm said. "They can play."

"The Hat'll have a good team," Hummer said. "They'll give those boys a run in the final."

"We'll see," said Norm. "We're not out of it yet."

Hummer started on the mound against Medicine Hat, and pitched the game of his life. He had once relied on speed, but as the years went by he switched to control and a type of knuckleball that he called his manure pitch. He claimed that, after he threw it, either the batter or the pitcher was going to stink. The Rattlers had never faced the manure ball before, and Hummer was a hero. Norm came in for the last two innings, and the big left-hander shut the door. We won 2-0.

On the other side of the draw, the Jr. Red Sox were playing the Shaunavon Badgers on the main diamond. We went over to see who our competition in the final was going to be. There were over five hundred fans in the grandstand.

"Get used to it," Norm said as we stood looking up into the stands. "We'll be playing the winner here tomorrow."

Even the Jr. Red Sox's infield warm-up was annoying. They hopped around, chattering like monkeys. The third baseman would scoop up a grounder, flip it behind his back to the shortstop, who would whip it sidearm to the second baseman. After every play, they fired the ball around the horn, each player giving a little yelp when he caught it and a hop-skip as he passed it on. After catching a few fly balls behind their backs, the outfielders huddled together and juggled a ball back and forth between them as they raced in to the bench. I wasn't one to prejudge, but I figured there were drugs involved somewhere.

The Badgers were the classiest team in the southwest. They always entered Provincials, and had in the past picked up Norm to play with them. An implement dealership and an oil company sponsored them, which meant money for equipment and uniforms. The Badgers were our fiercest rivals, but as they lined up to play the cocky visitors, I felt some pride that, like the Jr. Red Sox, the Badgers' hats and jerseys matched.

I was standing beside the grandstand, close to the on-deck circle where the Jr. Red Sox batters warmed up. Most of them came up with three bats and a cheek full of chewing tobacco, alternating between swinging and spitting. I had never tried chewing tobacco but did eat sunflower seeds, which Norm said was messy enough.

"Hey, Buckwheat!"

I looked up. It was Crusher, doing windmills with a bat in each hand.

"You still around?"

"In the final," I said.

He grinned. "We'll be seeing you, then." He tossed one of the bats toward the screen and slipped a dough-nut weight down the shaft of the other before taking a couple of full swings.

Crusher's prediction turned out to be a good one. There seemed to be no weak link, no one player who went up to bat and you could say, *At least here's an out.* Every baserunner took a big lead, bouncing back and forth, chattering at the pitcher. They stole second base by sliding in headfirst every time, even when there was no throw. They stole home in the last inning, already up seven to one. When they shook hands at the end of the game, they all turned their caps backwards before sauntering through the line.

There was a dance at the Shaunavon Hall that night. Scoop said there was one every year, and called it the Badger Bop. A few of the younger guys had brought extra clothes to change into from their uniforms. They had been planning to boogie the night away, betting we wouldn't be playing in Sunday's final.

"Just get a good night's sleep, boys," Norm said. "The Sox'll be tough."

Scoop quipped, "Sox, sox, sox. These guys just wanna dance!"

I caught a ride home with Dad because I hadn't brought a change of clothes. Also, I didn't want him to be going back to an empty house. Mom and my two sisters had been gone for six months by then. Dad's Christmas drinking binge had been the last straw, and Mom had packed the girls off to Grandma's big house in Moose Jaw on New Year's. I went along for the first week, but when it became obvious that Mom was staying put for awhile, I came back. I hadn't wanted to change schools halfway through the year and, since I was sixteen, could decide where I wanted to live. I had never known a time when Dad wasn't drinking, so his behaviour seemed somewhat normal to me. He never got violent with us, either. Mom said he lacked ambition, and getting sloshed every weekend was not allowing them to build for a positive future.

That first summer, Dad was still thinking Mom would be back. It was just a matter of time. I knew that he missed her, too. Whenever he was drinking and went on a walkabout, as he called it, our neighbours always answered the bell. He never turned mean, which was fortunate because of his fistic ability. He was more melancholy, a mellow drunk, apologizing for throwing up on your living-room rug, or for peeing in your sink instead of the toilet. Just before he passed out, the tears would come and he would say how he didn't deserve such a sweet wife or those fine kids of his. He was going to straighten up and make them proud of him. Maybe that's why Mom had stuck with him for so long; she had actually believed him.

The grandstand was two-thirds full for the Badger Bowl final on Sunday afternoon. It would have been packed if the hometown Badgers had been playing, but a crowd of six hundred people watching us was still huge. Most of the Jr. Red Sox team had stayed for the dance, and they continued to look a little worse for wear. They still managed to put on their fancy warm-up act when taking their infield. We just sat in our dugout watching them and waiting for our turn to take the field.

Norm started the game on the mound. His control was a little shaky, but he got stronger as the seven-inning game went on. Every inning the Jr. Red Sox had runners dancing around on base but we managed to get out of each jam with a pop-up or a double play. The score was one-zip for them in the top of the fifth when, with two out, their pitcher hit Scooter in the thigh. Scooter hobbled to first and stood on the bag, not even daring to take a one-step leadoff. Norm was up next and put the first pitch over the left-field fence.

We all streamed out and lined up to shake his hand as he circled the bases. Their catcher had his mask resting on top of his head. He leaned forward and squirted tobacco juice onto the handle of the bat lying beside home plate.

Scooter, who was hobbling home in front of Norm as the catcher spit, stepped onto the plate, picked up the bat and wiped the handle high on the catcher's pantleg, above his shinpads. There was a shout from their dugout as the catcher stepped toward Scooter. The umpire got between them and held up both arms.

"That'll do!" he roared.

The catcher sized up the situation and realized that our entire team was within five feet of him. Most of his reinforcements were either in their dugout thirty feet away or scattered around the ballfield.

"Stubble trash," the catcher mumbled.

Scooter grinned and said, "Check the scoreboard, kid."

The fans' cheering for the home run had turned to jeers for the catcher. It woke up the rest of his team, though. Their left fielder made a nice diving catch for the third out, and they seemed re-energized running in to their dugout.

Norm made it through the bottom of the fifth, but his arm was tiring. He had pitched in four different games over the past forty-eight hours. When we came in to bat for the sixth inning, he asked Hummer to start loosening up. I was warming the bench so I got the spare catcher's glove and caught for him. Hummer was fired up and by the end, the ball was smacking into the glove.

Our batters went out one-two-three. Scooter had been playing in right field, but the top of his leg had started to stiffen up where the ball had hit him. Norm nodded to me. "Rookie," he said. "Let's get some fresh speed out there."

I trotted into right field, Norm took Hummer's previous position out in centre field, and Hummer slowly took the mound. I looked up at the scoreboard and made a mental note: *2 to 1, playing the sixth. That's respectable.*

The Jr. Red Sox had become familiar with Norm's fluid left-handed delivery. It took a couple of batters for them to analyze Hummer's different, jerky right-handed style. He struck out the first guy looking at a high strike. Then a walk followed by a grounder to short and the subsequent double play meant that suddenly we were three outs away from winning the whole shebang.

Dad never hung around the bench much because he didn't really understand the game, and wasn't interested in learning. It was Norm's job to do the coaching. Dad was usually wearing his ball jacket and hat and mingling with the crowd, organizing future games, and making the odd bet. When we came off the field this time, though, he was right behind the dugout, banging on the roof.

"Way to go, boys," he shouted. "Three more outs and we're rich."

We should have been excited about our situation on the bench, but no one was. The fans may have interpreted our reserved nature as calm, cool professionals doing their job but in fact, we were all in shock. No one dared to say or do anything that might break the spell that this field had fallen under.

Hummer slung his jacket over his right arm to keep it warm, and Scooter clapped his hands, saying, "On the wood now, boys, let's get us some insurance."

The top of the seventh was short. I was up first and struck out on three straight fastballs. Luckily our next batter, Gerry Large, worked the count up to three balls and two strikes before fouling off another two pitches. He eventually popped up to the catcher but his lengthy at-bat bought us a few extra minutes of rest. Hummer was up next. He took off his jacket and hit the first pitch sharply down the first baseline. The first baseman picked it up cleanly but, instead of stepping on the bag to end the inning, fired it to the second baseman. The second baseman tossed it underhand in the air to the shortstop, who one-handed the ball and rifled it back to first. The throw beat Hummer by two steps. Some fans clapped and others booed.

"Cocky," I muttered.

"We've got them worried, Rookie," Norm said. "They're trying to rebuild their swagger. Grab your glove. Let's shut 'em down."

I raced out to right field and stopped ten feet in front of the fence. I turned and leaned forward, lifting each leg to ensure that my spikes weren't stuck on a clump of grass. I studied the terrain to see if there were any small rocks that I might slip on.

"Move in fifteen steps," Norm yelled. "First batter's right-handed."

They had figured out Hummer's pitching style. A double to the fence in left, a walk, and a bunt down the third baseline loaded the bases, with none out. They tried the squeeze play, bunting toward third base, but the ball swerved toward the pitcher's mound. Hummer scooped it up and threw to Gerry Large at home plate for the forceout.

The next right-handed batter choked up and tried to punch the first pitch off-field. The little blooper came sailing over first and second, exactly to the spot where I was standing. I didn't have to move but I did shuffle in and out a couple of steps while I waited for the ball to arrive. I kept thinking, *Catch it, squeeze it, catch it, and squeeze it.* As soon as I felt the ball safely in my glove, I pulled it out and fired it in to the first baseman. He was ready to peg it home, but the runners had tagged up on the fly ball and didn't have time to advance.

"Attaboy, Rookie."

"Good arm, Rook."

"Good catch, buddy."

The runners may have also been thinking that there was no need to risk it, because the next batter up was Slim, the walking refrigerator. He strode up to the plate and took two vicious practice swings.

"Time," said Gerry, our catcher.

"Ti-ii-ime," shouted the umpire.

Gerry trotted out to the mound and was joined by all of the infielders. I had no idea what strategy they were plotting. We couldn't walk the batter because that would tie the score at 2, and it was unlikely that we would get another runner on base in this game, let alone score another run. When I had caught for Hummer in the warm-up, he only threw two different kinds of pitches, a slow curve and his manure pitch, so I knew they weren't going over his wide repertoire of pitching selections. I figured that they were just stalling, settling Hummer down.

Gerry trotted back and squatted behind the plate. Slim took another nasty cut with the bat and the umpire said, "Plaaay Baaallll!"

Hummer went into his stretch windup and checked the base runners. They were all taking big leads, hopping back and forth, squawking at him. He pulled his back foot off the rubber and drilled the ball toward third. The runner dove back. The throw was high and our third baseman made a nice jumping catch. A lower throw and he would have had the runner cold.

The ball was tossed back to Hummer as their manager came out of the dugout and called *Time*.

"Ti-ii-ime," shouted the umpire.

The manager walked over to third base, where he huddled with the third-base coach while the baserunner listened in. The conversation was short, animated, and one-sided. As the manager walked back to the dugout, the third-base coach forcefully flashed rapid signals to the runners. I expected their leadoffs would now be a little less exuberant.

"Plaaay Baaallll!"

Hummer went into his windup, and from the way he was gripping the ball behind his back I knew it was going to be his manure pitch. He was either going to be the hero or he was going to stink. Slim stood at the plate, coiled like a heavy steel spring. All six hundred fans were yelling and cheering, and then simultaneously holding their breath as Hummer threw and Slim swung.

A bat solidly hitting the ball is either the most satisfying or most sickening sound in the world, depending on which side you are on. I didn't see the bat hit the ball, but I heard it. I spotted the ball up in the air, going straight out past second into centre field. Slim dropped the bat and stood there, both arms raised in the air.

Norm had started backtracking as soon as Slim swung. When he saw the ball coming his way, he turned his back and sprinted. The fence looked a mile away to me, but Norm's long legs ate up the turf. I was watching the ball sail through the air and Norm's dash toward the wall but Gerry said later that all of the baserunners suddenly started doing somersaults as they advanced toward the next base. The players on the Jr. Red Sox bench had come out, high-fiving each other and shaking like they were in a conga line.

Norm got to within five feet of the eight-foot high wooden fence and jumped. He grabbed the top of the wall with his free hand and pulled, spikes scrabbling up the side. Looking back over his shoulder, he reached as high as he could with his glove hand. The ball went *smack,* right into the middle of his glove. He tilted forward on the top of the fence but didn't go over. He kicked back and jumped down.

Silence. The baserunners were still obliviously somersaulting forward but the players around the dugout had stopped dancing. Then I distinctly heard Dad yell, "NOR-MAANNN!!" and a roar went up from the grandstand. Yelling, hollering, clapping, and hooting all swirled together as the crowd howled. I met Norm as he trotted toward the infield. I wanted to jump on him, like they do to the winning pitcher in the World Series, but I was too much in awe to touch him.

"Nice grab," I managed.

"Thanks," he said, and then grinned. "Follow close behind me, Rookie. I think I split my pants."

I stayed directly behind him while he was mobbed by the team, and also as we lined up to shake hands with the Jr. Red Sox. They all kept their hats on straight and shook Norm's hand a second longer than necessary, some grabbing his forearm with their free hand. They said things like *Great grab, Good wheels,* and *Outta sight, man.* When Crusher appeared opposite me, he said, "Nice catch out there, Buckwheat."

Dad had placed a few bets over the course of the weekend, including being given three-to-one odds against the Swift Current team. He had sweetened the pot with some of Norm's money, and they ended up winning over twelve hundred dollars. The total would have been more, but they had also bet that Medicine Hat would beat the Badgers in the 'B' final, but the local team had come through.

Even in the short time I'd been with the team, I had figured out that the one-beer rule went out the window when we were done playing. Beer was passed out to almost everyone huddled around our cluster of parked vehicles, and a plan was hatched. Whether our players watched more baseball or headed for the hotel bar, the final destination was, like always, Norm's farm. His home place was two miles west of town, and had a sound system in the Quonset. In rainy weather everyone sat inside that metal building, listening to the music and rehashing the day, but on most summer nights they sat outside on lawn chairs around the firepit. The Quonset was sheltered in the back by a long caragana hedge mixed with lilac bushes. Even when the wind was up, that area stayed calm. Norm was the only one allowed to touch the stereo and Ruth provided the food.

The team never arrived all at once, but by the end of the evening everyone showed up. If the tourney had been in a town far away, and a few of the guys had tied into a table of cheap draft at the Hotel, it was sometimes early in the morning before their lights came bouncing down the lane. No one seemed to want to call it a night though, until the whole team had gathered.

After we won the Badger Bowl, the Beer Gardens were still open, and Norm used some of the tournament winnings to buy a few rounds for the team. I was allowed in, as long as I didn't drink alcohol. Everyone was talking about Norm's catch, even the young barmaid who was serving us. She leaned over and wiped the wooden table, jiggling in her low-cut blouse.

"Hey, hotshot," she said. "Are you good at everything?"

Norm shrugged and gave her a good-natured grin.

"Boxing," Dad said loudly. "He's not the best at the art of fisticuffs."

"How about the art of handcuffs?" the barmaid asked, raising her eyebrows.

Everyone hooted and a few guys punched Norm's shoulder. Ruth sat beside him, patting his leg and sipping a vodka and orange juice. Drinks kept arriving for him, and he did his best to finish them. Dad was hovering beside him, describing the catch to everyone who walked by.

Eventually things quieted down as the fans and other teams started for home. Some of us decided it was time to head out to Norm's Quonset and dig into the food, including Ruth's famous egg salad buns. I was in good shape to drive, having had three Cokes and a bag of beer nuts. I wanted Dad to come with me but he insisted on sticking with Norm, who wasn't moving. Scooter had taken some painkillers for his swollen sore leg, so wasn't drinking much. He said he would ensure that they got to the party safely sometime before morning. A carload of partiers piled in with me, and our caravan followed Ruth to their farm.

Hummer was given the responsibility of operating Norm's stereo, and I was offered a cold Boh with my potato salad and sandwich. It was after midnight by the time Scooter drove Dad's car down the lane and parked beside the windbreak. Norm slid out of the front passenger seat and staggered closer to the lilac bushes to take a leak. Scooter waved Hummer and Gerry over, and all four of them huddled together, whispering and giggling. I went over to get the keys and ask where they had left Dad. As I got closer, I could pick out phrases and partial sentences and realized that they were talking about a woman.

24

"What's that?" I asked.

They all turned toward me and there was an awkward pause. I noticed some dried blood under Norm's nose.

"Well Rookie," Norm eventually said, "I can't really say. You're just going to have to ask your dad about it."

The other guys snickered and Norm elbowed Gerry, who was standing closest to him.

"Wait till tomorrow, though," Scooter said, tossing me the car keys. "Bruisin' Bob's turned into Snoozin' Bob." He nodded toward the back seat.

I felt the wind go out of me, like I had been kicked in the gut. My face flushed. Their reluctance to tell me what they had been talking about combined with the bits and pieces I had overheard gave me a pretty clear picture of what had happened. Dad must have made a grab for the barmaid as she wiped the table one last time, or maybe he had hooked up with one of the local women who had been as sloshed as he was. Norm had tried to stop him, and got popped on the nose for his efforts.

The sickly sweet smell from the lilac bushes invaded my nose and I gagged.

"You okay, Rookie?"

"You been drinking, you little bugger?"

"Lean into the trees if you're gonna puke."

I shook my head. "I'm okay. Just can't stand that lilac smell."

I was thinking that boys would be boys, but this was my dad passed out in the car. What would I say if Mom or the girls heard and asked me about tonight?

I drove the car home right after that and poured Dad into bed. I never asked him for his version of what had gone on that night. I just added it to the list of embarrassments. When Mom suggested that it would be best for me to take my grade twelve in Moose Jaw, I agreed. They never reconciled, and I hadn't spent more than a couple of days at a time with Dad since then.

I smiled and nodded at Hummer's question about remembering the Badger Bowl.

"I was playing right field," I said.

"No way, Rookie," Scooter said. "I played right field."

"You'd been hit by a pitch, and sat out the last inning," I said.

"Rookie's right," said Gerry.

They all started talking at once. The entire weekend was rehashed, including everyone's view of the famous catch. It was obvious that it had been discussed many times before.

"I was catching, and when it was hit, I stood up by home plate," Gerry said. "Then those guys started doing their somersaults. I'll never forget the guy who was tumbling home from third. He rolls over the plate while everyone's cheering, and he says, *They love us, Dude.* I say *He caught it — game over, Dude,* and he says *No way, man.* Then he looks up at the batter. That big guy who hit it is still standing there instead of trotting around the bases. The batter nods his head, says *Now that was something,* and walks away. I thought that baserunner was going to cry."

Everyone laughed.

"Now that I think of it again, maybe I wasn't in right field," Scooter said.

"We all know you weren't in right field, no thinking required," said Hummer.

"Well okay, but you guys won't know the rest. Most everybody went back to Norm's to party that night, remember?"

My smile froze on my face.

"For some reason I stayed back with Norm and Bob," Scooter continued. "At one point I went into the can and Bob was there, and...well, you know how he gets."

There were grunts and nods.

"He sort of cried, and was saying how much he missed Lilly and the girls. After maybe five minutes Bob settles down a bit and we come out. But we can't find Norm. He's gone."

"Gone?"

"His chair was empty. No one remembered seeing him leave." Scooter stopped for a second and tipped back his beer. "We waited, and I checked the stalls in the can again. Then Bob says *He'll be at the car*, so that's where we head. When we get close it looks like the car's empty so I start scanning the parking lot in case he's taking a leak somewhere. But Bob keeps walking straight over to the back door, flings it open, reaches in and, with one hand, hauls Norm out from the back seat."

"Snoozing?"

Scooter shook his head. "Norm roars and this little barmaid, can't be over nineteen, pops up from the back seat as well. Bob tells her to beat it, and she says in this whiney voice, *But we're going to Great Falls.* Norm says to stay where she is. Then he turns and starts toward Bob."

"Where were you?" I asked.

"On the other side of the car. I was hoping Norm didn't spot me. Anyway, he came at Bob and said *Back off, pal.* When Bob didn't move, Norm took a swing. Bob ducked, came in close and popped him twice on the nose – bop, bop. Norm went down on one knee. His nose was dripping blood. Then Bob goes back to the car and gently takes this girl's arm and guides her out of the back seat. He says *Lady, there's been a slight misunderstanding here. Do you need a ride home?* She shook her head and left. Then Bob told me to give him a hand getting Norm into the front seat. I listened, because now I was scared of Bob."

The guys chuckled.

"I drove and Bob sat in the back. Norm had his big head tilted up on the headrest, pinching his nose. Bob was leaning forward reminding him of what he had with Ruth. I remember Bob saying how everybody makes mistakes, and that the trick was to learn from them. Norm starts apologizing for the trouble and worrying that Ruth will find out and Bob says, *We'll take it to our graves.* Scooter stopped for a second to think about that. "And I guess we did, sort of. By the time we got to the farm, Norm was his old self and Bob was asleep."

I hadn't breathed through the entire telling.

"There's other stories, too," Hummer said, glaring at Scooter, "but I've swore not to spread any of it around."

"The man's dead," Scooter said.

"So what's the point in saying anything now?" Hummer asked.

"I had no idea," I said.

Everyone was nodding, some looking down at the ground and others looking around at the crowd. Only Scooter looked right at me.

"I expect, Rookie, that there are a few things in life you have no idea about," he said.

At another time I would have taken offence. Now I kept quiet.

"Ever wonder why your dad's garage stays open in times like these?"

"You guys look after him pretty well," I said. "I wanted to thank you for what you've done..."

Hummer held up his hand. "These days you have to look after yourself, get the best deal you can. Your dad's still the most thorough mechanic and has the most reasonable rates around."

I looked back up onto the deck, where Dad was passing around the frozen cookies. "I thought you guys just..."

"Tolerated him?" Scooter asked.

"Looked after him," I finished.

"Other way around," Gerry said. "Even Norm. Who knows where we'd be burying him today if it wasn't for your dad."

"Always been like that," Scooter said. "Your dad's still the manager. Look at him up there making sure everybody's got a drink, or something to eat. He looks after things."

"Everything except his own family," I said.

"He looks after the things he can," Scooter said. "And he hurts about the things he can't."

Gerry said, "I thought we weren't talking about this gloomy stuff today."

"We're not talking farming, or politics, or auction sales," said Scooter. "This is stuff Rookie should hear. We buried one friend today. We've got another one up there."

I looked around at the faces in the circle and then back up to the deck, where Dad was starting to cook a grill full of hotdogs. I reached behind Gerry and bent a lilac flower off the bush.

Gerry held up his bottle. "To Norm."

"To the Badger Bowl," Hummer added, holding up his bottle.

"To good friends," Scooter said.

We all clinked bottles and then I slipped the lilac into my top buttonhole. The group moved in a bit tighter. Anyone passing would have thought my tears were for the good friend we had just laid to rest.

TIN MAN SQUARE

I'm tugging on the zipper of my hockey bag. The guy sitting on my right glances over.

"Stuck," I say, jiggling the metal clasp.

"Pack 'em in, guys," my neighbour says. "Goalie can't get at his equipment."

Some chuckles come from around the dressing room.

"You could have said something earlier," says a guy sitting across from me wearing only his underwear. "I was planning on going to church with my wife this morning."

That brings hoots.

"I sure could've used another hour's sleep," the young guy sitting on my left says.

"Another hour, Romeo?" someone asks. "Or any at all?"

Romeo answers, "I'll have you guys know I was in bed by one o'clock."

More hoots, and a phrase pops into my head. I stop yanking on the zipper and say, "My old man used to tell me, 'If you ain't in bed by midnight, you may as well come home.'"

Silence. Some of the guys continue hanging up their clothes or setting their shoes under the bench. Others rummage around in their hockey bags, sorting out the equipment, looking for the pieces that go on first. No one looks at me. Then the guy to my right says, "What *was* it like cruisin' for chicks in the old horse and buggy?"

Everybody laughs and he nudges my arm.

Someone else says, "You can laugh, but my Grandpa said it was great. No cops on the roads back then. If he passed out from the moonshine, his horse took him straight back to the farm."

"No gas stations and no seat belts. Life must have seemed pretty good."

I shrug. I'm known for having a good sense of humour but don't know how to take this crew. It's my first time out with this team and there's not a single soul in the dressing room I know.

I received a phone call around 10:30 last night. I am usually in bed by ten, but had been absorbed in watching the CBC newscast about the Chinese students' demonstrations in Tiananmen Square. I had been following their bid for democracy over the past week. The TV had just replayed the clip where the Chinese man stands in front of the army tank and won't let it pass. The tank tries to get around him, but he keeps moving to stand in its way. Eventually the tank retreats. This show of courage and the army's retreat was interpreted by the talking heads as a symbol of the larger event. The analysts thought that the situation was coming to a peak. The students were the wedge that was going to crack open Chinese democracy.

"Fraser, how are you summering?" an overly friendly voice had asked over the telephone wire.

"Fine." I didn't recognize the voice but wasn't really concentrating, still half-listening to the news broadcast. "And how are you doing these days?"

"Good, I'm real good. Listen, Fraser, it's Pete. Pete Carter from Autobody."

The name clicked and I remembered his face from the college where we both worked. He had joined us a few times at our coffee table in the cafeteria last winter. We always seemed to end up talking hockey.

There was a pause. I searched my brain, wondering why this casual acquaintance was calling me when we were both on summer holidays. One word surfaced, *Amway.* I was already preparing my excuses as I asked, "What's new?"

"Say, Fraser, I was wondering what you were up to tomorrow morning?"

"It's Sunday, so I was going to sleep in and then I have some things planned. Why?"

"Well, I hate to be calling you, but I'm kind of stuck..."

In my fourteen years as a guidance counsellor at the college, I mainly listen to students' problems and help them cope with their issues. My psychology training kicked into gear and I intuitively sensed that my co-worker was reaching out, seeking my professional guidance.

"Hey, Pete, no sweat. It's what I'm here for."

"I wouldn't bother you if I wasn't desperate. I've tried everybody I know."

"Not a problem. Did you want to talk now or get together sometime tomorrow?"

"I'd like to talk now, because I'm at the end of the list. Not that I consider you at the end of my list, Fraser. Far from it, but I need to know, do you still play a bit of goal?"

It turned out that Pete's no-hit hockey team had a game at eight the next morning. Their goalie had sprained his knee going over a water-ski jump that afternoon and had left Pete a voice message saying he wouldn't be at the rink. Pete had spent the last four hours calling every goalie he knew.

I don't usually play summer hockey. In fact, when you're pushing the big five-oh, you don't usually play winter hockey, either. But Pete sounded desperate. I knew how boring it could be playing a game without a goalie at one end, having been the only one who showed up on a few occasions. The guys can aim for the post or crossbar, or turn the net around and bounce the puck in off the end boards, but it's just not the same. The intensity isn't there.

I told Pete that I would play, if I could remember where I'd stored my gear. Then I remembered that my goal stick had a big crack in the blade. Pete said no sweat, he could round one up. He was sounding so relieved that I could have asked for the moon, and he would have dragged it in.

"Don't expect miracles," I told him. "Remember what I told you at coffee. My nickname's Leaky."

Pete said that after all the calls he had made, he was glad to find a warm body. He even had a reward if I showed up.

"All the beer you can drink," he said. "It's on the team."

"At nine o'clock in the morning," I said.

"That's almost noon on the East Coast."

Pete hasn't shown up yet this morning, so everyone in the dressing room is a stranger. I'm sitting in my long johns, fiddling with the zipper and wondering about the horse and buggy crack. Then Romeo says, "I hope you're not as rusty as that zipper."

"It's caught on the cloth," I say, putting my head down and giving an extra-hard pull. The zipper slowly squeaks open.

I bend over to take the equipment out of my bag and Romeo says, "Whew," waving a hand under his nose. "That stuff hasn't been aired out since the Great Flood."

More chuckles. I set my catching glove beside me on the bench and start to take out my goal pads. My neighbour on the right glances down at the glove.

"Mind if I take a look?" he asks.

I shrug so he picks it up, turns it over a couple of times, then tosses it to Romeo.

"Take a look at that," he says. "Probably smaller than your baseball glove."

"Wow," says Romeo, sliding it on. "Now this definitely came over on the Ark."

More chuckles, and then someone says, "I'm pretty sure they didn't play hockey back then."

"Or even now," my other neighbour pipes up. "Name me two Jewish hockey players."

"Well, that Ark had two of everything, didn't it?" Romeo asks.

"That was animals, moron."

"Don't call me a moron. You guys saw the movie *Slapshot,* right? You can't tell me those Hanson brothers were human."

"He's got a point."

Romeo slaps his chest and spreads his arms wide. "I rest my case."

Just then the door opens and Pete waddles in backwards. He's pulling a hand trolley. On it are his hockey bag, two sticks and a large picnic cooler.

"Peeee-ttteeeyyy!"

"We can start getting dressed, guys. The beer's here."

Pete looks around and spots me. "Leaky, glad you could make it." He waves at his trolley. "I got you a stick. You know the guys?"

I shrug.

"Guys, this is Fraser Drummond, better known as Leaky. We work together at the college."

Mumbles all around. I shake hands with Romeo, which turns out to be his real name, and my neighbour on the right is Rich. A couple of guys pick their way across the floor and hold out their hands. I keep it to a minimum. Shaking hands with half-nude middle-aged men gets everything jiggling, which isn't a pretty sight this early in the morning.

After Pete finds a spot and they all sit down again, I count heads. Nine bodies now, including me. The talk around the room is that the other team is young, and we'll be relying on our experience to offset their speed. I don't find this logic reassuring. I have had ten to fifteen years more experience than anyone else in the room. Right now I would trade all of that savvy for the speed and reflexes I had in my twenties. It will be a long hour.

Pete is a catalyst, and all of the conversation now swirls around him. Everyone tries to catch his attention, and the sound level rises.

"Hey, Pete, what do you call a white guy surrounded by black guys?"

"I dunno. What?"

"Coach."

"Pete, did you hear about this old guy and his new, young wife?"

Pete smiles and shakes his head. The jokes go on, feeding off each other. He also appears to be the repository of the team's collective memory.

"Hey, Pete, remember when we played in that tournament in Minot?"

"Ahhh, our international hockey days."

"That year we picked up those guys from Weyburn, who played on defense with Rich here that final game?"

Rich hollers, "I tell ya it was Spelicki."

Pete giggles. "Spelicki was passed out in the back seat of the van. Remember, there was free kegs of draft at the dance, and Spelicki kept filling up that big mug he'd won as a door prize?"

"Hey, you're right," Rich says. "He didn't even sleep in his room that night, did he! Who was I paired up with then?"

"You were with Quint's buddy, that pylon he brought. Remember, the guy he told us played Junior?"

Everybody roars and starts speaking at once.

"Forrester, Red Forrester."

"Couldn't skate backwards...."

"Still wore ankle guards...."

"Remember when he turned to clear it from in front of our net and The Sieve had to make his best save of the game?"

"Red was a nice enough guy...."

"Bought all the pizza our first night there."

"Friendly."

"Yeah, but still he hadn't played Junior."

"Absolutely no way."

"Junior Bowling, maybe."

"Where *is* Quint this morning?"

Pete says, "I called and told him the game was at eight. He says he won't be here because he's got basketball Sunday nights. I say it's in the morning. There's this long pause and then Quint says, 'You mean there's an eight in the morning?' Swear to God, that's what he says."

"Quint's an idiot."

"Too much spare time. He needs a job."

"How long is he going to keep trying to be a fireman?"

"Don't know. He's still applying each time they advertise and keeps taking those tests."

"Sixth on the list last time, and they hired four. Figures he's got it made next time for sure."

"I've heard that before," Pete says. "There's always new applicants. There's even a course guys are taking now."

"At university?"

"Not sure." Pete hollers across at me. "Leaky, you know everything. What's that fireman's course all about?"

"It's a one-year certificate at Capilano College in BC."

"Right. That's what Quint should take."

"He'll never leave home."

"Thirty-one last month, and still eating Mom's cooking."

"Do they offer it through correspondence?"

I shake my head and Pete says, "They tried that, but sending those practice fires through the mail was tricky."

"Yeah, and when you sent your answers back, it got the other mail wet."

Rich pipes up, "I hear they really *hose* you on the tuition."

Groans rise up around the room. Then there's a bang and the door springs open. A hockey bag tumbles into the room, hitting the wall beside the door where most of the sticks are lined up. The sticks clatter down. The door swings almost closed again but jams where the sticks have fallen. One of the guys closest to the door hops up and half-opens it.

"Quint. Whatcha doing?"

"Hold open the door, will you? Got my hands full."

Quint comes in carrying two brown boxes, with the smaller one on top of the bigger. He's dragging his stick under one arm. He walks to the middle of the room and drops the boxes.

"New uniforms and socks," he says.

"I said to bring them Wednesday," Pete says. "That's a league game."

"What's this then?" Quint asks.

"Just ice time."

"I can't be there Wednesday," Quint says.

"Why not?" Rich asks.

"We're going to Cypress Hills, camping."

"We?"

"Yeah, we. What's wrong with that?"

"Not a thing. I suppose there's Bingo at night?"

Quint starts to unzip his fly and moves toward Rich. "Here, let me show you my dabber."

Everybody laughs, and Pete says, "I'll take the boxes home on the trolley and we'll hand them out Wednesday. Thanks for picking them up, Quint."

Quint waves an arm like it's no big deal. He goes over and collects his hockey bag, counting heads as he goes.

"Eight, nine, ten skaters, but no Sieve. I hate not having a goalie. Where's The Sieve?"

"Not coming," Pete says. "Some baby dedication thing at church. Then the guy I had lined up sprained his knee yesterday. I was on the phone most of the night. We got us a goalie, though. Quint, meet Fraser Drummond."

I half stand and we wave at each other.

Romeo adds, "Also known as Leaky."

"Hey," Quint says, "good to see you. You've gotta be better than The Sieve."

Rich laughs. "Since The Sieve gets better the more he drinks, he'd be pretty pathetic early on a Sunday."

"He doesn't really get any better," Pete says. "He just slows down so he can't get out of the way of the puck as quick."

Someone sitting across the room beside Pete says, "I've seen The Sieve standing in the shower and there's not a drop of water hitting him."

They chuckle at the old goalie jokes, and Quint sits down. Nine skaters now. Two full forward lines and three defence. I pull one of my goalie pads out of the bag and start strapping it on. I glance up and see three or four of the guys looking at my leg.

"What?" I ask.

"Those your regular pads?" Romeo asks.

"Yeah. Why?"

"Seem a bit...well, small."

I look down. The pad comes to just above my knee and sticks out about half an inch on either side of my leg. I flex my leg and the pad bends easily, since it's not very thick.

"These pads have seen a lot of hockey," I say.

"Before the slapshot," Rich says.

"Before the curved stick," Quint adds.

"Before the forward pass," Pete finishes.

They all laugh and I say, "That bulky new stuff's expensive."

"So are antiques," Pete says.

I reach down into my bag and tug out my white sweater.

"Hey, the Pats," Romeo says, recognizing the old crest.

I have been a Regina Pats fan since my Grandpa took me to see a game in the late forties.

Then Romeo frowns. "We're wearing black. Do you have a dark jersey?"

I shake my head.

"We could get you one," Quint says. "Sieve has a new sweater in one of those boxes. I could dig it out."

"I wear this," I say, and then stroking the crest, add, "for luck."

"Goalies can be any colour," Pete says. "Maybe after seeing us play for half an hour, Leaky'll put that white jersey on his goal stick and wave it over his head."

Rich finishes wrapping white tape around the ankle of his last skate, throws the roll into his bag with a flourish, and hollers across the room.

"Hey, Pete, big night for news, eh?"

Pete shrugs. "Didn't hear. What's up?"

"That old Ear-anian, religious bugger, Coal-mainie, he died last night. Died in his sleep, I think."

"Too good for him," Pete replies.

"Yeah, and what else.... Oh yeah, the Chinese, last night their army attacked all those students in Tin Man Square."

My stomach lurches and the leather strap I've been tightening slips from my hand. The students had been attacked? A hundred questions swarm into my brain. When and how? Arrests, retaliation? Had anyone been injured, or killed?

I sit up straight, turn my head to Rich and ask, "What else?"

He turns and looks me up and down. I see the annoyance cross his face as he wonders what I mean, why an old buzzard like me is even here and, finally, can I stop any rubber? His eyes travel down and stop at my thin, faded pads. A light appears in his eye.

"Oh yeah, that's right. Thanks. Nolan Ryan pitched a one-hitter."

"Go to Hell with ya!" Pete shouts. The room erupts as players wonder at that.

"He's gotta be close to forty."

"Forty-one."

"Amazing."

"A one-hitter!"

"They got a single in the eighth."

"Anything's possible these days, eh?"

I sit there, watching them put on their helmets and gather their gear before heading out to do battle. No one mentions the Chinese students again. Even Pete is talking baseball.

"Maybe that's an omen," Romeo says softly to me.

"What's that?"

"An old-timer like Ryan getting the one-hitter. Maybe you'll be getting the big 'S'." He crooks his fingers to show quotation marks around the S for Shutout.

"S as in Shut up, Romeo," Rich says.

"What?"

"It's bad luck to mention that until the game's over," Quint says as he pulls his jersey over his head. "Aren't you 's' as in superstitious?"

Romeo shrugs. "Sorry about that, Leaky."

I nod and raise a hand, but I haven't really heard him. My mind is still full of those students in the Square. I should scoot home to catch the latest news. I'm wondering if the Chinese government has given an explanation or a statement; what the world's reaction has been. If it's bad, then I can head to a church somewhere and pray.

The guys file out and I'm left alone in the room. Rich hollers back, "Hey, Leaky. Lock up and bring the key, eh?"

I look down at my fibreglass mask lying on the floor. After about thirty seconds, I bend over, pick it up and toss it into my bag. I'm not going to play anything with this crew. Why should I care if they are a little put out? What's that compared to people standing in front of tanks halfway around the world? I start to pull off my sweater just as Pete comes back into the room.

"Forgot the water bottles," he says, walking over to pick them up from the sink. "Hey, hurry up, Leaky. This game will be classic. The other team's picked up Eddie Staniowski in net."

"Ed Staniowski?"

The name is a trigger, flooding out my Tiananmen thoughts with hockey memories. It was 1974 and I was in old Exhibition Stadium, watching the Pats play. I had seasons tickets in section J, row eleven, seat eighteen. Two seats to the left of the big wooden pillar. I didn't miss a home game that whole '73-'74 season. To this day, their playoff series against the Swift Current Broncos is the best hockey I have ever witnessed. Bryan Trottier,

Tiger Williams, and Terry Ruskowski for the Broncos. Dennis Sobchuk, Clark Gillies, and my hero, Steady Eddie Staniowski between the pipes for the Pats. They won the Memorial Cup that year, a feat they haven't duplicated since.

Steady Eddie was drafted by the St. Louis Blues and went on to tend goal in the NHL for a decade. Now he was here this morning, playing opposite me?

"Steady Eddie?" I say.

Pete nods on his way back out the door. "I'm gonna put one by him, too," he says. "He's bound to have slowed down."

The game's about to start and I haven't even stretched out yet. I stand up, tugging the sweater back down over my belly protector. I grab my mask, glove, and blocker. The goalie stick is lying on the floor by the door. I'm about to lock the dressing-room door when the image of that Chinese student fills my head. He's standing in the middle of the road, directly in the path of the army tank, staring down the long barrel, not moving. Then I picture Eddie crouched down and gliding out of his crease to meet the Broncos, turning back wave after wave of the enemy with his acrobatic splits and dives. I could go home but, besides sitting on the couch and watching the news, there's nothing I can do to help. Here, at least, I can stand in the gap. I hear skate blades cutting into the ice and pucks banging against the boards. I click the lock shut and head down the corridor, toward the gate that opens onto an hour of pain and just maybe, seconds of glory.

Roll Your Owns

I first met Tony in late August, when I stopped to gas up my Bug at the Crown Valley Co-op. He was hunkered down on a wooden chair just inside the door, rolling a cigarette. Tony looked Norwegian, or Danish maybe, like a Viking. His grey-black hair hung down below his ears, curling where it met his thick, sunburnt neck. A grey moustache drooped like a heavy curtain to below his lower lip.

While I paid for my gas, I watched him look out the window at the gas pumps. Something about him suggested to me that he was always here. With his thick-veined hands, he massaged some tobacco out of a pouch onto a cigarette paper. He stuck the thin cigarette in one corner of his mouth and picked the stray tobacco strands from his faded coveralls, returning them to the pouch. To slide his pack of wooden matches from the front of his overalls, he needed to stand. Even with his stooped shoulders, he was close to six feet tall. He struck the match head with his fingernail and it flared.

"This is Kurt Richards, one of the new teachers," the Co-op manager explained to Tony and to two farmers sitting on metal chairs having coffee. "Just starting at the high school. Living up on the hill, in Ray's old house."

The farmers shook my hand and said hello, but not Tony. He nodded, then sat and turned back toward the window, the eye closest to me squinting as the smoke curled around it. I pretended not to notice any slight. I didn't want to give the silent old buzzard any satisfaction.

To tell the truth, I was feeling pretty superior to Crown Valley and all its people about then. I had just finished my Education degree at the University of Saskatchewan. My twelve weeks of practice teaching had been completed in the spring at A.E. Bowden Collegiate, Saskatoon's best high school. Four years of university and that high-level work placement had left me confident in my classroom teaching abilities. I thought I was more than well enough qualified to teach out here in the middle of nowhere.

I found the first few weeks of teaching in Crown Valley to be enlightening, in a dark, dismal sort of way. The principal was two years from retirement, and his appetite for change had been sated long ago. His favourite topic of conversation was the number of pensionable days he had left. At our second staff meeting, where I explained the obvious benefits of moving toward a semester system, he said, "Mr. Richards, you're a bright, energetic young man whose teaching career could well span thirty-five years." He stopped to clear his throat and I nodded, agreeing with his assessment. I was about to explain how we could start the new system at Christmastime when he continued. "Could you see your way clear to hold off rescuing the entire outdated education system until the last thirty-three of those years?"

Crown Valley's saving grace was two other brand new teachers in the high school, Fraser and Stevens. Having gone through university at the same time, we had been educated to believe in the same theories of teaching. Products of the same popular culture, we had similar beliefs about the world beyond teaching too. At the very least, unlike most of the other faculty, we were still breathing.

As the weeks in our small high school counted down toward Christmas, I satisfied myself with the progressive steps that I was making. I became an integral part of a new breed, an influential third of the group known as the "Cultural Revolution." We gave ourselves the name, but liked to think that someone else would have come up with it eventually. We gained more followers weekly. Students claimed it was eye-opening to hear a pro-peace view on the cause of the Vietnam War, refreshing to read poetry written by living Canadians, exciting to explore the possibility that Louis Riel could be viewed as a hero.

Every Friday afternoon, starting at 4 p.m. we held court at the Crown Valley Hotel and Steak Pit. Our regular table was on a raised level between two areas, with the pool tables on one side and the steak pit on the other. It was an ideal location to see and be seen. Here we hoped to meet and interact with our students' older siblings, including some of the opposite sex. Single young women in Crown Valley were as scarce as paved roads.

It wasn't as easy as we had planned to link into the area's pool of young farmers and labourers. As a group, they were intimidated. They would say hello or nod if I happened to be alone, waiting at the bar to order a drink or standing at the urinal, but when the three of us were together at the table, they went out of their way to avoid us. Stevens said it was like we were radioactive. The next week he made a sign and propped it on one of the empty chairs, declaring the area a nuclear-free zone. I signed it, as did Stevens and Fraser. Some people stopped to read it and when, after a few Scotch, Fraser drew on a happy face, they smiled. We asked them to add their signatures and that accomplished two things. It was a good conversation opener, breaking the ice, and we also found out their last names. If the name was familiar, we would ask if they were related to one of our students, and it flowed from there.

We ate our Friday night supper at the Hotel, cooking our own steak on the grill. We tried playing pool but the two tables were in hot demand on the weekend, surrounded by keeners who must have slept with their pool cues. We played partners, challenging whoever held the table, but our games were over quickly. By eleven o'clock the place was packed and the music loud, not an ideal environment for conversation. That was when we would retire to "Fort Whoop-Up."

Fort Whoop-Up was what we had renamed my rented home on the hill. We let it be known that, after the Hotel closed for the night, Fort Whoop-up's gates were always open. The night that Stevens put the "Nuclear-Free Zone" sign on the empty chair, we had our first visitors. The three farm boys were so drunk they had to lean in together like a tripod to stay upright. We treated them well, giving them food and a place to safely finish drinking their 24-pack of Bohemian. The next Friday they were back, a little less drunk and with friends in tow.

The Fort was envisioned to be a meeting place for freethinkers, where discussions were held on everything from the merits of *Playboy* magazine to the practicality of a Saskatchewan revolution. Soon people were stopping by on Saturdays and Sundays, too. Our goal for the end of our first winter in Crown Valley was that there would be more people at the Fort on a Saturday night than at the rink watching the senior team, the Royals, play hockey.

We kept carrying our Nuclear-Free sign back and forth every Friday evening, collecting more and more signatures. One night we forgot to take it home and Stevens went back the next afternoon to claim it. He called me from the Hotel.

"Richards, I'm at the Hotel."

"I'm happy for you, Stevens."

"Can you come down?"

I was in the middle of moving my cinder-block stereo stand from along one wall to the other, and told him so.

"It's important," he said. "I've got something to show you."

I went down and there he was, standing beside our table. I was halfway across the floor when I saw what had caught his interest. Our sign was firmly tacked up on a pillar behind our table, high enough to be out of the way but low enough to be read. It was still within reach for others to add their signatures by standing on a chair. A pen hung on a string below the sign. We heard later that the Hotel manager had nailed it up, and there it stayed.

We came up with more local plans, like raising money for newer textbooks. The money-raising scheme involved hosting a day of snowmobile races over the school's football field. The Administration wasn't crazy about the machines roaring around the schoolyard and the football coach complained about damage to the field. They also frowned on the odd nip of rye consumed in the crowd and the gambling that went on, but they did like the two thousand dollar profit. We used the money to purchase history texts with sections dating after the Second World War.

On the first Friday of spring, assisted by six bottles of wine, our group voted golf as the greatest game ever invented. Fraser had played as a teenager, and said that it was good exercise, developed coordination, and could be enjoyed on your own or in a group. Stevens pointed out that it was also a sport that could be played for most of your adult life.

The following afternoon the three of us ventured into the city and purchased golf bags, filling them with all of the essential paraphernalia: driver, irons, putter, balls, tees, ball retriever. We even bought genuine golf hats and spiked shoes. After that, we talked of nothing else but golf. We discussed the pros and cons of sand greens versus grass, drivers versus irons, Titleist versus Canada Cup. We told only golfing jokes and cherished quotes from Arnold Palmer and the Golden Bear, Jack Nicklaus. We started planning a tour of Saskatchewan's golfing hotbeds for our summer holiday. Evidence of how influential we had become, golf memberships at the Regional Park's course were soon selling briskly.

As teachers recently arrived from an urban area, the three of us understood that rural isolation had a lot to do with our popularity and influence. I had never before experienced such power, this feeling of limitless possibilities. I imagined that it was similar to how Alexander the Great felt as he decided which country to conquer next.

Not everyone approved of our efforts, but most of those people were either frightened of change or over the hill. I placed Tony in the second category. Whenever I gassed up the Bug at the Co-op, he ignored me. If I addressed him with a specific question, his answer was to nod or shake his head. His silences seemed to speak loudly of his ignorance.

My one source of information about Tony was Mel, the manager of the Co-op, who claimed that on rare occasions, usually after a few whiskeys, Tony talked his ear off. Mel said that he couldn't make hide nor hair out of most of it, because whenever Tony got excited, he switched into French or German to explain himself more clearly. Mel claimed that Tony spoke six different languages. Tony had fought in both World Wars and a couple of other minor skirmishes, as he called them. Mel couldn't remember if Tony had ever mentioned whose side he had been on. Up until Tony had retired five years earlier, he was working as a section man for the CPR, maintaining the railroad tracks all over southern Saskatchewan. He now lived in a one-room shack across the alley from the gas station, heating it with a wood stove all winter long.

Tony's yard was neat as a pin, surrounded on all four sides by a trimmed caragana hedge. Half the yard was vegetable garden. Mel had witnessed Tony placing railway ties around the garden's edge all by himself. Occasionally two strong men could do that, one at each end, but normally it was a three-person job. Tony was pushing eighty-five, or at least that was as close as anyone could come to his real age, since he claimed he had never owned a birth certificate.

Tony must have been on my mind because, at the next Saturday gathering at Fort Whoop-up, I brought him up. The topic was the importance of family, and Fraser was suggesting that in Aboriginal cultures they respected and venerated their senior citizens, their elders, while we hid ours away, waiting for them to die. It was all very profound and we drank a toast to the statement. A few minutes later, I said that Tony would probably be a neat person to get to know, if we were planning to get to know any of Crown Valley's older people. The others toasted my idea, thinking that once Tony came to know and understand us better, his aloofness would fade.

The next day at noon I made a special trip to the Co-op to buy cigarettes. I usually bought them at the

Lucky Dollar downtown, where they were a nickel cheaper, but I decided the investment was worth it. When I walked into the lobby, it was empty except for Tony in his chair by the window. I headed for the Coke machine and slipped in the correct change.

"Want a Coke, Tony?" I asked.

He shook his head. "Bad for guts."

I cracked mine and sat down on the metal chair beside him. He continued to look out the window. I could see the view he had – the road, the railway tracks, and then the open fields.

"What do you see out there?" I asked. "Anything ever change?"

His mouth was hidden behind the moustache, but I saw his cheek twitch. "Same every place. Things change an' stay the same."

I tried to remember about being respectful to elders.

"A couple of friends and I might drop over to your house for a visit tonight," I said.

He shrugged and spread out his hands, taking in the Co-op lobby. "Visit here."

"It's just that we're golfing nine holes right after school, and this place closes at six. How about seven or so?"

He shrugged again. "Hokay, may be I'm home."

I didn't expect that Tony would have trouble fitting us into his social schedule. I decided to give him an option. "Fine with me, Tony," I said. "We'll stop in and, if you aren't home, we'll drop by some other time."

He shrugged again just as Mel came in from the back, where he had been fixing a tractor tire.

"Hi, guys," Mel said, heading for the Coke machine. "Anybody care to join me?"

"Sure thing," Tony said. "Throat's drying up."

I placed my empty in the Coke box and left, completely forgetting to buy cigarettes.

That night we drove over to Tony's shack straight from the golf course. When we pulled up, Tony was standing in his doorway with a cup in his hand. We climbed out of the car and walked to the wooden gate. I introduced my two compatriots, Fraser and Stevens, and Tony nodded.

"Seen 'em," he said. "Everybody needs gas."

Tony motioned us in. He was drinking straight rye whiskey from a porcelain coffee cup. He offered us the same, along with a splash of water from the pail by the sink. The drink was warm but the cups were clean.

Tony settled into the rocker, leaving two chairs for the three of us. I leaned against the cupboard while Tony dug out his papers and started rolling a cigarette.

"Can you roll them with one hand?" I asked. "You know, like movie cowboys, while they're riding their horses."

He squinted up at me but didn't reply. I thought he might be hard of hearing so I started to ask again, only louder. He held up a hand and shook his head.

"I've never seen anybody do it, either," I said. "Must take years of practice."

He lit the cigarette and it hung from the corner of his mouth with the smoke drifting into his left eye.

"Man with one arm learn pretty damn fast," he mumbled.

Fraser and Stevens laughed. I am, without bragging, an authority on wit. Verbal jousting is my specialty. This old bugger wasn't about to get the last word.

"So you roll your own," I said. "Is it homegrown or Colombian or what?"

That brought another chuckle from Fraser and Stevens but no reaction from him. My wit was lost on him, I supposed. He got up and refilled our glasses. The second cup made everyone feel a little more comfortable and the conversation picked up.

"Tony," Stevens asked, "what's your last name?"

"Bjornstad," Tony answered.

"Good to know," Fraser said. "We have this habit of calling each other by our last names."

Tony looked puzzled. "Last names?"

"Stevens, Richards, and Fraser are our last names," Stevens explained.

Tony shrugged. "Sound like first names. Bjornstad, that's a last name."

For the next ninety minutes the three of us carried the conversation, but every so often we managed to get Tony's opinion.

"Mel says you were in the war," I said at one point.

"Couple," he said.

"Which side were you on?"

"Side?"

"Did you win or lose?"

"Nobody wins," he said.

Tony's concise, frank tone pleased us. We were tickled with ourselves for thinking of getting to know him. As we were leaving, he seemed uncertain when I asked if we could return the next night.

"You have other things," he said, stretching his arms out to almost touch the walls of his shack. "You will want to be doing them."

I told Tony that I could think of nothing more interesting than visiting with him.

"This golf," Tony said, "it keeps your interest."

"It's great exercise," Stevens said. "Hey, why don't you join us for a round, Tony?"

Fraser and I nodded but Tony shook his head.

"I like to walk in quiet," he said.

"There's lots of walking in golf," Stevens said. "That's one of the best parts."

"Why pay to walk?" Tony asked.

He eventually agreed to another meeting for the next evening. This time I brought cheese, Fraser, red wine, and Stevens, crackers. Tony loosened up a bit more and after two hours, we left singing a dirty French song he had learned during World War One.

A few days later, waiting our turn to hit on the par 3 seventh, Stevens mentioned that in Banff, everyone was hiking. Over drinks at the Fort later on, we went through the benefits of hiking and discovered that it had all of the advantages of golf with none of the delays. And there was no heavy bag to carry. That night I put my clubs in the basement, beside my tennis racquet. I bought a really neat backpack to go with my new boots.

The visits with Tony continued. I had assumed that he would open up a little more with each visit and we would discover interesting nuggets from his colourful past, but progress was slow. Some nights he just sat there, like he had nothing to say. Stevens suspected he was hiding a huge secret from one of the wars and Fraser agreed. We just needed to gain his trust and the floodgates would open.

Because of our influence and our tendency to talk liberally about whatever we were doing, interest in Tony began to pick up. This happened first among the young, then throughout the whole community. Students on their way home from school dropped by the Co-op for a Coke and then hung around waiting for Tony to speak. Farmers had a rash of tires with slow leaks that they wanted checked. Mel had to put out more chairs. Quotes attributed to Tony were repeated and memorized. Someone said Tony had been at the Armistice signing in 1919. Someone else said he had been hired as a youngster by Van Horne and was there when Lord Strathcona pounded in the last spike. Mel grumbled about how people should either buy something or hang around someone else's lobby.

After quite a few visits to Tony's, we went shopping in the city for a present for him, something to seal our budding friendship. We looked all over and had settled on a huge belt buckle with the outline of a bulldozer on it. But then we spotted the big white Stetson. It was sitting firmly on the head of a cowboy mannequin, who had a plastic hand-rolled cigarette dangling from the corner of his mouth. A thin black leather band circled the hat with a small feather stuck in the side. It was one of a kind, the perfect gift for Tony.

When Tony saw the hat, he was speechless. It was exactly the right size and added five inches to his height. It made his face look longer and thinner. He poured us all a drink, thought for a second and then raised his cup.

"Gifts," he said. "Friends."

We all agreed heartily with his toast and tossed back the warm rye. Tony appeared to be thinking hard. He sat back in the rocker, tilted up the Stetson's brim and scratched his forehead.

"What's on your mind, Tony?" Stevens asked.

"Gifts should be," he said, waving his hands back and forth, *"échanger,* you know, swapped."

"This was our gift to you, Tony," Fraser said. "We don't expect anything in return."

"You feel good, no? Me, too, I need to give."

I looked around at Tony's small, clean shack. I could see the cot where he slept. It was tightly made, corners square like they learn in the army.

"Tell you what, Tony," I said. "Why don't you roll us each a cigarette?"

"That would be fair," Stevens said, and Fraser nodded.

"Maybe I learn to roll them in one hand, just for you," Tony said, and we all laughed.

"No," he continued, "I think I know. Something from my past."

I saw Stevens tense up and Fraser lean forward.

"What's that, Tony?" I asked.

Tony started to stand up and the Stetson nudged the light, caused the cord to swing. He took the hat off, set it on the cupboard beside the water pail, and walked over to his cot. He knelt down and reached underneath. His hand came back out with nothing. He bent down lower to look underneath and stretched his arm a long way in. He brought out a tin can, stood up, and came back to his rocker. He sat down, put the can between his knees and reached over for his hat, which he set on top of his head again.

The can was an old tobacco tin. Fraser and Stevens' eyes were glued to the lid that Tony was slowly twisting. He seemed to be thinking of what to say.

"Something from my early time," he said. "When I'm younger than you."

He took off the lid and put his big hand into the can. There was a clunking sound as objects on the bottom slid around. Tony's hand came out and he counted whatever he was holding. "One for each," he said, reaching toward us and opening his hand. There were four brass buttons lying on his palm.

"From my first uniform," he said, shaking his hand for us to take them.

We each took one button and Tony closed his hand around the fourth. The button had fancy etchings on it, and the letters HRH printed in script. His Royal Highness, maybe.

"Where's the uniform?" Fraser asked.

Tony shrugged. "Wool, dirty. Too hot. Cut off the buttons and left it on the pier in Halifax."

"You've had these a long time," Stevens said.

Tony nodded.

"We can't take them, Tony," Fraser said.

"They remind me of that time," Tony said. "But one

is enough." He held up his hand with the button in it. "Now you have something to remember me."

I carefully put the button he had given me in my pocket. Later that night, fiddling with it at the Fort, I hooked it onto the Bug's keychain.

On Monday, Tony wore his Stetson to the Co-op. When Mel asked where he got it from, Tony said the wind blew it into his yard, caught on his caragana hedge. He was waiting for the owner to come by and claim it. That night he repeated the conversation to us, and we all laughed as he described how some of the farmers hung around to see who would come in to claim the hat.

Though many in and around town had taken an interest in Tony by now, the three of us were still the only ones who visited Tony at his house. One day in late spring, we dropped by when Tony was planting his garden and saw he was wearing his white hat.

"When vegetables grow big, I make special stew for you," he said, looking up and smiling from where he knelt between the rows.

He started to get up but I said we couldn't stay long. We had just taken over coaching the ladies softball team and were doing some research into their proper batting stance, taking into account the female physique. If we could get the girls hitting well, it wouldn't matter how poorly they fielded. The best defence is a good offense.

"Our first league game is here in three days," I said, "and they want to spend the first practice trying on uniforms."

"Hey," said Stevens, "why don't you come and watch?"

I looked at Stevens, and Fraser said what I was thinking, "Come watch them try on their uniforms?"

Stevens chuckled. "No, come to the game."

Tony shrugged.

"Six-thirty at the high school diamond," Fraser said. "Catch a ride up with Mel. The Co-op's sponsoring the team and he's coming to watch."

"Yeah," Stevens said. "We'd pick you up but we have to be at the diamond early, liming the field and working on the batting order."

Tony didn't appear very interested in the idea but he did show up with Mel for that first game, and then every other home game the ladies played. We complimented ourselves on getting the older generation more involved in the community. Seeing the white Stetson in the stands was like a good-luck charm for the team. The batting theory also worked well. By practicing three times a week, the ladies record in league play was seven wins against three losses by late June. They had won all five home games. Crowds picked up and the team had more players on their bench than ever before.

Then school was done for the year and we were faced with a dilemma. There were two more league games and a playoff tournament yet to be held, but our minds had moved on to another sport. We had been researching sport fishing and Fraser's cousin knew a place up north where you could canoe and tent with a real Indian guide. We thought that would be a neat experience, and getting up there early would ensure better fishing. We decided to go the first week in July.

Mel took over the coaching reins for the last two games and the playoff tournament. I heard that Tony sat on the bench and they got second in the playoffs. Up north, our Indian guide turned out to be a bit of a dud. We knew more about the North's history than he did. It rained on three of our seven days, and the fishing was mostly sitting around. The water was cold and the portages seemed longer than the brochure had said. Fraser was sure that the guide was taking us the long way around on purpose.

It was near the end of August before I saw Tony again. I was back to teach for a second year and had stopped to fill up the Bug. There he was, in his usual spot.

"Hi, big guy," I said. "How's it going?"

He shrugged and looked out the window. I noticed he was bareheaded, but didn't say anything.

"How's the whiskey holding out?"

"Always whiskey," he said.

Mel said, "Tony's been sick. Had this cough for over a month and he can't seem to shake it."

"I know what you mean," I said. "I caught something up North. My nose ran for a week."

Mel clicked his tongue and shook his head.

"How's the garden producing this year?" I asked.

"Better," Tony mumbled, and then grunted. "More better."

I paid Mel and turned to leave.

"See you around, Tony."

He was concentrating on rolling a cigarette.

"You know, maybe you need some papers with a filter on them," I said.

Mel chuckled and Tony said, "Maybe."

I drove away and had turned down the side street past Tony's shack when something white caught my eye. I slowed down. It looked like the top of Tony's big white Stetson, maybe caught in the caragana hedge. I pulled over and got out for a better look, thinking he would be pleased if I found it for him. When I got close enough to see over the hedge, I saw the Stetson was planted firmly on top of a straw scarecrow in the middle of Tony's lush garden. Little bells were hanging around the edges of the hat's brim, and they tinkled as the wind rocked the scarecrow back and forth. The head swayed and the bells shook.

I bent down and searched the ground. The first stone missed and so did the second, but the third plunked that hat good and hard right on the crown. The bells jangled, the hat tilted back, but it stayed on the scarecrow's head. I could see the twine holding it in place. The scarecrow's button eyes stared straight through me.

THIRD AND LONG

If Gil hadn't liberated his grandmother's bird-watch-ing binoculars for the Rider football game, and if they hadn't then fallen underneath the end-zone seats in Taylor Field, or if LeClair hadn't picked them up while taking a shortcut under those same stands to the men's can, then the 1981 Texas Mickey Classic might never have occurred.

"Hey," Gil had hollered at the back of the guy who picked up the binoculars, "those aren't mine." It wasn't the most articulate statement, but it was the best that Gil could muster. The three-hour drive in to Regina had included Hairball's infamous *backslider* con-coction – iced tea laced with white rum and vodka. Taken in large doses, it interfered with Gil's speech and motor skills.

The other man had turned around, lifted the glasses head-high by the strap and walked back. "I just see them on the ground, man." His French accent cut up the words. "Was looking to take 'em to Lost and Found."

"No sweat."

"Not much to watch anyways today, hey my friend?" He handed the binoculars back to Gil.

"Yeah, the Riders suck."

"I was thinking cheerleaders, and those long green suits."

"Yeah, that, too." Gil waved the binoculars by the strap and turned to navigate the tricky maze of wooden pillars back to his seat.

"Hey man, I know you," the French thief said.

"Hey man, yourself. Don't think so, I'm from outa town."

"Oui, me too. Which way?"

"Southwest about a twelve-pack." Gil started to tilt, so he propped himself up against a pillar for support.

"I knew it. Rawling, right? I played basketball in school. Raoul LeClair."

"Good mammaries," Gil said, squinting at LeClair. "Too bad you're not my type."

"You got the Rawling mouth, too," LeClair said.

Gil recognized LeClair but didn't let on in case the guy really had been trying to steal the binoculars. "Where're you from, man?"

"Ladieux. A carload of us come in every game."

"Suckers for punishment."

"We like the game," LeClair said. "Besides, it's sump'ting to do."

Gil knew that feeling. Their short baseball season had ended in mid-July, and nobody got serious about hockey until November. A Saturday afternoon football game in the city was an attractive September distraction.

"Ladieux," Gil said. "Heard your hotel burned down."

LeClair nodded. "Been a thirsty year. Opens again real soon."

The crowd roared and both men turned toward the field.

"Better find my seat," Gil said. "Maybe we got a first down."

"Yeah, I'm floatin' here," LeClair said, and continued on toward the washroom.

Gil spotted a game-day program on the ground in front of him. He looked up to see where it might have fallen from, but caught himself tipping backward. He picked up the program and slowly made his way back up the steps to his row, wedging in between Hairball and Stilts.

"Where you been?" Hairball asked.

Gil lifted his binoculars. "Scored this program down there, too," he said. "Bet it's got the lucky number in it."

"Yeah, well, you missed our field goal."

A guy sitting in front of them holding a pom-pom made out of green and white plastic strips turned around. "No more numbers," he said, looking at Gil.

"What?"

"Lucky numbers. They stop announcing them after the third quarter."

"It's the fourth quarter already?" Gil asked, looking at Hairball.

He nodded. "Yup, down by sixteen and going into the wind."

"Piece o' cake," Gil said.

Hairball said, "Those Eskimos have always had horse-shoes up their..."

"Anal canal?" Stilts asked, and Gil snorted.

The wave was underway on the far side of the stadi-um, and when it came roaring around the corner into their end, Hairball jumped up on one side of Gil and Stilts stretched up on the other. The program fell off the bench and landed by Gil's foot. He studied it as the human wave flowed around Taylor Field and past them once again. Then he used his runner to edge the pro-gram through the gap and it floated back to the ground under the stands.

Hairball looked at him, and Gil said, "Simplify."

"Right on," Hairball said. "Reduce clutter." He threw his half-full box of popcorn far ahead of them, onto the track between the stands and the playing field. Stilts peeled off his ball jacket, wadded it up and threw that. They watched it slowly unravel in the air, floating above the heads of the fans below them and then disap-pearing down past the edge.

"You'll be cold," Hairball said.

"When we cross that bridge," Stilts said, then paused. "Well, you know...."

Gil and Hairball slowly nodded. Gil sometimes thought that the thinner air Stilts was forced to breathe because of his extra-long legs must somehow affect his thinking. Today though, he knew that Stilts was plain ticked off. In fact, the suggestion about where the Eskimos' horseshoes were located had been the first sen-tence he had spoken for hours.

Stilts's strange behavior was caused by what had happened during the drive into the city. At noon they had been cruising down the Number One in Gil's yellow Nova, singing along with Goose Creek Symphony on the cassette and passing around the red water jug with the backslider in it. Gil was concentrating on looking ahead for radar traps when a blue Chev sedan roared by, straddling the centre line and then cutting in so close that Gil couldn't even see the license plate. He was about to remark to Hairball regarding the necessity of such quick lane changes on a four-lane highway, but the guy pulled ahead so fast that Gil wasn't sure how close the car had actually been. Within a minute it was out of sight. Then five minutes later they caught up to the Chevy again. It had slowed considerably, and Gil was going to pull out and pass when Hairball said, "What's with that guy?"

Gil slowed down, and they watched the Chevy sway back and forth, the weaves getting wider each swing. Soon the car was swerving from one lane into the other. Stilts, with his legs stretched out in the back seat, said that maybe the driver was having a heart attack. Gil slowed down even more. Hairball put the lid on the water jug. The blue Chevy pulled over onto the shoulder and stopped. Stilts said maybe the guy was dead. Gil checked his mirrors. There was a semi coming up behind them. It moved into the passing lane and zoomed past. There was nothing else behind them. He slowed the Nova almost to a stop, and as they rolled by the Chevy, they could see the driver's head slowly drop onto the steering wheel.

BEE–EEEP.

Gil jumped and hit the gas. The Nova surged forward and they were all thrown backwards. Hairball yelled *Horn* and Gil eased off the gas pedal. He pulled the Nova over and slowly backed up. As they got closer, Stilts was peering out the back window and said the other driver was moving and rubbing his forehead.

"Must've fallen asleep," Hairball said.

Gil swung the Nova's back end out so he could pull up beside the Chevy's driver-side door. Hairball rolled down his window as Gil put on the four-way flashers. The driver tried to open his door but it bumped the Nova.

"Hey!" Gil said.

The fellow's bloated, pasty face looked confused. He left the door open, rolled down his window and stuck his balding head out. He was maybe twice their age, crowding forty, and was wearing a lime green leisure suit. Gil could see that at least the top three buttons of his red flowered shirt were undone, the collar overlapping the suit all around the neck.

"Are you okay?" Hairball asked.

"Seen any cops?" the guy asked.

Hairball shook his head. "Not since Swift Current. Need their help?"

The guy shook his head and slowly smoothed the hair from above his ears to the back of his neck. He looked back inside the car and reached to pick up some eyeglasses. He put them on but one of the arms was bent, and they wouldn't sit straight. "Got a beer on ya?"

Gil saw Hairball look to the floor, where the water jug was sitting between his feet. Gil coughed and shook his head. "No, too dangerous," he said. "Police all up and down this road."

"Where you heading?" Hairball asked.

"Football game." He held up one arm and then rested his hand on top of his balding head. "Go Riders."

"Hey," Stilts said from the back seat. "That's where we're going, too."

"How much farther?"

They were still 150 kilometres from Regina, and traffic would get a lot heavier in the last 60, once they passed Moose Jaw. Gil was thinking that this guy might not make it much farther, and also that he was a danger to other vehicles on the road.

"Maybe he should catch a ride in with us," Gil said to Hairball, but loud enough for everyone to hear.

The other driver shook his head. "Rental. Gotta get it back to..." He paused, looking around, searching, "the, uhh, airport in the morning."

A half-ton went by in the passing lane, followed closely by a Volkswagon Beetle. Stilts leaned forward and hit Gil on the shoulder. "Punch-buggy, no return."

Gil ignored the punch. "We should get moving," he said, and Hairball nodded.

The guy hollered over, "Any of you drive?"

Gil rubbed his shoulder, looked at Hairball and smiled. "Yeah, one of us could help you out."

Stilts wasn't happy about being volunteered.

"What if he's, you know," he said, and then lower, "a wacko?"

"You lead, and we'll follow right behind," Gil said. To reinforce the point, he backed up the Nova and pulled onto the shoulder of the road, directly behind the Chevy.

"Hairball could drive," Stilts whined.

"No, he's my navigator."

"We'll save you some backslider," Hairball said, "but you can't take it with you."

"It looks cold out there," Stilts said. He was always complaining about the temperature, which Gil attributed to the constant Saskatchewan wind swaying his slight frame, like the Nova's whip aerial bending in the breeze.

"If you drive, you can wear my jacket," Hairball said, tossing it into the back seat.

Stilts was stymied. "Okay, but stay right behind us. If I put on the flashers or slow down, don't pass me and keep going."

Hairball got out and pulled his seat forward so Stilts could climb out of the back. Stilts shrugged into Hairball's jacket and then walked over to the Chevy's driver-side door.

"Move over," he said to the man, "and stay on your own side."

Gil and Hairball watched as Stilts slid the seat back to accommodate his long legs, put the Chevy into gear, and pulled out onto the highway without signaling or shoulder-checking. Another semi was right there and roared by in the passing lane, warned by the Nova's flashers.

"Better stay close on his tail," Hairball suggested.

Ten kilometres up the road, they could see that the guy had passed out, with his head pressed against the passenger-side window. Gil noticed that every few minutes the Chevy would swerve to the left and then quickly straighten out. When the Chevy swerved, the guy's head leaned away from the window. When Stilts straightened out, his head smacked into the glass and bounced.

"He learned that from you," Hairball said, "trying to sleep with you driving."

They both laughed and Hairball spun the top off the water jug.

Since Hairball knew the quickest route to their secret parking spot three short blocks from Taylor Field, the Nova took the lead on the city's outskirts. They liked to show up early, find their seats, get settled, watch the teams warm up, and check out the crowd. When Stilts pulled up beside the Nova and turned off the key, it was an hour before game time. He pointed to a pay phone down the street at the Seven-Eleven and told the guy in the green suit, "You can call a cab or something from there now or after the game."

His passenger held out his hand and Stilts reached to shake it. It held a business card that read:

ELECTROLUX/RAINBOW SYSTEMS
Fred (Whipper) Watson
Western Sales Manager
Winnipeg, Manitoba
(204) 555-7491

"If you ever need anything, any little thing at all, just show them that. Guarantees you the Whipper discount."

Stilts seemed impressed and showed the card to Gil
and Hairball before sliding it into his wallet for safe-
keeping. Whipper said that he was going to stay in the
car for a while, listening to the pregame show on the
radio. He would head over to the stadium closer to
game time.

"Lock your doors," Gil said. "Not the best neigh-
bourhood."

"If you boys are ever in Winnipeg," Whipper said
before closing the driver-side door Stilts had left open,
"look me up. I owe you a night on the town."

Gil had raised the Nova's hatchback and they
grabbed their backpacks full of licorice, peanuts, and
barbeque chips, along with their green plastic rain pon-
chos and seat cushions. No one noticed that Stilts was
still wearing Hairball's jacket.

Watching the jacket float down out of sight, something clicked in Hairball's brain and his grin
faded. "Hey, you bastard. That was mine."

"No wonder it felt small," Stilts said.

"You're an idiot," Hairball said.

"But a warm idiot," Stilts answered, tugging his
sweater from his backpack and pulling it over his head.

"That was my League Champs jacket."

"With your name on the sleeve," Stilts said, "I expect
we'll be able to ID it."

Gil looked through his binoculars at the spot where
the jacket had gone over. He shouted "Hey" as the jacket appeared in the air above the ledge. A fan in the front

row wearing a hard hat painted green with the Rider logo in white on the side grabbed for the jacket but missed as it dropped out of sight again.

"It was there, man," Gil said, pretty sure he hadn't been seeing things. Then it was there again, and this time the fan caught a sleeve, hauled it in and waved to someone down below.

Hairball stood, waved his arms and yelled, "Hey, up here."

The fan turned around and waved back. They were sitting twenty rows up, so instead of having Hairball walk all the way down, the fan started the process of passing the jacket up, row by row. As it passed each row, fans turned around to see who it was going to. When it reached Hairball and he put it on, they cheered.

"It's a miracle," Gil said.

"Now you can sit down, moron," someone behind them shouted, and Hairball did.

"Check the sleeve," Stilts said. "Make sure it's the right one."

"You're dead meat, Highpockets," Hairball said.

Stilts had pushed too far whenever Hairball started calling him by his old nickname. "Hey, Hair," he pleaded, "no harm done."

"It *was* funny, Hairball," Gil agreed. "First he throws it, and then that look on your face when you realize it's yours. Then it floats right back up here. You the *man.*"

The Eskimos had moved the football inside the Rider fifteen-yard line, and Gainer the Gopher started the crowd chanting *Dee-Fence.* Gil nodded toward the old fellow sitting two seats down from Stilts. He was droning DEE-EEE-EEE so hard that his face had turned red. A dribble of drool shook on his chin. Stilts snorted, Hairball rolled his eyes and all three high-fived as the pass went incomplete.

With five minutes left in the game, two shirtless fans ran onto the field, trotting around in the end zone.

"Hey, we should do that," Stilts said and Gil cuffed him.

One of the fans was waving a sign that said *Esks Suck*. The remaining crowd cheered. The other fan reached the goalpost and jumped up, trying unsuccessfully to touch the crossbar. He landed and twisted his ankle, making him easy prey for the three Yellow Jackets with SECURITY printed in big black letters on their backs. The other trespasser evaded capture with some quick footwork and surprising speed.

"Sign him up," the red-faced man hollered.

The game ended with the Rider backup quarterback throwing a Hail Mary that bounced off one Rider receiver's hands, hit a second receiver's helmet, and plopped into the arms of an Eskimo defender.

"Figures," Hairball said as the final gun sounded. "Horseshoes every game."

"We were down by twelve," Gil said. "That last play didn't matter."

"It's the principle," Hairball said. "It builds momentum for the next game."

They slowly packed up, watching the rest of the crowd stand in line and shuffle down the steps toward the exits. After about ten minutes, they stood and walked down toward the sidelines. The two closest security guys were busy talking to five fans still trying to get onto the field. Gil recognized LeClair. The Rawling trio slipped between the iron railings and walked quickly up the sidelines, toward the player benches.

Four years ago, in a light October blizzard and before security had become so tight, the three of them had made it all the way up the alley to the dressing rooms. They had seen the visiting coach, Hugh Campbell, being interviewed by radio station CKRM just inside the dressing-room door. He was wearing only a towel and they had high-fived each other, marvelling that even the coaches showered after a game. Gil hadn't seen anything else because the coach was blocking his view, but Stilts witnessed two black defensive tackles emerge from the shower's steam without even towels on. He turned pale and stammered, "L-l-let's go." Later, when Hairball pressed him for details, he said only, "You have *no* idea."

"Hey! Where you think you're heading?"

Gil looked over his shoulder, waved and they kept walking.

"Stop! Get back here."

Up ahead, another Yellow Jacket had turned and was watching them, waiting to see if they would make a run for it.

One of the two security guys who had stopped LeClair's crew was now walking toward them. He pulled his yellow jacket away from around his jiggling belly. A radio swung from his belt and his hand hovered near it, like a gunslinger's. Hairball laughed.

"Hi, man," Gil said. "We're just cutting across to our car. It's away on the other side."

"No one on the field," the security guy said. "You know the rules."

"Yeah, but it's shorter," Stilts said. "We'll stay on the outside."

"Can't," the guy said, jabbing his thumb back over his shoulder in the direction he wanted them to go.

"We're here now," Hairball said. "What's the harm?"

"Then everybody'd do it," Yellow Jacket said.

Gil gestured around the near-empty stadium. "There's nobody left."

"Rules are rules."

"Hey, cut us some slack," Hairball said. "We're from out of town."

"Yeah, Alaska," Stilts added. "Never seen a game before."

"Alaska or not, I'm told *no exceptions.* Let's go."

They all started moving back toward the gate where LeClair and his crew stood with the other security guard. Gil nodded at LeClair.

"These ones are from Alaska," the first Yellow Jacket said to his partner.

"Alaska?" He turned and looked them over. "Bring the dogsled down? That's not as good as these guys. They're part of the French-Canadian radio broadcast crew. Just left their passes with their equipment while they went to the can."

"Hurry up," LeClair said. "We're back on air in ninety seconds." The other guys mumbled *oui* and *trés bien.* Gil was impressed.

"I may have been born at night," the guard said, "but not *last* night."

Gil made a mental note to remember that one.

"Now get moving. All of you."

They were herded back out the gate and started walking toward the stadium exit.

"Idiots," LeClair said to the backs of the Yellow Jackets.

"These guys are from Ladieux," Gil told Hairball and Stilts.

"We come a long way to be treated like that," Hairball said.

One of the group asked, "Alaska?" and LeClair laughed.

"Non, these boys are from Rawling."

"Far enough," the guy said and they all nodded.

There was a silence as the two groups moved along side by side but separate, like water and oil. Even though Rawling and Ladieux were only twenty kilometres apart, it might as well have been a thousand. Ladieux was a French stronghold, and Rawling was of mainly British and German stock. Rivals was too tame a word to describe how these two towns felt toward each other. Hockey matches, baseball games, and even the high schools' track-and-field meets had the aura of a battleground. Ladieux calling their hockey teams the Canadiens, and wearing the "rouge, blanc, et bleu" uniforms also indicated where their loyalties lay. Gil knew first-hand the sympathy to be gathered in Rawling after receiving a Canadien elbow to the head, and the accolades to be garnered for deking their Jacques Plante-style goaltender.

The surrounding towns felt that Ladieux got special treatment from the government, like an addition to their French immersion school and a hospital that remained open while others closed. Relations between the two communities might have been less strained if Ladieux's citizens had acted grateful or even slightly embarrassed by the special treatment. Instead, to Gil, they seemed proud, as if it was their right. Mingling could have helped but they stuck together, a breed apart. That big brick church in the middle of town with the forty-foot steeple told everyone passing by on the highway that they were superior, as if their mumbling, wine-drinking priests had cornered the religion market.

Gil felt the uneasy silence building as they walked along, Then, because LeClair had found and returned his binoculars, he asked, "You heading back tonight?"

"Non, we got rooms at the Seven Oaks. You guys?"

"Landmark."

"You go to uhhh, what you say, that place around the back?"

"The Nightclub? Yeah. It's always packed."

Stilts added, "We always eat at that Smitty's in the morning."

"Babes and booze for the taking," Hairball said, more to himself and Gil than to the Ladieux guys, "and Stilts dreams of restaurant food and cable in the rooms."

Everyone laughed, then one of LeClair's buddies asked, "You get a movie channel?"

"You bet," Stilts said. "Pay-per-view for the newer movies and then a different channel has older ones for free."

"Commercials in them?"

"Yeah, but some of these shows haven't even come to the Odeon in Swift Current yet."

A few of the guys shook their heads at the wonder of it, and they walked on in silence.

After another fifty yards of walking, LeClair said, "Two road games for them now."

"BC and then where?"

"Hamilton. Then the Stampeders back here in three weeks."

Hairball bumped Stilts off the sidewalk and he clipped a fire hydrant. Stilts rubbed his knee and glared at Hairball. "At our next Black and Blue game, we're gonna be on opposite teams," he said.

"Careful what you wish for, my boy."

Gil saw the Ladieux crew exchange looks, and he wished that Stilts could learn to keep his big trap shut.

"You guys play football?" LeClair asked.

"Not really," Gil said, offhand. "We go out to the ball diamond, you know, the outfield and toss the ball around."

"We scrimmage," Stilts said. "Sometimes there's ten or twelve a side."

"Tackle?"

"No," Gil snorted.

"You bet," Hairball said loudly.

The school division had never arranged football as a high school sport. The cost of equipment and continually dropping enrollment had made it a low priority. The boys had picked teams and played at noon hours, after school and on weekends, but never against another town.

One of LeClair's sidekicks said the words that Gil had been dreading. "We play that game, too, pretty damn good."

The challenge hung in the air for an eternity. Hairball glanced at Gil, who slightly shook his head. Gil tried to catch Stilts's attention too, but he was looking over everyone's heads, back at the stadium. Gil breathed, thinking that maybe Stilts hadn't even heard the comment.

"We should have a game sometime," Stilts said, loud enough for no one to mistake.

LeClair smiled. "Two weekends open, could be home-and-home."

"Right on," Hairball said. "Winners get a twenty-four pack of Canadian."

"Non, twenty-six of white rum, and bottled Coke."

"All right, thirty-six Labatts."

"Whoa!" LeClair held up his hands. "Tell you what. The new hotel's big opening is next weekend. Play in Ladieux on Saturday, and they sponsor the winners with a Texas mickey."

"Are you sure?" Gil asked.

"Owner's his brother-in-law," another one of the Ladieux-ites said.

"No problem," LeClair said. "You show up and it's a go."

"We'll be there," Hairball said.

"We don't have any equipment," Gil said, his head swirling with the details. "We need to decide on the rules, the number of players, the size of the field, referees...."

"You don't know the rules?" LeClair asked.

"We know the game," Stilts said, shaking his head and glaring at LeClair.

"You try to get enough for nine-man," LeClair said. "If not, we play six-man."

"How about twelve-man?" Hairball replied. "I'm sure we can round up a dozen or so."

"You'll be wanting some as replacements," LeClair said.

Stilts jumped in. "We always play both ways, offence and defence, so no substitutions required for us, thank you very much."

"We, too, but I'm thinking someone might get hurt," LeClair said slyly, and his buddies chuckled.

"Especially if they aren't all wearing the same amount of equipment," Gil added.

LeClair spread his hands. "We have no equipment." He looked to his group for support. "Eh?"

"Non.... No equipment."

"Well, some do wear the shoulder pads, but small ones, from hockey."

"Mais oui, and there's the cleats."

"Ah, but you need cleats. It's for the grip."

Hairball held up his hands. "Hold on. Nix the shoulder pads. And I'm not getting stepped on by no steel cleats. Runners."

Stilts nodded. "Those ones with the rubber knobs on the bottom are okay."

LeClair turned to Gil. "I call you, Monday night. If you still want to play, we talk details on the phone."

"Oh, we'll want to play, bud," Hairball said. "Count on it."

Gil told LeClair to call him at work during the day, and gave the number for the Pioneer grain elevator.

They split up at the intersection. After walking another block toward the Nova and well out of earshot, Stilts hollered, "Bring it on, baby."

They could see Whipper Watson's Chevy was still parked beside the Nova. Hairball said, *Waiting for his chauffeur, maybe?* then exchanged a grin with Gil as Stilts blurted, *Forget it!*

The car was empty anyway. They looked back toward the stadium, but didn't see Whipper weaving his way down the street. While Gil unlocked the Nova, Hairball checked the back alley and peeked into the dumpster, partially as a joke.

Saturday evening at the Nightclub, Sunday morning over Smitty's pancakes, and finishing the back-slider on the afternoon drive home were all secondary events to the speculation about who could play in the game and who wouldn't. Gil had, without a vote taken or a word said, been appointed as the organizer.

"Call the Snyders," he told Hairball. "See if the twins are back from working the rigs."

"Yeah, they'll knock a few heads," Stilts agreed. "We'll have to get a message to Joey, Ted, and Slime in Saskatoon, too. Make sure they come home from school for the weekend."

"Slime won't play," Gil said.

"No, not unless Marilyn's out of town. He'll say his knee's sore, or his back."

"Marty'll play and hey, what about that cousin of his? What's his name? He hangs out and helps with harvest."

"You mean Ed?"

"Yeah, Ed from Swift Current. I've seen him wearing a Colts jacket."

"Everybody makes the high school football team, Stilts. There's about forty players every year. The question is *did he play?*"

"Let's ask Marty."

"He'll say Ed was the starting quarterback, drafted by the Riders, but decided not to go."

"Yeah, he wanted to help Marty with harvest instead."

"No, I think Marty'll come clean, especially if we say we're looking for Ed to play with us," Gil said. "The proof's in the pudding, as they say."

"The proof's in the pudding? You sound like your Grandma."

"We may need to recruit her yet. Okay, counting us that's seven, maybe nine if the twins are around."

"Nathan will play," Stilts said.

"He's only in grade ten."

"But he runs like an antelope. Remember last time we played?"

"Yeah, he's still in shape," Gil said. "Nathan's in. And what about those two buddies of his?"

"The Harrisons? That younger curly-haired one seemed kind of whiny," Hairball said.

"That's 'cause you beaned him with the ball after the play," Stilts said.

"Gotta be awake at all times," Hairball said.

"We'll get Nathan to ask them," Gil said. "That makes twelve."

"You guys know Roland Stenson?" Stilts asked. "He rides for the PFRA."

Gil shook his head but Hairball said, "That cowboy?"

"Yeah. I think maybe he'd play."

"He's gotta be pushing thirty."

"He's not as old as he looks. I heard them say that he signed a scholarship to play college ball in Missoula, but broke his collarbone rodeoing that summer."

"Even if he doesn't want to play," Gil said, "he can ride his horse up and down the sidelines after we score a touchdown."

Hairball laughed and slapped Stilts on the back. Stilts didn't see the humour. "Make fun if you want. He's American. He could be the quarterback."

When Gil showed up for work on Monday morning, he was thinking about how this Thursday, September 18th, would be his second anniversary at the Pioneer Grain elevator. He was still the helper, the third man on the totem pole, behind the manager Red Fraser and his assistant Howie Richards. When Gil had started, his plan was to work for one year, earn some money while taking a break from the boredom of school and determine his future direction. There weren't many well-paying job openings around Rawling. Red had stopped beside him in the aisle one day as Gil was checking for the Co-op's firmest red tomato. Red said he was getting a helper position and asked what Gil's plans were for the winter. That winter had stretched into a year, then slid into two.

Red and Howie were sitting in the office having a coffee. Red said he had listened to the game on the radio, and asked if it had been any better in person. Gil said the game was no hell but that it had been a memorable trip. He told them about the crazy blue Chev on the highway and them coercing Stilts to drive Whipper Watson in to Regina. He didn't say anything about the Ladieux challenge. He couldn't see any percentage in playing a game they were sure to lose. He figured that, if he could stall and delay, slow things down, then in a few weeks it would be too cold to play. Maybe it would even snow early. Both towns would then have all winter to bluster about the couldas and shouldas and wouldas. By Spring, they would all be talking about the hockey playoffs and then baseball coming up.

Gil had forgotten the Hotel opening, though. LeClair called the Pioneer at three p.m. sharp. Gil was loading hopper cars at the back when Howie came around the scale and hollered, "Phone!"

"Who is it?"

"Don't know. Some guy who asked 'Allo, ees Geeell dere?'"

"Can you take over for me, Howie?" Gil asked. "Just weigh out what's in this last bin and dump it into the hopper car."

Gil scooted into the storage shed where they kept the fertilizer and chemicals, closing the door before picking up the telephone extension.

"Gil here."

"Hello. It is Raoul LeClair. We meet at the Rider game. You remember?"

"Yes. Yes, I do."

"We are ready to make prepares for the game."

"Well, Raoul, if you're having any trouble getting players on this short of notice, we can always..."

"We have twenty-two sign up today."

Gil felt the walls closing in. "Well, ah, that should be enough. Have you heard if it's going to turn cold?"

"Maybe next week. Long-range says the same for weekend as now."

The ceiling was lowering, too. "Hmmm, that's great. I'll have to check to see if our field is available...."

"We play first in Ladieux, 'member? Saturday, with the Hotel grand opening."

Great, Gil thought, a big crowd getting each other's hot French tempers riled up.

LeClair continued. "Roast pig supper, with Happy Hour prices all afternoon."

Even better. A large, hostile crowd, fuelled by cheap liquor. Gil took a deep breath, reviewing the angles and options. "Okay, but let's start early. How about 1:30?"

They settled some of the basic rules: nine players a side; two-hand touch on the ball carrier; immediate rush on the quarterback with blocking allowed at the line of scrimmage. They would each provide a referee and the game would consist of two thirty-minute halves.

"After the game, you guys stick around for some pig at the Hotel, eh?"

"For sure," Gil said. "That's where we'll be presented with the Texas mickey, right?"

There was a pause, then LeClair laughed. "That Rawling joking," he said.

Gil phoned Hairball, who was supposed to be haul-ing bales but would be inside for the half-hour that *Jeopardy* was on TV. Hairball was unbeatable when it came to trivia, unless a time limit was involved. Then his throat tightened up under the stress, and sometimes he almost gagged trying to get the answer out. It was in grade nine Social Studies, the time the class was playing Reach For The Top, when he made that sound like a cat with something stuck in its throat, that his nickname was born.

"I heard from LeClair."

"It's a go?"

"Afraid so. Saturday at 1:30."

"Here?"

"There. Hotel grand opening."

"No sweat," Hairball said. "We should have a practice sometime this week. Go over some plays and positions."

"We've got just enough bodies," Gil said. "If some-body pulls a muscle or gets hurt at practice, then we're screwed."

"You're saying skip practice and just wing it on Saturday?" Hairball asked.

"Why not? It's just for fun."

"Right. This is Ladieux, Gil."

They went over the players list again and split up the people to call and tell about the game. They left the long-distance ones for Stilts. They also decided to meet on Wednesday night at the field. They wouldn't actually practice but they would talk strategy over a few brews. Hairball said he would bring a football in case anyone wanted to toss it around with him.

Gil hung up the extension and went into the office. Red looked up from the desk where he was filling in some paperwork.

"How's loading that car coming along?"

"Howie's finishing it off."

Red nodded, put down his pencil, folded his arms and waited.

"I'll go back out and help him seal it up and move it."

"Nothing else?" Red asked. "You seem a little tense these days."

Gil wondered what Red was after. He hoped that Red hadn't heard about Gil's Swift Current job opportunity. He didn't want Red to think he was ungrateful for this job and was sneaking around looking for another, and also why stir things up if he didn't take it? Or maybe Red had a Ladieux connection who had filled him in on the upcoming match? Gil knew that Red didn't have much use for the elevator agent over there, so it wouldn't be through him. He had heard Red say that if the guy couldn't speak French, he wouldn't even still be employed.

There had been a contest last Spring where the districts tried to meet certain targets selling fertilizer. The Ladieux elevator entered in the individual category while Rawling registered with the other towns under the group portion. Sales were good and it was getting down to the wire. Red was finalizing a big sale with the Hutterites that would have put the district over the top, but he was short of inventory. The Hutterites were seeding through the night and needed the fertilizer for the next morning. Red called around and the Ladieux elevator had enough of what he needed. *Tell them to come up here,* the Ladieux manager had said, *and we can load their trucks with all they need tonight.*

What he didn't say was that he planned to book it as his sale. During the week that it took Red to find out what had happened, he lectured Howie and Gil on how the Ladieux area had been misjudged for years, and really, who wouldn't want to maintain their own culture and identity? Then Headquarters called, with what Red had anticipated being congratulations on their district surpassing the group target. Instead, he was told that his last fertilizer claim was rejected because it was a duplicate of a sale counted by Ladieux in the individual category. That was the first time Gil had seen Red's temper match his name. A calendar still hung over the hole he had punched in the wall by the phone.

Gil decided that talking football was safer than saying he had been hunting for a new job.

"We're organizing a little football game," Gil said.

Red nodded. "Playing the high school kids?"

Gil shook his head. "Just some of the guys."

"You seem a bit jittery over a pickup game. Is there money on the line?"

"Not yet."

Red kept looking at him with that little smile of his, twirling the pencil between his fingers. "What are you cooking up, Gil?"

Gil looked at the calendar and paused, remembering Red's rage as he drove his fist through the gyproc.

"How old are you, Red?"

"Be fifty-three in November."

"Did you ever play football?"

Red shook his head and tilted back his chair. "We had baseball in the summer, hockey in the winter. Not choices like now, with the kids choosing between soccer, volleyball, football, basketball, and even lacrosse."

"We're playing another town."

"Who?"

"Ladieux."

The pencil snapped. "Need a manager?"

By Wednesday night they had fourteen confirmed players. Red was the team manager and his assistant Howie had signed on as the trainer. A dozen fans were also committed to travelling to the game. Eight of the players had been able to get to the strategy session, and were sitting on the bleachers at the ball field.

"Is this it?" Roland Stenson asked.

"All that could make it tonight," Hairball said.

"There's six more coming for the weekend," Gil added.

"I heard at school that Ladieux's having tryouts," Nathan said. "There's gonna be cuts."

"That's just like them," Red said. "Probably bringing in imports."

"Let's have a look at the playbook," Stenson said.

Stilts and Hairball looked at Gil, who looked back at Roland. "Playbook?"

"You know, the plays we're going to work on for the weekend."

"Uhhh...that's a good idea, Roland. We haven't played much before, so..."

Hairball spoke up. "We like to keep it simple on offence, Roland. Nathan here's our speedster, so he goes long. Stilts cuts across the middle 'cause he's so tall, and my specialty is the buttonhook."

"Who's the fullback?"

"We don't usually bother rushing the ball with two-hand touch."

"Two-hand touch? We're playing two-hand touch?"

Roland was shaking his head so Gil tried to explain. "We just thought that for this first time, since we don't know what it'll be like, we'd try it this way."

"Only for the ball carrier," Hairball added. "There's blocking and full contact on the line and stuff."

Marty, who was built more for stability than speed, said, "Yeah well, I still wish we could wear a helmet or shoulder pads or something."

Roland looked at Marty like he had just claimed the Riders could whip the Green Bay Packers. "There's no equipment?"

Marty shook his head and Hairball said, "Equipment's for wimps."

Roland was silent for ten seconds, thinking things over. Then he grinned. "This'll be like rodeo," he said. "No protection between you and the bull."

Hairball tossed Roland the football. "Want to warm up the arm?"

"Why?"

"You're quarterbacking, aren't you?"

"I wasn't planning on it."

Hairball looked at Gil, and then back to Roland. "But you're from the States, you played in college."

"I was a linebacker," Roland said. "I can help with the defence."

"We're dead meat," Nathan said.

"Hold on a minute," Gil said. "Let's just toss the ball around for a bit. Maybe one of us has a stronger arm than we remember."

They moved into the infield and started throwing. Players took turns running routes and the football would be delivered in the vicinity. Hairball yelled *Not so far* when it was his turn to throw it to Nathan. There were a couple of sprawling catches but other than that, it was pretty dismal.

"Hey Marty," Stilts asked, "what position does Ed play?"

"Oh, he can play anywhere. He was with the Colts for three years."

"Great, he can start at quarterback then."

"Start at QB? Well, he hasn't played in a couple of years. I'll have to check. He may have hurt his shoulder in their last big playoff game. He was taken off in a stretcher, I think. Can't raise his arm above the shoulder any more."

"He is coming though, isn't he?"

"Oh, for sure. There's still that roast pig thing afterwards, isn't there, and happy hour prices?"

Gil shook his head. They *were* dead meat. "Guys, let's meet back here again Friday night. We'll try to have everybody out and talk about positions."

Roland said that he would write down some things that the defence would have to know, like the difference between zone and man-to-man coverage, and the signal for the blitz. Nathan said he would check out the throwing arms of the guys at school and Stilts mumbled that his sister Debbie could throw pretty well.

"It's snowed in September before," Gil said. "We're not getting paid to play, so if it's cold or windy, we'll have to postpone."

"But if we wait for a day when it's not windy," Hairball said, "we might never play."

Gil grinned and said, "No flies on this Hairball."

Ever since early summer Gil had felt restless. He knew he could transfer to another, smaller point within Pioneer and be an assistant manager, but he didn't like that option for two reasons. Firstly, taking a job in another elevator would mean moving away from Rawling, the place where he had grown up and still looked after things. Some of his friends had left to earn good coin on the oil rigs or to further their education, but they all had a specific purpose. Gil couldn't move to another town just for something to do. Besides, who would look after these goofs if he left? Secondly, he wasn't really excited about making the grain-buying business a career. Being the helper was one thing, but getting into management would involve more training and time, committing him to a dying business. The CPR and CNR were systematically shutting down rail lines, forcing elevator closures, and eliminating jobs.

Unfortunately, Gil didn't have a burning desire for any other job or trade. Hairball's future was mapped out for him, taking over his dad's farm. He was renting a half-section and had twenty cows of his own. Stilts was a year younger, but had started as an apprentice with Big Sky Electric. He worked full-time for nine months, then went to school for three months in the winter. After four years of this, he could write a test and become a journeyman electrician. Hairball said it was a natural career choice because Stilts could change light bulbs without a ladder.

Gil's looming second anniversary at the elevator, plus the speed with which that time had gone by, scared him. Two weeks ago Gil had lied to Red, told him that he had a doctor's appointment in Swift Current, and took the day off. He spent the morning driving around and looking at the various businesses. He had gone into the mall and imagined it was him serving customers at Work Wearhouse, or behind the counter in Canadian Tire's automotive section. He said he was looking for a car at D.J.'s Honda Sales and pictured himself as the salesman in his brown suit and scuffed oxfords. He even went into the Southwest Credit Union and sat in one of the soft vinyl chairs by the window, watching the tellers handle money and smile at the customers in the lineup that never dwindled.

In the afternoon he had an appointment with a career counsellor at the Cypress Hills Community College. That had been his mom's idea. The counsellor, a woman in her fifties who kept checking her watch, had a stack of magazines from different colleges and universities. She started by asking Gil what he was interested in. Gil thought, if he knew that, he wouldn't be sitting across the desk from her. He shrugged and said he was uncertain. The counsellor gave him a pencil and four sheets of paper with various questions on them. She marked each one as he moved on to the next, and in the end she said it showed that he had an aptitude for numbers and logic. She suggested accounting or something with computers, tapped her watch, stood up, and wished him luck.

After that, Gil had stopped at the Canada Employment Centre, again his mom's idea, and checked the job board. There was a posting for a junior accounting clerk with the auditing firm of Stanley, Stanley & Kirk. The qualifications were grade 12, attention to detail, and the ability to work overtime. Gil had started to fill out an application form but couldn't remember his Social Insurance Number or his Saskatchewan Hospitalization Number. He took the form home and left it on the kitchen counter.

On Friday, the day before they went to the Rider game, he had been surprised by a message to call CEC for an interview. His mom had filled in the missing information and mailed the application. He had arranged to go this Thursday but, when the day came, they were swamped at work and he didn't feel right about asking Red for another day off so soon. Instead, Gil had called back and changed the appointment to 4:30 next Tuesday.

Gil had planned to talk with Hairball and Stilts about careers and futures over the weekend in Regina. When discussions like that occurred, it was always late at night, after the bars had closed and everybody was loose. Gil remembered the conversation they had had a year ago when Stilts first mentioned going to work for Big Sky. They were driving down the dirt road south of town, the one that joined the two grids. The moon was full and shining so bright that Gil had turned off the Nova's headlights. Hairball had opened them a second Canadian with his teeth and scoffed when Stilts told him they were those new twist-off caps. "Twist-offs are for wimps," he had said.

"I'm signing up," Stilts had told them.

"What for, the army?" Hairball asked.

"Big Sky. They're looking for apprentices."

"How do you know that?"

"I went in and asked. Talked with Mr. Cooper."

Hairball snorted. "You went in?"

"Yep."

"And talked to the owner?"

"Affirmative."

"And I suppose he said, 'You're just the guy we're looking for!' Stilts, you kill me, you really do."

"It's the truth," Stilts said. "I start on Monday."

"Good for you, Stilts," Gil had said, turning slightly and hoisting his bottle up over the front seat so that Stilts could clink it from the back. "Initiative. Who'd have thunk it?"

"Thanks for the tip, Gil. They're looking for one more, too," Stilts had said. The sentence hung in the air while Hairball took a long pull on his beer and Gil concentrated on turning the Nova into the abandoned Jacobsen farmyard, which Hairball's dad rented from the widow. When no one spoke, Stilts continued. "I plan on starting my own company someday, you know. I could use a partner. Old man Cooper's retiring in a few years, and we'll be the only show in town."

"There's a reason for that," Hairball had said.

"Whaddaya mean?"

"Electricians, carpenters, plumbers, they all have this one habit — they like to eat. That's why they have their business in the city, where there's growth. Name the last building that went up in Rawling?"

"People don't just build, they replace and upgrade," Stilts had said. "Big Sky's been here twenty-five years."

"Cooper's got everything paid for," Hairball said, "and he's built up his customer base. When people move into the City, they still get Big Sky to do some of their work."

"We'll learn from that, and make the contacts working for Big Sky," Stilts countered. "Then when things turn around, BAMM! we'll be here."

Hairball laughed. "It's not gonna turn around. This is as good as it gets."

Stilts had looked at Gil for support but Gil shook his head. "It's third and long, buddy."

Stilts mumbled, "What do you guys know about anything, anyway?"

It was Hairball's turn to reach back and clink Stilts's bottle. "Look, it's your life, man. I'm stuck here on the farm, going nowhere. So I'm not going to complain about the company — the more the merrier. You just need to be realistic."

"Electrician's a good trade," Gil added. "You can learn it here and then go someplace else when work dries up."

"Maybe it *is* third and long, and you guys would punt," Stilts had said. "But that makes for boring football, right? To hell with you, I'm going for it."

That had been a year ago and Gil had never heard Stilts complain about the work. When things slowed down in the winter, he had school to attend. Gil had been hoping to talk with them this past weekend about his pending interview. Unfortunately, Whipper Watson had interrupted the drive in and, ever since, Gil had been thinking about the upcoming tilt against Ladieux.

O n Friday night they had fourteen bodies. Roland Stenson brought another cowboy from the PFRA. He hadn't played football before but Roland said the quickness he showed when steer wrestling could transfer into useful blocking on the line.

"Oh, and he'll need to borrow someone's runners," Roland said.

The Snyder twins were there in their leather jackets and itching to play. "We had to switch a couple of shifts and drove straight from Lloyd this morning," Travis explained, "but we couldn't miss out."

Trent clenched his fist and said, "Yeah-yeah, I haven't hit a Frog since volleyball playoffs."

Nathan and the two Harrisons, the only ones still in high school, were all ears.

"In volleyball?" Curly Harrison asked.

"He'd crossed the line," Travis said, and Trent jumped in with, "Yeah-yeah, you gotta stay on your own side o' the net."

Joey and Ted were down from Saskatoon. Slime had caught a ride back with them but had taken Marilyn to the show. He would absolutely, definitely be at the game, though.

"He's been working out," Joey said. "He'll be good at middle linebacker."

"What he's up to tonight won't be good for his legs," Roland countered.

Gil explained to the high-schoolers, "It's the butter in that movie popcorn. Not good for you."

Hairball clenched his fist and stuck his arm straight out. "Ba-da-bing," he said, and everybody laughed.

Roland continued. "He won't know our signals, either. No, I'd better play the middle."

Marty had brought along his cousin Ed, who was wearing his Colts jacket.

"Hey, Ed, good to see you again," Gil said, shaking his hand. "Thanks for coming."

"He wouldn't miss it," Marty said. "And...he was the backup quarterback."

"Well, backup after the starting guy broke his leg," Ed corrected.

Gil turned to Marty and grinned. "Good to see you, too, big guy. That's excellent news. What's the injury status?"

"Why ask me?" Marty said. "He's standing right there."

Ed lifted his right arm up level with his shoulder. "That's as high as it goes, boys."

Gil groaned and Roland said they had better get working on some blocking schemes for their running game. Stilts said that his sister Debbie was still a free agent.

Marty held his hands up above his head. "Hold on. That was the bad news. Who wants to hear the good news?"

"Ladieux forfeited?" Gil asked hopefully.

"There'll be snow by morning?"

"Ronnie Lancaster's your uncle?"

"None of that," Marty grinned. "Anyone else? Okay, the bad news was that Ed's right shoulder's buggered. The good news is that he's left-handed."

Ed pumped his left hand in the air and everybody cheered. Hairball tossed Ed the football and then ran out on his favourite pattern, the buttonhook. Ed pumped once and then threaded the ball right into Hairball's stomach. Hairball grunted but hung on. He trotted back and tossed the ball underhand to Ed while Stilts went long. Ed threw this one over Stilts's head but everyone cheered that, as well.

Hairball slapped Gil on the back and said, "Now we've got a game."

Travis Snyder laughed and punched his twin in the arm. Trent grimaced then hit Travis in the shoulder. Marty got between them and suggested they save it for the other team. Trent said yeah-yeah, and Travis told him there was a lot more where that came from.

Gil looked around and noticed that Roland was the only one not smiling or laughing. He walked over to where Roland was sitting on the bleachers, studying his handful of papers, drawing circles and arrows and making notes.

"What's up, Roland?" Gil asked.

"You know what wins football games?" Roland asked. "I'll tell you what. It's defence that wins games. We now have a QB and that's good, but it's eighteen hours before game time and I haven't even shown the defence the different formations, let alone practice them."

"Well, let's do it," Gil said. "What's the first step?"

"How about deciding who's going to play where?" Roland asked. "Then my defence can kick your offence all over this sorry field."

Saturday morning's weather was clear and calm. Red had asked that they all meet in front of the Co-op store at 11:00 a.m. sharp. When Gil showed up at 10:45, the three high schoolers were the only other players there. Gil wasn't surprised because they had been the only ones not old enough to get into the bar after last night's practice. The rest of the team showed up in dribs and drabs. At eleven, Red came out of the Co-op and asked Gil how many they were missing, which was half. By 11:20, Slime was the only absentee.

"Did he know when we were meeting?" Gil asked Ted.

"I left a message with his mom last night," Ted answered, and then snapped his fingers. "But maybe she's at that craft sale in the Hall now."

"I'll go get him," Stilts said.

"No," Red said. "Let's keep every player who's here, here." Red turned to his wife. "Donna, I left our camera sitting on the outside steps. Could you take the car and grab it? And then swing by and see what's keeping the Collick boy?"

Donna said, "Aye, aye, Captain," and left.

Red then climbed up into the back of Marty's half-ton and raised his arms.

"Ho-kay, can I have your attention, please? Gather round, guys. I don't know if Gil told you or not, but I'm the team manager today. Howie's the trainer. Raise your hand, Howie. Ho-kay. Now we got thinking, you guys are out there practising and stuff, so what could we do to help? I called head office and they gave the thumbs-up for Pioneer Grain to sponsor the team. So Howie went into Swift Current this week and got some shirts. Toss one here, Howie."

Howie reached down into the cardboard box at his feet, pulled out a T-shirt and tossed it up. Red caught it and held it out in front of him. It was white with *Rawling Rebels* spelled out in orange letters. People clapped.

"We tried to get orange shirts with yellow writing, but they wouldn't have got here in time," Red said. Some of the crowd cheered at that. Red continued. "Howie also talked to Edith and the Co-op's going to sponsor the team's refreshments."

Howie walked over and opened the door to the Co-op. The store manager came out carrying a case of Gatorade. "Give Edith a hand, guys," he said. Gil and Stilts took the case from her and set it in the back of Marty's truck, along with some energy bars, oranges, and dill pickle chips.

"Everybody grab a T-shirt and make sure it's big enough," Red said. "They're all extra large or double-extra. Let's all be wearing them when we show up at the field. Howie, we got one for Edith, too, so make sure she gets hers."

Gil picked out an extra-large and pulled it on. It hung down to the middle of his thighs but had short sleeves, so they wouldn't get in the way. He watched Roland hold his cowboy buddy's hat while he pulled on his T-shirt, and then had the favour returned. There was a small cheer to the side as Slime wove his way through the crowd toward the shirts. He was wearing a ball cap to cover his uncombed hair.

When he passed by, Gil slapped him on the shoulder and said, "Good to see you, Slime. You need any toothpicks to keep those eyelids open?"

Slime shook his head and then hollered up to Red, "Mr. Fraser, I have to confess that I found your wife in my bedroom."

Red laughed. "I hope you had better luck than me."

A school bus pulled out from the alley behind the Co-op and stopped on the street behind Marty's truck.

"Oh, one last thing," Red said. "We'll all travel together on this bus. Jake here's volunteered his time to drive and the Co-op filled up the gas tank. So grab your stuff and let's go. Fans, too, there's lots of room."

There was a buzz of excitement as the extra T-shirts, drinks, and food were loaded onto the bus. People carried on their own supplies in coolers, and lawn chairs were loaded in the back through the rear doors. Gil and Hairball got front seats, along with Red and Howie.

Red's wife Donna sat back with the other fans.

By noon the school bus was ready to go. Red counted heads and got fifteen players, two management, a driver and eleven fans. Edith stuck her head in the door and hollered, "Good Luck, Rebels!" There were whoops, "Thanks" and "Go Rebels" shouted back. Edith told Red that she was catching a ride to Ladieux with some fans who were leaving closer to one o'clock.

"We'll be going over to the Hotel's grand opening after," Edith said, "if you and Donna want to catch a ride back with us."

"The bus'll be stopping, too," Hairball said, aiming his voice at Jake the driver.

Jake looked at Red for confirmation and then nodded. "At your service, guys. I'll make two trips but I'm not staying all night. This baby turns back into a pumpkin at about 9 o'clock."

"Even if we win?" Hairball asked.

Jake laughed. "If you guys win, someone else may have to drive us all home."

The football game was being played behind Ladieux's new school, on the soccer pitch. When the bus pulled up and Gil saw the field, he knew that Rawling's pride would have the guys spending next week's precious practice time fixing up their own ball diamond's outfield. LeClair and his crew had outlined the field with lime and also put lines at mid-field and across the goal lines. They had taken the netting off the soccer goals and strapped 16-foot two-by-fours to the posts to make uprights. They had even stapled some red plastic triangles to the top of the lumber, which fluttered in the wind.

The Ladieux team was already on the field, stretching and loosening up. They were wearing Canadiens hockey jerseys. Gil thought they must have borrowed a set from the senior hockey team, which was a thrifty idea. However, when he walked to mid-field in his new T-shirt to meet LeClair, he noticed that the jerseys were made of a light nylon with lots of holes, and everyone had their name on the back.

"Gil, good to see you made it after all," LeClair said, holding out his hand. Gil shook it.

"Nice job getting the field ready," he said.

"Oui. Calais our rec director handled it," LeClair said. "These old bones found it tough to just make the practice every night."

"Looks like you got a full squad," Gil said, motioning to the two dozen bodies on the field.

"Lots of interest," LeClair said. "May be we using some of our other guys next game."

LeClair waved to the sidelines and a man wearing a black and white jersey trotted over. This was a real hockey referee's sweater because it had the SAHA patch sewn on the shoulder, ensuring that the owner had his officiating certification.

"Gil, it is Jean Calais. He will blow the whistle."

"Pleased to meet you," Gil said. "Good job on fixing up the field."

Calais shrugged but smiled, shaking Gil's outstretched hand. *Never tick off a referee* was Gil's motto.

"See, they bring a bus," LeClair said to Calais.

"I see that, but a school bus, not the town's," Calais said.

"We'll talk," LeClair mumbled.

Calais pointed out his assistant on the sidelines, who would be the timekeeper.

"That's Paulhus. And your referee is...?" Calais asked.

Their referee! Gil had forgotten to recruit one. He looked over at the sidelines, scanning the fans setting up their lawn chairs. He didn't feel comfortable asking any of them to help officiate the game. One of their players could do it, but they were already short of bodies.

"Uhhh, there's a few more people coming. If no one volunteers, I'll do it."

Calais held up his hand. "If it's agreeable with your side, monsieur, my assistant Paulhus could help, if someone from your side ran the stopwatch?"

"Whew! Sounds good to me. Thanks," Gil said.

Paulhus trotted out on the field carrying a plastic bag. As Calais went over the rules with Gil and LeClair, Paulhus pulled a referee's sweater out of the bag and over his head. The bag also contained a whistle and a starter's pistol. He gave Gil the stopwatch and showed him how it worked.

"T'irty minutes a half, stop time," Paulhus said. "They need to pay attention, 'cause it's the official time." Gil had Edith in mind for handling the timekeeping duties, and he felt comfortable that she would be responsible enough. Then Paulhus handed Gil the starter pistol and said, "Shoot into the air, not by anybody's ear."

Calais tossed a coin in the air and Gil chose tails. It was heads. He took that as a sign of things to come.

"We start in twenty minutes," Calais said. "Rawling to kick off to Ladieux."

When Gil went back to the sidelines he saw that Stenson had some of the defence gathered around him, reviewing his sheets of paper. Hairball and Stilts were talking with Ed, no doubt reminding him of their favourite pass routes. The Snyder twins were lying flat out on their bellies, deadlocked in an arm wrestle. Slime was beside the bus, combing his hair in the mirror. Red came over and said, *What's up?*

"We kick off," Gil said. "They'll ref and we'll run the clock."

"Typical," Red blustered. "Their field, their refs, and they get the ball first."

"It's on the level, Red. I'll fill you in later."

Gil saw that Edith had arrived and went over to ask her to run the stopwatch. Meanwhile Red reviewed the lineup and let everyone know they'd be on defence first. Hairball was the kicker and he insisted that Curly Harrison pin the football for him. Curly had been the only player at practice too scared of Hairball to try the Lucy-Charlie Brown trick, pulling the ball away just as Hairball's foot was about to strike leather.

Gil and Ed stood together on the sidelines as the teams lined up for the kickoff. They both looked around at the fans sitting and standing along the edge of the field. There had to be fifty on the Ladieux side. They also had a banner which read "Texas Mickey Classic." Underneath, someone had taped on a smaller sign that read – "1st Annual."

Ed took a deep breath and grinning, said, "Ahh, to live in a small town."

"It's not that bad," Gil said.

"I'm not knocking it," Ed said. "There's more fans here than ever watched a Colts game. I liked hanging out at Marty's 'cause we always did things around the farm and downtown or at the rink."

"What are you up to these days?" Gil asked.

"Going to Tech in Moose Jaw," Ed said. "Taking Electronics."

"Like it?"

Ed shrugged. "Two weeks, two cabarets."

Gil nodded as he watched the kickoff wobble in the air for twenty-five yards. "Attaboy, Hairball," he hollered after the Ladieux return man was touched following a five-yard return.

Calais used a green beanbag to mark where the ball was. Paulhus paced out ten yards toward the Rawling goal line and dropped a yellow bag, the first-down marker.

Both sides were tentative to start with. Ladieux was trying short passes and running sweeps, and Stenson was guessing correctly. They moved down the field, but didn't get any big gains. Stenson's D held them on the twenty, and they punted the ball through the end zone for a single point.

Gil had felt butterflies watching from the sidelines, but as he went in with the offence to scrimmage the ball for the first time, he couldn't breathe very deeply. His neck muscles were tight and he felt nauseous.

In the huddle, Ed said, "Let's get our feet wet, boys. Travis, don't punch anybody, just keep the rush outside long enough for me to deliver the mail to Hairball on the buttonhook. Marty, give me a good snap on 'two.' Everybody take a deep breath. Okay, let's break."

Ed clapped his hands and everyone trotted to their positions. Gil suddenly felt like a cog in a well-oiled machine as he lined up beside Slime and a few steps away from Hairball. A small ray of hope glittered off the Ladieux soccer net.

Ed stood behind Marty and hollered, "Down, Set, Hup, Hup," and the ball was snapped. The defensive lineman charged in and bowled Gil right over. If Slime hadn't reached out and tripped him, the lineman would have been on Ed before the quarterback could set up. From the ground, Gil saw legs moving upfield so he assumed Hairball had caught the pass.

Gil slowly got back to his feet after he heard the whistle. His head felt woozy.

"Tripping!" the defender hollered at Calais.

"Clumsy," Travis Snyder growled.

Hairball had made their very first first-down, and was strutting back to the huddle.

"That's what *I'm* talking about," Stilts hollered, pumping his fist in the air.

"Settle down, guys," Ed cautioned. "It's gonna be a long game."

Gil was ready for the next rush, and as the game wore on he learned to be more flexible, to bend but not break. After the first adrenaline high, the Ladieux defence tired as well. Midway through the first half, Nathan caught a long pass and the drive stalled on the ten-yard line, close enough for a field goal. Then Ladieux came back on the next series and went the distance on a sweep to the left. At halftime it was 8–3 in favour of the Canadiens.

Calais came over to the Rawling sideline and asked Edith to set the stopwatch for exactly ten minutes. Then they would get the second half underway. Gil looked around at the team, all either sprawled on the ground or bending over with their hands on their knees, trying to breathe.

"Ho-kay, good first half, guys," Red said. "Excellent D, Roland. Now we just gotta get the offence humming, and we're home free."

"What do you want us to hum, Red?" Hairball snarled.

"It was just an expression. You guys are doing great, too."

Roland agreed. "A couple of breaks, a bounce our way for once, and you'd have already blown this wide open. Right, Ed?"

Ed nodded. "We've got 'em right where we want 'em, boys."

Howie had noticed that Travis Snyder's t-shirt was torn around the neck and dug out a new one from the box. Travis refused to switch.

"But there's blood on the shoulder, too," Howie said.

Trent piped up, "Yeah-yeah, but it ain't his."

When Howie gave Red the injury report, it wasn't as bad as Gil had feared. They would all be stiff and crippled tomorrow, but for now only Joey had a pulled hamstring and Roland's cowboy friend had a knee acting up. They were both icing their aches and wanted to keep playing. The cowboy said the borrowed runners were uncomfortable and he promised to play better in his boots. Howie convinced him to try a series in just his socks.

Gil saw LeClair coming across the field so went out to meet him.

"Gil, it is a close one, *oui?*"

"Yeah, we're hanging in there," Gil said.

"But it's what I would expect," LeClair said. "Rawling, it is full of competitors."

"As is Ladieux," Gil said.

"Mais oui, but our real sport is the hockey," LeClair said smugly.

Gil squeezed his lips together and counted to eight. He was grateful that no one else from the Rebels had heard the comment. "Is that hotel thing still on?" he asked.

"Cer-tain-ly. We have one whole section saved for you. I already tell them you're coming."

"We're planning on it," Gil said. "That's the first stop on the bus route."

"That's good. Is there anything else you need?"

"No, I think we're okay." Gil thought for a second. "Oh, maybe a few more points?"

LeClair pondered that and chuckled. "That's good," he said as he walked away.

Red grabbed Gil's arm back at the sidelines. "What did Frenchie want?"

Gil looked at Red's strained face. "He said that they were protesting the game because our middle linebacker's an American. We were only supposed to play with Canadian citizens."

"I knew it," Red said, crumpling his black leather Pioneer Grain cap and flinging it onto the ground. "You get close and they pull every dirty trick they know." His face was almost purple, and for a second Gil was afraid to tell him the truth.

"Sorry, Red," he said, picking up the cap and handing it back. "I was just stringing you along. He wanted to know if we were going to the hotel after the game."

BANG! Edith fired the starter pistol to signify the end of the half-time show. Red put his cap back on his head and called for everyone to huddle around him.

"Okay, they kick off to us now," he said. "Nathan and Stilts are back to receive. Let's go get 'em." Everyone put an arm into the middle except Hairball, who put in both arms and a leg. They yelled "One, Two, Three, Rebels!" The Rawling fans cheered as the offence ran out onto the field to accept the kickoff.

The second half got rough. The break had allowed the players to catch their breath and to remember, or overhear others talking about, cheap shots taken by the other side in the first half.

"Did you see that shove on Eddie after he threw the ball? They know that's his sore shoulder."

"We gotta protect him."

"Yeah, and that guy wearing the bandana, he elbowed me every time he blitzed. He's not getting through next time."

"Their receivers run right at you off the line. They'd knock you down if you didn't move."

"Let 'em try. You've got a right to defend your space."

On the kickoff, one of Ladieux's speedier guys was

cutting around to touch Nathan, who had caught the ball, when the cowboy showed good steer-wrestling form by grabbing him around the neck and twisting him to the ground. The tackle sprang Nathan for another five strides but referee Calais called it holding and Rawling was moved back ten yards from the point of the infraction. On the next running play, Nathan on a sweep to the left, Monsieur Bandana sliced through the blockers and performed a shoestring tackle. While both players were down, Marty lost his balance and fell, elbow-first, onto the bandana. Players from both teams tumbled on, and it looked like an old-fashioned dog-pile. Calais and Paulhus were running around the edge of the pile, blowing their whistles and trying gingerly to separate players. It was a scene from a bad wrestling match.

Gil was helping get the players apart when he saw Red and some of the defence start onto the field. He moved to intercept them.

"Hold on there, Red. We've got it under control."

"Yeah-yeah, just want a closer look," Trent Snyder said, pushing forward.

Red looked at Gil, who said, "Outnumbered and on their turf. This is not the time, Red."

Roland Stenson said, "Sorta reminds me of the Little Bighorn."

Curly Harrison mumbled, "Into the Valley of Death rode the fifteen."

"Not today, Curly," Gil said. "Maybe next weekend, for the return match."

The guys chuckled at that and some of the tension drained.

"Ho-kay, back up and get off the field, defence," Red said.

When Gil turned around, he saw that LeClair was shooing the Ladieux extras off. He also noticed two Mounties standing in the Ladieux crowd. There was a detachment stationed in town, so it may have been coincidental that they showed up right then. One of the players could even have been an off-duty RCMP. Maybe Monsieur Bandana's red kerchief was hiding a Mountie buzzcut.

Everyone unpiled and the two teams split apart. Calais blew his whistle again, loud and long.

"Captains!"

Gil and LeClair jogged over to where Calais and Paulhus were standing.

"Guys, you've got to get control of your teams."

"The game's two-hand touch," Gil said. "Not tackle."

"We don't start," LeClair answered, "but we can finish."

"Both sides have been too aggressive at times," Calais said. "Anything more like what we just saw and I'll call the game."

"We all have to work tomorrow," Paulhus said. LeClair and Gil both looked at him so Paulhus continued. "Well okay, tomorrow's Sunday, but you know what I mean."

"And if this game is called, the score stays like now?" LeClair asked.

"No, it'd be a tie," Gil said.

Calais nodded. "Draw."

"I tell my team, don't start anything," LeClair said. "You guys watch penalties better, and we play the game fine."

"Then do it," Calais said. "We'll take a break and start again once that's understood."

Gil waved his offence to the Rawling sidelines, where they mingled with the defence.

"You okay, Nathan?" Curly asked.

Nathan was rubbing his scraped arm. "I was until Marty landed on me."

"I tripped. Lucky I landed on their guy first."

Travis Snyder growled, "Next time, we're all going in."

Gil held up his hands and Red, standing right beside him, hollered, "Ho-kay, quiet!"

"Guys," Gil said, "there can't be a next time. Any more of that and the ref will call the game."

"Yeah-yeah, so?"

"So," Hairball said, "we came to play football, not brawl."

"Easy enough for you, Hairball, you're a receiver," Slime said. "Try blocking on the line for a play or two."

"Hey, anybody who wants to switch, just say the word," Hairball said.

Ed said, "They're after me every time I take the snap, guys. I say the best way to rub their noses in it is to beat them."

"Right on," Stilts said.

"On their home field, too," Roland Stenson added.

"Okay, let's do it," Gil said. "But remember, keep a cool tool."

One, Two, Three, Rebels!

The game started again, with each team not quite as intense as before. Monsieur Bandana had stopped blitzing and, by hanging back in the secondary, picked off a pass that Ed had meant for Stilts over the middle. He might have returned it all the way but Gil had the angle and forced him out of bounds at the twenty-yard line. A quarterback draw and two short passes later, they crossed the goal line to give Ladieux a 15-3 lead. In the very next series, Ed pitched the ball to Nathan on what looked like a normal sweep left. However, Nathan held up and threw a wobbly pass back across the field to a wide-open Stilts, who galloped all the way into the end zone. Hairball missed the convert and it was 15-9 for Ladieux.

While the teams were getting organized for the kick-off, referee Calais checked with Edith on the time. Then he told each team captain, "Six minutes left in the game."

Gil was off with the offensive unit and heard Red shout, *Let's hold 'em, D.* Fans on both sidelines were standing and clapping. The upcoming job interview floated into his mind and hung there like a dark cloud, and he wished that he could freeze time forever.

Marty came over and said, "Ed wants to talk with all the offence."

Gil moved to where the players were gathering around Ed. "We're not gonna have much time," Ed was saying, "so let's hustle out there. First sequence we won't even huddle, see if we can catch them off guard. Here's what we'll do." He outlined a running play and Hairball's buttonhook. "They'll be expecting the long bomb," he said, "but there's still lots of time if we're prepared and don't waste it."

Slime had been keeping an eye on the field and now said, "They're punting."

"Okay, let's keep our composure," Ed said. "Don't panic. Remember, it's ours to win, theirs to lose."

After a short punt, the offence took over around midfield. When they lined up the first time without a huddle, the Ladieux defence was ready for them, but when they did it again on second down, Gil could see some confusion. Hairball was open on his buttonhook and made the first down.

The next play called was another pass to Hairball. Gil was sliding back, getting set to block his man when Monsieur Bandana cut through again on the blitz. Gil turned, trying to push him outside, and their knees banged together. They both went down and Gil's original block ran past them untouched. Ed tried to evade the rush by turning back, but was eventually nabbed for a big loss. Monsieur Bandana hopped up and limped back to his side of the line. Gil tried to stand but his left knee gave out and he crumpled.

"Man down," Slime yelled.

Calais blew the whistle. Howie came out onto the field and knelt beside Gil.

"Can't put any weight on it," Gil told him.

"Better sit out a series," Howie said.

He helped Gil up and as they slowly made their way off the field, Travis Snyder trotted past them to take Gil's spot. At the sideline, Gil let go of Howie and turned back to watch the game, leaning against Roland instead. His knee wasn't numb anymore, it was on fire. He tried to put some weight on the left leg and stumbled. Red's wife Donna came over with her lawn chair and insisted that he sit in it.

On second down and twenty-five to go, Ed tried to cross up the Ladieux defence by running the quarterback draw. He got five back, but then was shut down.

Red hollered over at Edith, "How much time left?"

"Two-eighteen," Edith said.

"Time out," Red yelled in to Ed. "Call a time out."

Ed ran up to Calais and signaled for a time out. The referee shrugged and said, "Why not? I count to thirty real slow."

Normally on third down Ed and Curly Harrison came out and Travis and Roland went in as added blocking for Hairball's punt. Travis had already gone into the game as a replacement for Gil, so someone else would have to go in. Gil looked over to see who Red would send. Red was waving the team in towards him. Gil pushed himself up using the arms of the chair. Roland grabbed him by the armpit and helped him hop over on his right leg.

There was silence for a few seconds while Red gathered his thoughts, so Gil stated the obvious. "Third and long, guys. Punt and hold 'em deep."

Red looked around at the team. "Thanks, Gil, but I'm thinking of something else."

"What's that?"

Red grinned and put one arm around Gil's shoulder and the other around Roland, pulling them closer. "Ho-kay, let's razzle-dazzle 'em," he whispered, and started explaining.

Roland walked onto the field with Gil holding onto his arm and hopping along beside him. As they passed Calais, who was concentrating on the time out countdown, they stopped.

"26...27...28...you going back in?"

"Gonna give it a shot, ref," Gil said, and then added quietly, "Heads-up out here. Trick play. Keep an eye on our sidelines."

Calais shrugged and then blew the whistle to signal the end of the time out.

Gil heard Red yell, "Ho-kay, let's get that punt deep and hold 'em."

Then they were in the huddle. The players all had their heads down. Gil said, "Third and long, guys, with two minutes left. They think we're punting."

Hairball quickly looked up at him and said, "But we're not?"

"Well, Red figures punting makes for boring foot-ball."

"All right," Stilts said.

Gil cleared his throat. "Listen up. When we break the huddle, Stilts and Ed help me off to the sidelines. Curly, you stay in to block in my spot. Everybody needs to move around so we're harder to count, and line up like we're going to punt. Stilts, don't step out of bounds and don't go over the line of scrimmage. The refs are on the lookout. When Hairball gets the snap, he fakes the punt and hits Stilts on the streak pattern down the sideline."

"The bloody sleeper," Travis whispered.

"I can't throw it that far," Hairball said.

"You have to," Roland said. "Anyone else back there's gonna make them suspicious."

"How about I pitch it to Nathan? He can throw."

"That'll take too long," Ed said. "You're way back there getting the long snap."

Stilts grinned. "I like it," he said.

"Me, too," Marty said. "Gutsy."

"Let's do it," Slime said.

"Yeah-yeah, I'm in," Trent echoed.

"You know what to do?" Hairball asked, poking Stilts, who nodded.

"Hairball, on what count do you want Marty to snap?" Ed asked.

"Right away, before they figure it out."

"Okay, as soon as you're in position, holler *Hup,* and Marty snaps."

Marty nodded. "Let's do it."

Gil hopped to the sidelines, held up between Stilts and Ed. Stilts stopped just short of stepping out of bounds and turned to watch the play like everyone else on the sidelines. Gil kept his hand on Ed's arm, feeling heavy and helpless. He knew he should be out there on the field, taking care of things. But today there was nothing more he could do. The goofs were on their own.

Rawling's players on the field were jostling each other and switching places in confusion. Nathan moved back and forth from one side to another. Hairball yelled "HUP." Marty snapped.

Gil had an excellent view from where he stood on the sidelines. There was no rush because the Ladieux players were all retreating to set up their blocking for the punt return. They stayed clustered in the middle because that's where Hairball had been punting the ball all day. Stilts started trotting downfield along with a few other players, looking like part of the sideline crowd. Hairball took three steps, holding the football out like he was going to kick it and then stopped. He took another two steps, turned the football around and cocked his arm, looking down the sideline.

Gil saw LeClair look back over his shoulder to where Hairball was standing and then over to the sideline, where Stilts was now streaking. "Sleeper!" LeClair yelled. "The damned sleeper!"

Hairball stepped up and released the most perfect spiral that Gil had ever seen. It floated and spun like you sometimes see in a movie. Time did stand still. Stilts had those long legs gobbling up the yards, and no one was going to catch him. When he stretched up both arms toward the floating ball, his fingers broke through the dark clouds and Gill felt so light he could have floated right out of town.

HURDLES

Randy was one of the boys from Milroy who discovered that the deserted railway station's wooden platform was ideal for shinny. It was fairly smooth, assuming they kept the weeds pulled from between the planks. The playing surface easily held a dozen players, and there was no road traffic so the nets never had to be moved. They could yell and holler as much as they wanted, re-enacting the exploits of their favourite NHL stars, especially Bryan Trottier, the local hero from Val Marie.

Trains still rumbled down the tracks past the station twice a week, pulling boxcars to and from Milroy's single Pool elevator, but the railway station itself was closed forever. Freight was hauled by truck and Randy couldn't remember ever seeing a passenger train.

As Randy stood on the platform under the shade of the peaked roof today, though, he wasn't preparing to play ball hockey. He was alone, waiting for his gym teacher. Mr. Petrie had said he would drop by sometime after two o'clock. Randy had been at the abandoned railway station since one.

Randy finished bending at the waist and touching his toes. He brushed some small stones away from a spot on the platform and sat down. He bent one leg behind him and slowly leaned forward in the hurdler's stretch, clasping his hands around the front foot. He brought his forehead down to touch his knee and held the stretch for a count of ten. Then he switched legs.

This was Randy's first year at Kendal High School. School in Milroy only went to grade eight. Students from grade nine and up were bused the eighteen kilometres to Kendal. Here in Milroy, Randy had been the only boy in his grade, along with five girls, but at Kendal there were enough students to fill up two classrooms of grade nines. Randy had been nervous the first morning his bus pulled up to Kendal High, but then he saw something that made him smile – a real gymnasium. Back in Milroy the schoolyard had only a ball diamond, swings, and two teeter-totters. During the winter they had to play dodge ball in the basement. Randy was awed at the thought of organized physical education classes and playing sports indoors, where the games could continue rain or shine, and the ball could be thrown overhand without hitting the ceiling.

The first thing he noted on the class schedule his homeroom teacher handed out was that the school routine included two physical education classes every six-day cycle. While the boys from both classes combined to take Phys. Ed., the girls were taught health, and vice versa.

Before the first Phys. Ed. class, Randy had waited until most of the other boys left before changing into his T-shirt, gym shorts, and runners. He wasn't used to taking his clothes off in front of a room full of strangers. Lately Randy had been noticing peach fuzz in embarassing spots on his body. What if someone else noticed, and pointed it out to the rest?

By the time he got out to the gym, the Phys. Ed. teacher was already talking. Randy had pictured all Phys. Ed. teachers as tall, tanned, and muscular, but Mr. Petrie was short, skinny, and pale. He had strands of hair looping from beside one ear over the top of his balding head to the other side. His T-shirt hung on him like it was still on the hanger. Watching him explain how to properly stretch before and after jogging, Randy had a vision of doing that himself – teaching the proper techniques, bringing out the best in the players, and coaching championship teams.

At the end of class, Mr. Petrie had gathered them together in the centre of the gym floor.

"Since you're all new to our school, either from Elementary or out of town, we have a couple of teams that you may be interested in trying out for," he said. "This year, the grade nines and tens will both play on our junior volleyball and basketball teams. You play other towns in the division. It's good preparation for grade eleven, when you can try out for the senior squad."

There was a buzz of excitement.

"Volleyball starts first. We're having a tryout practice after school this Thursday."

Then he looked right at Randy, smiled, and as if he was psychic, answered a question that had been nattering in the back of Randy's head. "If you've never played before, don't worry. We're here to teach the skills." Mr. Petrie put his hands above his head, jumped straight up, flicked his wrists and watched his phantom jump shot swish through an imaginary basketball net. "Athletic ability and a desire to learn are enough. We can teach you the rest."

Randy smiled back, feeling he had made a friend. Mr. Petrie barked at everyone to hit the showers.

When Randy tried out for the junior volleyball team, he wasn't the only one from Milroy. Gerry Wall from grade ten was also at tryouts. Gerry's mom gave them a ride home after the first practice because she worked in Kendal's Royal Bank. At their second practice, Randy was one of three boys trying to jump up at the net and block shots while the lineup on the other side practised spiking the ball. Coach Petrie blew the whistle and everyone stopped.

"Mister..." he said questioningly, looking right at Randy.

"Carter. Randy Carter, from Milroy."

"Mister Carter," Mr. Petrie said, slowly walking out onto the middle of the gym floor. "You *are* allowed to jump in Milroy, aren't you? I mean, there's no law against it, is there? Nothing in the water that turns your feet into cement lumps?"

"No, sir."

"Well then, jump, dammit! No use going up if your hands don't ever get above the net. Now, jump, jump. Everybody, to the net and jump."

Mr. Petrie came over behind Randy, put both hands on Randy's waist just above the hips, and growled, "Bend those knees a bit for a better push. Now jump."

As Randy jumped, Mr. Petrie boosted him another three inches, so both Randy's hands were fully above the top of the net. "That's the height you need, if you're going to successfully block a ball coming over. Now let's do it again...and again."

On the way home, Gerry was sitting in the front seat beside his mother and turned around to say, "Personal attention. I think Mr. Petrie likes you, Randy. That's good. You've got the team made."

"He made me look stupid. *Do you have cement feet?* I don't get it. What's he trying to prove?"

"I played basketball for him last year, and my advice is, don't bother trying to figure him out," Gerry said. "Just keep your head down and work hard. He has his favourites, and maybe you're one of them, but I like it fine being ignored."

"I wish I was as tall as you. You can almost touch the top of the net without even jumping."

Gerry's mom said, "You'll get your growth spurt yet, Randy. Gerry just shot up last winter. Every time I turned around, he needed another..."

"Pair of shoes," Gerry and Randy both finished for her.

"I hope you're right," Randy said, "but I think a lot of it's in the genes. Since none of my uncles are over five foot six, I think my spurt'll be a fizzle."

For the next two weeks Randy took Gerry's advice. He practised hard, listened to everything Coach Petrie told them, and tried to please. When the sheet listing the team roster had been posted, his name was one of the twelve.

Mr. Petrie had seemed in a very frisky mood during Randy's first Phys. Ed. class after the team had been named. He divided the class into three groups, and had them rotating through three stations: a half-court volleyball game, tumbling on mats, and doing calisthenics. Every seven minutes the groups would switch, with Mr. Petrie clapping his hands and herding the boys from one location to the next. At the end of the class, he said, "All right, everyone hit the showers. Mr. Carter, can you give me a hand with the mats and balls?"

The storage room was at the back of the gym. The mats were stacked at the back and all balls were kept in big wire containers along the side wall, divided according to sport: basketballs, volleyballs, soccer balls, footballs, softballs. Randy was carrying three volleyballs into the storage room when he accidentally bumped Mr. Petrie. Mr. Petrie chuckled and gave Randy a small push on his way out. By the time Randy had tossed the balls into their proper place, Mr. Petrie was back at the door with a mat.

"Grab the other end, Carter," he said, smiling as he swung the mat so that it thumped Randy's chest.

Randy said, "Hey, watch it," as he staggered back a step. Mr. Petrie wiggled the mat as they carried it, making it hard to hang onto.

"What's the matter, Carter?" Mr. Petrie smirked, sounding like a kid himself, "Can't take it?"

Randy tugged and then quickly pushed on his end, causing Mr. Petrie to stumble. "Touché," Mr. Petrie said as they laid the mat down along the back wall. "Let's carry two next time."

They pushed and jostled through the five minutes of cleanup. Mr. Petrie fired the last volleyball into the storage room at Randy's head. While Randy was ducking, Mr. Petrie moved in, grabbed him around the shoulders, and tried to wrestle him onto the pile of mats. Randy squirted loose, sliding out the door and into the gym.

"Hit the showers," Mr. Petrie said, swinging the door shut and clicking the combination lock.

Randy looked forward to the after-school practice that afternoon. Now that he had made the team, he was obviously *in*. Coach Petrie was a good guy, and Randy was lucky to have a teacher like him. Playing volleyball and being seen goofing with the coach would help Randy fit into his new surroundings.

After school, everyone was changed and out on the court before Mr. Petrie appeared, clapping his hands. "Okay, get warmed up, stretched out. You know the drill, let's move it."

Randy tried to catch Mr. Petrie's eye as he strode by, to give him a smile or a wink, but didn't get a chance. The boys were divided into two teams and simulated game situations, with Mr. Petrie stopping the play regularly to comment.

"Set, Set, Spike. That's two sets, then the spike. Associate this fact with something that your little brain can remember. How many hands? Two. How many feet?

Two. How many eyes? You got it. How many sets? Two. Okay, let's start over."

"The serve goes *over* the net. Forget that fancy stuff. We'll work on power and placement later. It's pretty basic: if that ball doesn't go over, you've eliminated any chance we have to score."

"*Mister* Carter. A bump needs both arms hitting the ball at the same time. You could snap one of those toothpicks if you're not careful. Worse than that, we get called for a double hit. Everyone over to the wall; practise your bumps."

At the end of an hour, they were ordered to run around the gym fifteen times each way. Anyone not done in twenty minutes had to do it again. Randy finished with a minute to spare and collapsed near the door to the locker room. Gerry, who had sprained his ankle after drilling home a particularly nasty spike, was the only one still hobbling around when the twenty minutes were up. As Gerry limped in and slumped down the cool cindercrete wall beside Randy, Mr. Petrie hollered over, "Mister Wall, since your ankle is obviously hurting, and you did manage to complete the run, I see no point in making you repeat. Fifty push-ups will suffice. Mister Carter, please count them off as he pumps."

Mr. Petrie headed for the door without looking at anyone, throwing over his shoulder, "Practice again tomorrow, same time, same channel."

That day's pattern was typical of Randy's relationship with the teacher. One minute Mr. Petrie was friendly, playful; the next he was an iceberg. Regardless of his mood, Mr. Petrie was always fair during the games. They played other junior teams in their school division, and everyone got on the court for at least one set each game. By the end of the season, Randy had turned into an above average setter, and a reliable server. Still, on the days when the coach was friendly, Randy sometimes felt more like the mascot along to amuse rather than a valuable member of the team. The times that Mr. Petrie was distant, Randy wondered what he had done to annoy the coach and what he could do to reverse the treatment.

R andy stood up from the railway station platform, brushed the dirt off his bum. His green sweatpants had a yellow stripe down the outside of each leg, with TITANS printed in white letters. All the boys teams at Kendal High were called Titans, and the girls were Titanettes. Randy peeled off the sweatpants. Underneath he wore green gym shorts with KHS printed on the front of the left leg. He stood with his legs shoulder-width apart, arms in front of his body, and twisted his shoulders and head as far as he could, first one way and then the other. As he was twisting, his shorts started to slip down his skinny hips. He stopped to undo and then retighten the string inside the waistband.

The sun was hot at the station, beating down on the platform. The shadows were shrinking as it got closer to mid-afternoon. The smell of oil and tar rose from the wooden ties, and grasshoppers whirred in the long grass alongside the tracks. Randy picked up his sweatpants and put them on the window ledge. He put his right foot up on the ledge while he tightened the laces in his runner. He could see his calf muscles bulge, and he ran his hand up and down his lower leg. Then he switched feet to tighten the other runner. Moving out of the shade over to the edge of the platform, he stepped down onto the gravelled edge of the track. He lifted and shook each leg as he stepped over the first rail and moved to the middle, directly between the two rails.

The weeds alongside the railway tracks were tall for so early in the year, some up to Randy's knees. Weed control along this stretch of track wasn't a priority for the CPR crews, and yellow clover and sowthistle arched over the dandelions and speargrass.

Randy started stepping on each tie, walking faster and faster in the direction of the Pool elevator. As he picked up speed, the ties were too close together to step smoothly on each one, so he started landing on every second one. He then practised jumping a couple of times, leaping forward over two ties. As soon as he got into a running rhythm, he started to count: one, two, three, four, five, jump; one, two, three, four, five, jump. Once he reached the elevator he slowed down to a walk, catching his breath while still moving. He checked his watch: one thirty-five. He should have brought a canteen of water from home. He felt the top of his head, how hot it was. He should also have worn a hat. He turned around and started running back toward the station.

The week that volleyball season ended, with a convincing loss in the semifinals, the notice had gone up for junior basketball tryouts. When Randy went to the gym, he was joined by twice as many hopefuls as had tried out for volleyball. Gerry was there again, and whispered to Randy that most of the guys thought volleyball was wimpy. Randy stuck with it throughout the entire camp, but knew his chances of making the final twelve were slim. The basketball appeared to have a mind of its own, hopping away whenever he tried to look up from his dribbling. The hoop seemed to shrink when he got ready to shoot. Mr. Petrie provided some guidance, but Randy understood that the coach needed to spend time rating the more skilled players. Randy's lack of skill, combined with being a dwarf in a giant's sport, had him prepared when his name wasn't on the list when the team roster was posted.

"Practise your shooting," Mr. Petrie told him in class after the roster had gone up. "You'll be there next year. You've got good hand-eye coordination. Practise dribbling with your head up. You could be the guy bringing the ball upcourt for us next year."

Randy told his parents that he had decided not to play basketball because it interfered with the hockey season. He also said that it would be better not having to travel so much on the winter roads. His mother agreed, saying she was pleased that he had put so much thought into the decision. His dad looked up from the newspaper at Randy and mumbled, "Cut, eh?" Randy had nodded.

Gerry made the team, along with three other guys from volleyball, so Randy sometimes stayed in after school to watch. On Saturdays, if he wasn't playing hockey, he came in with the Walls to watch the team play.

"How's school going, Randy?"

"Fine, Mrs. Wall."

"I do believe you're growing."

"I'm not so sure, Mrs. Wall."

"Well, you'll soon have your growth spurt. Why, when Gerry started his, it seemed like every time I turned around..."

"I know, he needed a new pair of shoes."

Mr. Petrie started asking Randy to help out during the games, especially with tournaments. Randy either kept score or ran the clock. Mr. Petrie soon discovered that Randy was amazingly accurate at keeping statistics: shooting percentage, free throws, and penalties in the opposition's end. Randy found it fun being involved. Instead of being a student in Mr. Petrie's class, or a player on the team, he was like an assistant coach, providing information that could help their team win. This practical experience would be useful when Randy went on to become a Phys. Ed. teacher himself.

Of course some of the team members were jealous of his position. Sometimes when he walked by the bench he could tell they had been talking about him. He could feel their eyes following his progress over to where Coach Petrie was standing. Once while Gerry and he were waiting at the front entrance for Mrs. Wall to give them a ride home, Randy had asked why the guys always talked about him.

Gerry said, "They're wondering why you hang

around all the time, that's all. They just don't know you. I tell them you're okay."

"Thanks, Gerry."

"Why *do* you come along? I didn't know you liked basketball."

"I'm thinking of being a Phys. Ed. teacher."

Gerry thought for a few seconds. "That's good. Coach Petrie has a lot of knowledge, regardless of what people say."

"What's that mean?" Randy had asked, but Gerry wouldn't elaborate.

"Forget it," he said. "Rumours."

On the Saturday of the mid-season tournament, Randy scorekept three straight games. Mr. Petrie came over and told him to go into the teachers' lounge and pick out a pop from the fridge. The lounge was just outside the gym doors. It was normally off-limits to the students, reserved as a place where teachers could go and relax between classes. Randy hesitated at the door, then knocked loudly before turning the knob and walking in. The bright fluorescent lights showed him that the room was empty. Even though it was a lot smaller than he had thought, Randy was still curious. There were two La-Z-boy recliners in corners, four old couches in the middle of the room surrounding a coffee table loaded with ashtrays, and stacking stools along the wall. Even the six padded metal chairs around the arborite tabletop seemed special. Randy walked to the back, where there was a little narrow kitchen. It held a hotplate, fridge, cupboards, and coffee maker. Randy made an effort to remember everything he saw, so he could repeat it to

Gerry on the ride home. He opened the fridge, pulled out a root beer, and was looking for a bottle opener when the door opened and a man came in.

Randy moved out of the kitchen to where the man could see him better. He was just sitting down on the couch and lighting a cigarette. He had wavy blond hair and was wearing a Saskatchewan Roughrider jersey. He glanced up and saw Randy.

"Well, hello there. Thought I was alone. Are you the new principal?"

Randy shook his head and held up the root beer. "Mr. Petrie sent me in here for a pop. Would you have a bottle opener?"

The man pointed back to the kitchen. "Try the drawer by the coffee pot. If it's not there, bring me a spoon and I can open it for you."

Randy turned around to look while Mr. Roughrider continued talking.

"You must be one of the basketball players. No uniform, though. Are you injured?"

The bottle opener was in the drawer. Randy opened the bottle and turned around. "I was keeping score. I play volleyball."

"What's your name?"

"Randy Carter."

"Hmmm, I don't remember teaching any Carters," he said, sucking on his cigarette. "I spent the last three years at the Elementary. You must be new."

"We live in Milroy."

"Well, that explains it. I'm Mr. Warriner. I teach Chemistry from grade ten up."

"Nice to meet you," Randy said.

"Say, there wouldn't be another root beer in the fridge, would there?"

"I could look," Randy said.

"If there is, could you open one and bring it to me?"

As Randy handed Mr. Warriner the pop, the teacher said, "So how are things going for you at Kendal High?"

"Pretty good."

"Bit different than Milroy, I expect."

Randy nodded.

Mr Warriner took a sip and said, "So you're helping with the tournament?"

"I help Coach Petrie wherever I can."

"He's a good strategist," said Mr. Warriner. "The senior boys basketball team won Provincials last year. He coached them all the way."

"Do you coach the football team?" Randy asked.

Mr. Warriner laughed. "No, I'm just a fan. See, I'm wearing number 23. That was Ronnie Lancaster's number, the greatest quarterback the Riders ever had." He took a drag on his cigarette and the smoke curled up to almost cover the eye that was still closely watching Randy. "So, things are going okay, then?"

Randy nodded. "I should get going. There's one more game."

"See you around, Randy," said Mr. Warriner. "Thanks for the drink."

As Randy closed the door, he could tell that the teacher was still watching him.

The players were on the court warming up, passing the balls and shooting baskets. Mr. Petrie came over to

Randy's table at centre court just as he was sitting down.

"Everything set, Mister Carter? Have you received both teams' lists for the official game sheet?"

"Yes, sir, I got yours. The other coach just told me to copy it from the last game."

"Technically they must provide a list before each game. However, if you've already copied them onto the game sheet for him, we'll let it go." He turned away, saying over his shoulder, "Remember next time, it's his responsibility."

Randy tried drawing the conversation out. "I met Mr. Warriner."

Coach Petrie stopped. "Where?"

"Just now, in the teacher's lounge."

"Those people *do* need their nicotine fix, don't they. And?"

"Nothing," said Randy. "He was nice. He said you were a good strategist."

"That's good. He can be a bit too nosy for a science teacher. He didn't ask why you were in there?"

"No. He had a pop, too. He kept a close eye on me, though."

Coach Petrie said, "Oh well, no harm done." Then he turned and walked toward the home team bench.

"Good luck, coach," Randy said to Mr. Petrie's back.

The junior Titans basketball team won the midseason tournament. Later that spring they won the divisional championship on a nineteen-point game by Gerry Wall, and an aggressive new defensive scheme that

Coach Petrie introduced during the last month of the season.

With basketball season over, the school's jocks had turned their focus to track-and-field. Phys. Ed. periods and noon hours were spent evaluating the students' natural talent and determining which events they should compete in. Most students were interested in the evaluations because they were allowed to miss some classes while they practised their events, and also be away the entire day of the track-and-field meet.

Like the other sports, these events were a first for Randy. In Milroy they had held a Field Day that everyone participated in, with events like ball throw and the 60-yard three-legged race. If you won, you got a red ribbon and if you lost, you got a white ribbon. At Kendal High it was the big time, with real events like discus, javelin, hurdles, and relay races using official metal batons. Kids from other schools in the Division came to compete and if you placed in the top three in any event, you got a crest and competed a week later at Districts. Placing in the top three at Districts meant a trip to Provincials, and a guaranteed place in School Legends.

When Mr. Petrie asked Randy what events he was going to practise for, he didn't mention that for the past two years his team had won the Egg-on-the-spoon Relay. Randy had given some thought to where he should devote his training time, and had decided on the longer races. He thought they might require more dedicated training and discipline rather than natural ability to be successful. When he said he was interested in the 440 and the 880, Mr. Petrie nodded and suggested he also try the hurdles.

"You're fast, have good balance, and a sense of rhythm. You're also low to the ground, which is an advantage. Remember, we only qualify our top four students in each event, and there's already a dozen names signed up for both the 440 and 880. But they all avoid the hurdles because they think it's too difficult. It only takes proper technique and dedicated practice time. We can provide one if you provide the other."

Randy thought it over and came up with three things he liked about the hurdles before jumping over a single one: first, there would be fewer competitors so he might actually qualify for the meet; second, it was possible that he could excel in an event others thought difficult; and number three, Mr. Petrie would spend some time focused on him.

"I'll do it," Randy said. "I'll give it my best shot."

"Good. Now change into your sweats and get out to the track. Go over to where the hurdles are set up. Do your stretches and then warm up by jogging along *beside* them. Get the feel for the spacing, the timing, the rhythm you'll need. I'll be out before the end of the period to give you some instructions, and we'll run through them a couple of times."

The track circled the football field, on which most of the other events had been set up. As Randy cut across to the far side where the hurdles were standing along the edge of the track, he recognized two boys from the other grade nine class walking ahead of him. He hoped they would stop at one of the other practice sites. They walked past the long-jump pit, the high-jump stand, the discus and shotput circles. They stopped at the javelin, but only long enough to each heft a spear, run up to the line and fake a throw. They dropped the javelins at the line and walked on.

When Randy reached the hurdles, the other two were sitting on the grass, legs spread apart, reaching for their toes. Randy had no idea what muscles needed to be stretched for hurdling. He felt uncomfortable, inadequate, yet was unwilling to ask the other two for advice. He moved down a couple of hurdles, bobbed up and down touching his toes, and then put the heel of his left foot on top of a hurdle. He noticed the boys watching him as he twisted back and forth. By the time he switched feet, they had each moved to their own hurdle and were also doing the one-legged twist.

At final count, five boys including Randy jogged up and down the track, timing the steps between the jumps, and ignoring each other. Only four would qualify, so one of them would be dropped. Randy watched the others. Two of them had legs the length of a giraffe's neck, and another jumped as smooth as a gazelle. Randy clung to the hope that being built low to the ground, combined with determination, would be enough to earn him a spot.

Mr Petrie came over and showed them the proper stepping rhythm to use between hurdles and the correct form to follow when jumping over. Then they all ran through the hurdles one at a time, with Mr. Petrie giving advice.

"Mr. Hughes, this is a race, not a lollygag convention. Try it again, as if winning meant a week off school. That's better."

"Bend at the hips, Jackson, don't be so straight up and down when you jump. Stretch way out with your left hand, like you're reaching for the red ribbon."

"Mr. Carter, always jump from your right foot — that's the purpose of counting steps: one, two, three, four, five, jump. One, two, three, four, five, jump. It avoids that shuffle step at the hurdle. Back in line and try it again."

Randy liked it, and for the next week practised every noon hour and Phys. Ed. period. If he had prepared a scouting report, he would have written that two of the guys were quite a bit better than him, but the other two had about the same ability. With practice, he had a shot at third and definitely at the final spot. Mr. Petrie agreed as he talked to them on Friday, a week before the track meet.

"You're all really coming along. Unless my stopwatch has slowed down, we could be in line for a record if the track's dry and the wind's behind us. Remember, we have our qualifying races on Tuesday. I'll time everyone, give you all three chances, and then take the four fastest runners. Is that fair?"

Everyone nodded.

"One last thing. Some of you have been using the hurdles after school. That's fine, but when you're finished, don't leave them spread out on the track. Carry them back over underneath the bleachers."

Randy almost choked. Practising after school? That wasn't fair for the kids from out of town. How could he compete when the others got extra practice time? He knew from experience on the volleyball team that whining to the coach would get him nowhere.

"Mr. Petrie?"

"Yes, Mr. Carter?"

"I was wondering, since I don't live in town so I can't use the hurdles, if there was anything that could help me over the weekend."

Rick Hughes piped up, "A leg transplant," and everyone laughed.

Mr. Petrie clicked his tongue at Rick's joke and said, "Time to head in and change." As they walked back to the school, he slowed to walk beside Randy and said, "What do you mean, anything to help you over the weekend?"

"Well, I can't come in to use the hurdles like everybody else, so I thought there might be some type of training or practising I could do in Milroy that would help me get ready for Tuesday's races."

"No hurdles at the Milroy school you could borrow?"

Randy shook his head. He didn't really expect a solution. He just wanted Mr. Petrie to know he was at a disadvantage regarding practice times, in case the races were really close. Then Mr. Petrie could say to himself, *If Carter can stay close to these guys after having practised so little, imagine what he could do if he had the same chance.*

"Well, you can run. Running and speed are still half the race, and you can...I know, for your timing, you can use the railroad tracks. Run along the ties, and every sixth tie, jump over one. That's a good way to work on your rhythm. Don't go too fast on them, don't practise your speed there because you could slip and twist an ankle, but it's great for timing."

Randy nodded unenthusiastically.

"I'll tell you what," Mr. Petrie said, his arm brushing against Randy's shoulder. "Assuming dry weather, I'm planning to take my convertible for a spin this weekend. If you're practising on Saturday after two, I'll stop by Milroy to see how it's going."

"Really? Where should I be?" Randy's voice sounded shrill. "I'll practise by the old railway station, at the end of Main Street. It's empty, anyhow."

Mr. Petrie shrugged and smiled. "Wherever. I'll find you."

Randy had heard about Mr. Petrie's candy-apple Mustang convertible but had never seen it. He usually walked to school. Legend had it that the convertible never came out of the garage except on special summer occasions. Randy was ecstatic. Not only would he see the coach, but also his car. If he played his cards right, he might even get a ride. More than that, Mr. Petrie was coming out to see him – *him* – on a Saturday. Sure, maybe he had planned on being in the area anyway, and maybe he felt obligated because Randy had helped out so much with basketball, but still it had to mean that he thought Randy was a bit special. How many other kids were visited by their teacher on a day off, especially when there wasn't a problem?

On the bus ride home, Gerry asked Randy why he looked so happy. Had he made the hurdle team? For a second, Randy thought of telling Gerry about the next afternoon's visit. Gerry would be surprised, and happy, but he would want to be there, too. He might even bring others. No, Randy decided he wanted Mr. Petrie to himself. He shook his head in response to Gerry's question and didn't elaborate. He sat on the bus, humming and smiling, all the way home.

Randy settled into a pattern of twenty-five jumps between the railway station and the grain elevator. He was so hot that he felt like taking his T-shirt off. He would have, if he hadn't been expecting company. Randy hopped up onto the platform and then over to the side of the railway station, under what little shade it provided. He checked his watch – two-o-eight – and no sign of the red convertible. He wondered if Mr. Petrie would bring along someone for the ride, like maybe a girlfriend.

Randy peeked around the corner of the station and down Main Street. Nothing stirred out there, no vehicles, no people, not even a dog. His mom had once said that it was the only main street she knew where you could fire a cannon down it at almost any hour, and never hit anything. *He'll be here,* Randy said to himself, *there is no doubt, he will positively show up.*

And then he did. The red convertible turned onto Main and headed straight for the station. What should Randy do? Jump out and wave? Ignore him? Go back to the tracks and keep practising? Hide? He just stood there watching around the corner as the car drove slowly toward him. It was a beautiful two-door that seemed to shimmer in the heat. The top was down and Randy could see only one head. Mr. Petrie drove down the two blocks of gravelled Main Street, going very slowly.

Randy thought he would stop the car out on the street and walk the rest of the way, but he turned up the weedy, cinder-gravel driveway. Instead of stopping at the corner of the station, Mr. Petrie gunned it and the car roared right up the ramp. It thumped over the wooden planks to the middle of the platform and came to a stop. Mr. Petrie turned off the motor.

"Good day, Mr. Carter." Mr. Petrie was wearing a Seattle Seahawks cap, and he lifted the beak up and down.

"Hello, Mr. Petrie. Sure is hot, hey?"

"The weather or the car? Ha. Both, I expect."

Mr. Petrie seemed a bit giddy. Randy wondered if he had been drinking, or if it was from the sun, riding with the roof down for too long.

"I've been practising for about an hour."

"And how's it going?"

"It works okay for the timing. The ties aren't always the same distance apart, though. I've got no idea on the height of my jumps, either."

"No." Mr. Petrie opened the car door. "Visualizing's okay as far as it goes, but there's nothing like the real thing, is there." He got out, closed the long door and patted the hood. "Want to go for a ride later?"

"Sure, a ride home would be great. Should I show you what I've been doing?"

"It's a touch warm, don't you think? Maybe we'll just sit in the shade and discuss strategy." Mr. Petrie walked over to the wall and squatted down in the shade.

"Sure thing. Do you drive through Milroy very often?"

"I drive straight through every chance I get." Smiling, he patted the ground beside him.

"I meant, when you visit here, Coach, do you drive around town very much?"

"Randy, come over here. When we're not in school or around the other students, you can call me Tim, okay?"

Randy moved over closer to where Mr. Petrie was squatting. The hat was tilted back and Mr. Petrie was squinting up. A line of sweat was slowly trickling from the hairline above his ear down toward his jaw.

"You've got the build of a runner, Randy. Slender, quick." He wiped at the sweat. "Has anyone ever told you that?"

Randy shook his head.

"I was a runner. Did I ever mention that?" He didn't wait for an answer. "Cross-country was my specialty, but I ran a respectable mile, as well."

"I'd like to try out for cross-country in the fall," Randy said.

Coach Petrie nodded. "You remind me a lot of myself as a youngster," he said, stretching out his arm. "And that look in your eye whenever you need discipline, that wanting to please, willing to do almost anything to be accepted." He stroked the calf muscle of Randy's closest leg.

Randy half-laughed and slid back a step. Mr. Petrie inhaled, stood up and lunged toward him. Randy was ready, having played this game before. He sidestepped, laughing, and ran around to the other side of the car. As Mr. Petrie came after him, Randy moved around the car, always keeping the vehicle between them. When they had made a complete circle, Mr. Petrie stopped at the drivers-side door and held up his hand.

"Okay," he said, "enough. You're leaving handprints. It really is too hot for this. Get in and we'll go for a spin."

Mr. Petrie opened the driver's-side door, got in, lifted his cap and ran his hand, front to back, through his wet hair. He tossed the cap onto the front dash and held out his right arm, hand open, toward the passenger seat, inviting Randy in. Randy was exhausted from running in the heat for the past hour. He tugged on the door handle, imagining a tall, cold glass of water. The door was big and heavy, and creaked as it swung open. He slid onto the warm white leather seat and then leaned out, using both hands to pull the door shut. It slammed and he turned to apologize. Mr. Petrie had slid over right beside him. He slipped his arms around Randy's shoulders. Mr. Petrie's face was very close, and Randy could see that even though he was still smiling, his eyes were cold, serious. His breath smelled of peppermints. Randy twisted and squirmed around so his back was to Mr. Petrie, and started throwing elbows behind him. Mr. Petrie moved even closer, stretching one arm across Randy's chest, holding down both of Randy's arms. The other arm slid down to Randy's belly. Randy shouted *Hey* and squirmed harder as he felt Mr. Petrie's fingers digging at his waistband.

The big railway station shielded the car from the rest of town. No one, not even Greg Wall, knew that he and Mr. Petrie were there. Randy's hollering, if it was heard at all, would be dismissed as a loud game of ball hockey. He was on his own. Mr. Petrie's arm across his chest was tight, much stronger than he would have thought. The other arm's fingers were pushing, wiggling, trying to get under the string holding up Randy's shorts. Randy pushed out his stomach as far as he could, trying to keep his stomach tight to the string. Mr. Petrie exhaled and pulled his hand back. Randy thought he was giving up, but the arm around Randy's chest, pinning his arms to his ribs, didn't loosen. Too late, Randy felt the palm of Petrie's other hand on the small of his back, then slide under the string. Randy kept squirming, with his legs pressed together.

The tight string rubbed and grudgingly stretched as Mr. Petrie's hand wiggled around the side and to the front. The only sound was their breathing, the small grunts as they squirmed, the squeak of the leather seats. Mr. Petrie's hand slid lower. Randy stopped his useless struggling and they both held their breath. Randy's eyes were squeezed shut, his legs pressed tight, his bum pushed as far down as it could go into the car seat. Mr. Petrie's fingers touched the curly fuzz, sliding from side to side, feeling, exploring. Randy's body was tense, waiting, waiting.

"Damn."

Mr. Petrie wriggled his hand out from under the string of Randy's shorts. He lifted his arm off Randy's chest. Randy was wary, slow to move. Was this another trick, with Mr. Petrie waiting for him to unwind, uncross his legs? He turned his head and saw that Mr. Petrie had slid back to his own side, under the steering wheel.

"I'm late," Mr. Petrie said. "Hop out, please, Mr. Carter, I'd best be going."

Randy grabbed the door handle and pushed open the door with his shoulder. He turned to keep an eye on Mr. Petrie as he slid out and shoved the door shut. It didn't close completely, but Randy made no move to push it again. Mr. Petrie didn't ask him to. Looking straight ahead, Mr. Petrie put his cap back on, started the car, put it in gear, and moved slowly forward, the uneven boards of the platform jiggling the car and rattling the passenger door. Just before going down the ramp at the far end, he raised his right hand and held it even with his shoulder for a few seconds. Randy could see that he wasn't looking in the rearview mirror for a return wave. Then the red convertible turned the corner and was gone.

Randy stayed out in the sun, the heat slowly working its way from the top of his head down through his cells one at a time, loosening the knots. As the shock melted down into his feet and drained out his toes, he started shaking. Only then did he notice the train coming out of the hazy, heat-rippled distance. He hadn't heard it earlier, when the horn would have blown loud and long at the crossing outside of town. He stayed by the edge of the platform as the train got closer, as it honked again approaching the station. People had been known to get sucked under the big steel wheels as a long train roared past. Randy noticed the boxcars swaying as they blindly followed the powerful engine down the rickety old track.

The train barely slowed as it clickety-clacked past

Randy standing at the edge of the abandoned station's platform. The engineer stuck his arm out the window, holding up his hand with fingers spread wide.

Long after the train and its noise had faded, Randy gathered up his sweats and started down the platform. His foot kicked a small stone. He stopped and looked down for a second, and then nudged it again. "Gillies," he mumbled, "has it on the wing."

Randy scuffled the stone back and forth between his feet, then booted it across the platform. "Over to Trottier streaking across centre, toward the Oiler blueline."

Randy could hear the excitement in the announcer's voice. He felt the hair on his neck move as he trotted up to another stone and kicked it.

"Trottier across to Bossy, who one-times it, kicked out by Fuhr, right in front."

He saw a third, larger stone and kicked it as hard as he could toward the corner where the red Mustang convertible had disappeared.

"They scooore. Trottier, on the rebound."

Randy raised his arms high, shouting, "Yaaahhhh, Yaaahhhh," jumping and sobbing. The sky brightened as the hot sun dried his wet cheeks. His body loosened under the embrace of Clark Gillies and then Mike Bossy, and finally the entire Islanders team as they surrounded him, shielded him, protected him.

Chickens

It was looking like another scorcher the morning Dad plotted to kill Ben. He couldn't bring himself to do the deed all by his lonesome, so he called for reinforcements.

"Corporal MacDonald, please," he said into the phone.

I was eating Corn Flakes at the kitchen table, five feet from the phone. Dad turned his back to me, as if that set up a soundproof wall between us.

"Sean? It's Lorne Jones here. I'm fine, thanks. Listen, I need a favour. Remember that problem I was telling you about? Yeah, that's him. Well, it's been getting worse. I think the time's come. Could you drop over today? Noon would be fine. See you then."

He hung up the phone but kept his hand on the receiver for a count of ten. Then he turned to me and said, "Roger, tell Mom I've gone for a run."

We lived just off the paved highway, on the old Calder homestead. Mom had grown up in Toronto and always dreamed of living in the country. Dad had started out on a farm but his family had moved in to town when he was seven. A vacant two-storey house across from the school, complete with running water and indoor plumbing, had convinced Grandma that town was the place to be. Grandpa travelled two miles out to the farm nearly every day, and that turned out to be a wise family move. Grandpa liked his solitude and would stay in the old three-room house during seeding and harvest, with Grandma shuttling meals to him, using the children as couriers. Perhaps that's where Dad first discovered his love of running, hauling a lunch bucket back and forth over those two miles of dirt road.

Dad hadn't wanted to become a farmer. He said he didn't like the uncertainty, being so dependent on out-side influences like the weather, insects, weeds, and world grain prices. He went to university instead and studied to be a teacher. He now taught math at the high school. He said that with mathematics, you always knew where you stood. The answer is the same on a hot Monday as it is on a windy Friday. Since he was the only one on staff who ran, they also appointed him coach of the school's cross-country track team.

This farmyard was as far as Dad would compromise with Mom's dream of being out in the country. We raised chickens but rented out the cultivated land. He wouldn't have agreed to even that if it hadn't been for the freedom those miles of dirt back roads could bring to his aching knees. Mom was allergic to exercise, and would tell people that the only thing she ran was a tab at Big Bob's Groceteria. She was also allergic to fur.

The first time Mom had dragged Dad out to see the Calder place, he said, "Be a shame to have a big farm-yard like this without a dog."

"As long as it stays outside," Mom answered, "that would work out fine. It can keep the chickens safe from the coyotes."

"Chickens?" Dad asked. "Coyotes?"

After walking around the yard once and refusing to step inside the Leaning Barn of Pisa, Dad had looked in the direction of town and said, "We'd need another vehicle."

"Just an old clunker," Mom answered. "It's only five miles."

"We won't be able to afford a setup like this, not on the one salary."

At the time of this conversation, I was "in the oven," as Mom explained whenever she told the story, and they had decided she should give up her Post Office job and stay home to look after me when I was born.

"They'll let us rent to own," Mom said. "It won't cost much. Mrs. Calder's in Pioneer Lodge now and wants a family living out here. If we try it for a while and don't like it, we haven't lost anything. It'll still be cheaper than the apartment we're in now."

Dad was not convinced. "You shouldn't be doing any packing and moving in your condition," he said. "Let's think about it again after the baby's born."

"It's so quiet out here," Mom had said, looking around with her arms spread wide. "Not much traffic, is there."

Dad nodded and said, "Probably get snowed in every winter."

"School bus drives right past on the highway," Mom said. "It could pick you up." Dad was frowning as he bent down to pick burrs out of his socks. She tried again. "A person could run for miles back there without seeing a soul."

Dad looked up. When Mom innocently asked, "Would those dirt roads be any good for your knees, or is the pavement better?" he shook his head, smiled, grabbed her shoulders and said, "Hush up, already."

The next afternoon when Dad got home from teaching school, Mom was sniffling on the apartment's futon. She was holding a box of Kleenex, eyes watering. In the middle of the hardwood floor, standing on the weekly newspaper, stood a ten-week-old golden retriever.

"There was a sign up in the post office," she said. "He's a purebred, but doesn't have the papers."

Dad had looked down at Mom, sitting there all smiles trying not to sneeze, and over to the dog, wagging its tail. It kept looking up at him and then over to Mom, whining softly.

Dad sighed and squatted down. "I've always liked the name Benjie," he said, petting the dog's head.

Eight weeks after Benjie arrived, so did I. We grew up together on the Calder place and somewhere along the line as he stretched into a full-grown dog, Benjie had shortened to Ben. Over the next eleven years, Mom had always made two things clear: Number one, Ben was Dad's dog and number two, he stayed outside — Ben, not Dad.

Whenever Dad was training for a race, he and Ben would disappear on the back roads for hours at a time. I was too young to tag along, but I watched the road for their return from my second-floor bedroom window. When I saw specks of movement in the distance, I ran downstairs and rode my bike out to meet them. Dad would be striding down the middle of the road while Ben switched from ditch to ditch. When they saw me coming, Ben would stretch out and race up to the bike, then turn back to Dad, speeding back and forth as the distance closed between us. I would stop the bike, plant my feet, hold out my hand and get a high-five from Dad as he glided by. Then I would turn the bike around and follow them home.

When they got back into the yard, Dad's tall, thin body would be drenched in sweat and Ben's tongue would be almost touching the ground. They both flopped, panting, onto the front veranda. I made sure that Ben's bowl was filled with fresh, cool water while Mom hand-delivered an iced tea to Dad.

Ben had grown into a large, hairy dog whose bark kept the wild animals away from the chicken coop. We tried to keep the chickens inside the wire fence that surrounded their little house. This was partly for their safety and partly so that we could find the eggs they laid. Two of them had been hit on the highway during broad daylight, and there were weasels and foxes roaming at night. Even with Ben patrolling the yard, if a hen decided to nest in the surrounding trees and bushes, it soon became the daily special at the Wildlife Café. Mom and I collected the eggs in the henhouse every morning, but she refused to search the trees in case she came across some remains. Nor did she let me.

"You learn about that side of life soon enough," she would say, "without going looking for it."

Ben turned out to be useless as a watchdog for humans. Whenever someone came into the yard, Ben bounded up and leaned against the visitor's leg, waiting to be petted. That was pathetic enough, but once he received any sign of affection, Ben would lie down and roll onto his back, begging for a tummy scratch.

I was the first one to discover a lump. Ben was lying on his back on the veranda, feet in the air as I scratched his belly. He was panting and drooling with his eyes half-shut as I scratched his stomach and watched the highway traffic. I was playing a game with myself, guessing the colour of the next vehicle that went by. If I got it right, then I could take a drink. Suddenly Ben yelped and scrambled to get up, knocking over my glass of lemonade with his back leg.

"Bad dog, Ben," I said, sliding over to avoid the puddle. He hung his head. "What's the matter, big fella?"

I thought maybe he had tangled with a porcupine and I had touched a quill. Or perhaps there were some burrs stuck in his fur. I coaxed him into lying on his back again and felt around. Using both hands to part the hair, I found a lump the size of a marble on the left side of his belly, just below the ribcage. When I touched it, he jumped again.

That night Mom told me to show Dad. By then Ben

was leery of being poked and prodded, and he didn't want to lie down. It finally took Dad to say in his sternest voice, "Ben, sit," before he would be still. Ben kept his eyes on Dad as Mom and I gently pushed him down, smoothed out his fur and pointed to the small lump.

"No problem," Dad had said. "Plugged hair follicle, or maybe a boil. He needs a good wash."

I was relieved, but Mom looked doubtful. "Maybe the vet...."

"We don't need any vet telling us our dog has a pimple," Dad said. "Not at fifty bucks a visit, we don't." Then he petted Ben's head and the dog scrambled to his feet. "Good dog, big fella," Dad said. "A good wash'll do wonders, won't it, boy?"

The next morning Mom and I washed him in a big tub, out in front of the veranda. His light brown coat shone from the shampoo. We cleaned the mud from his paws and Mom even clipped a couple of his nails. It was hard to wash his belly, though, because he flinched and whined whenever we touched that area. Mom cut some of the belly hair with scissors so we could see better.

"That's no boil," she said, her eyes watering.

"I'll dry him off, Mom," I said. "Your allergies are acting up again."

She nodded. "I'll get us some iced tea."

That evening Ben was bounding around the yard like a puppy again, pouncing on grasshoppers, drooling on Casey the cat.

"What'd I tell you," Dad said. "A clean bath and he's got a fresh lease on life. Let's go for a run, Ben."

A week later I found Ben around the side of the house, sprawled in the shade. He was whining and gently licking his belly. I could see the enlarged lump through Ben's matted hair.

I ran into the house. "Mom, Ben's got those plugged hair follicles again," I said.

Mom sniffed. "Your father will have to deal with this," she said.

Mom wanted Dad to take Ben into a vet clinic in the city on Saturday. Our local vet Doctor Barber was a large animal doctor, with what mom called *no pet compassion*. Dad said that bedside manner didn't count for much with animals, and the fee would be more at the city clinic.

"I've already made the appointment," Mom said.

I helped Ben into the front seat of the half ton, where he sat up straight and looked at us through the partially rolled-down window. Usually he rode in the back of the truck but the trip to the city would be longer than his normal ride into town or to the neighbours. Sitting in the front was also a bit of a treat. From the way he was walking now, rolling from side to side with his back legs wide apart, even I knew it wasn't plugged hair follicles.

I spent the morning patrolling around the chicken fence on my bike, making noises to scare off unwanted visitors and tossing chickens back over the wire if they escaped. Dad returned that afternoon with the news we already suspected. Tumours had spread throughout Ben's belly. The vet had taken a sample for testing, but was ninety-five percent sure it would be bad news.

"Forty-eight dollars for the exam," Dad said to Mom, "and sixty for the biopsy. He said he'd put him to sleep for another one twenty-five. I said I'd think about it."

"What's to think about?" Mom asked. "He's in pain, Lorne."

"I'm thinking what's the cost of a bullet?"

"And who's going to do that?" Mom snorted. "You? We've got gophers in our back pasture older than Ben. Cows would be safer on our farm than in India."

"Okay, Edith."

"You don't even help butcher the chickens, and not a single one of them has ever gone for a run with you."

"I get your point, Edith, but this is different." Dad thought for a second. "Besides, I'd like to bury him here."

We waited a week before the vet called back to confirm the bad news. He gave Dad two estimates — six weeks, tops, and a hundred and fifty dollars, taxes included. The next morning Dad had phoned Corporal MacDonald, whose son Sean Jr. had recently struggled with algebraic equations. Dad had stayed after school for a whole week, giving Junior extra attention. One night after supper, I had overheard Dad telling Mom that Junior reminded him of our porch light with its forty-watt bulb. Everything looked normal, but there wasn't much illumination. At parent-teacher interviews, the Corporal had said, "You ever need a favour, Mr. J., you just ask." And then he had chuckled, tugging on his big brown belt. "As long as it's legal, that is."

The RCMP cruiser pulled into the yard just before noon. All three of us went out onto the veranda to greet him. Corporal MacDonald uncoiled from behind the driver's seat and another Mountie came out the passenger's side.

"Morning, Mr. J.," MacDonald said, nodding his head in our direction. "Edith. And I suspect this is Lorne Junior."

"Roger," Dad said.

"I thought so. My first son's a Junior, too. Sean Jr."

"No," Mom said, "his name's Roger."

"Oh. This is Constable Stewart. The Jones's."

"Pleased to meet you," Mom said.

"My pleasure," said Constable Stewart.

"Stewie's a crack shot," MacDonald said, and then lowered his voice. "I thought he'd be useful."

"Appreciate that," Dad said.

"Dog's around back," Mom said, and turned to go into the house. She held out her hand to me. I was torn between following Mom and ignoring what was going to happen, or staying to support Dad. In the end I stayed, but moved away to sit on a stool. Ben's water dish was at my feet and I slid it over under the porch swing.

"What's the dog's name?" Corporal Stewart asked, unbuttoning the flap on his holster.

"B...," Dad coughed and swallowed. "Ben."

"Don't worry, sir," Stewart said. "We understand. I'll be quick."

"Behind the barn," Dad said. "Back in those elms there's a good spot."

MacDonald tilted his chin sharply toward the back

of the house. Stewart nodded and walked around the side. I heard him say "Here, Ben" and then chuckle. I could just imagine old Ben leaning into the Constable's leg and stretching into the pat. Then there was a long pause.

"I...we really appreciate this," Dad said, and coughed again.

"No problem," Corporal MacDonald said. "We may sometimes seem cold and unapproachable," he held up both hands and made quotation signs with his fingers, "but we're human, too. If we can help out in a tough or awkward situation, we will."

CRAA–ACK.

I looked up at Dad, who was staring out past the highway. His face was still and his lips were pressed together. I felt a lump in my throat but was also curious about what Ben would look like, and where we would bury him. I could visit his grave every day, and Mom could plant flowers. Maybe we would build a marker. It might even say something special, like "running on the clouds."

Constable Stewart appeared from the side of the house and nodded at MacDonald. "It's done," he said.

"Thanks, Stewie," MacDonald said, wiping an eye.

"Yes, thanks for your help, Constable," Dad said.

Corporal MacDonald walked forward and held out his hand to Dad. "I feel for you, Lorne. It's never easy, but it's over and done with now. If there's ever anything else..."

A thin howl rose from behind the house, causing us all to jump. It stopped but the sound echoed in my ears.

Then it started again, closer and stronger. Dad and I moved to the edge of the veranda and peered around the corner of the house. Ben was lying on the path between the house and barn, dragging himself toward us with his two front feet. There was blood running down his nose. A whine seemed stuck in his throat.

"Jeez Murphy," MacDonald said from below us. He quickly flipped up his holster flap and pulled out his big black gun. He held the pistol out at arm's length with both hands and pulled the trigger, BANG, BANG. I jumped with each sound, just as Ben's body jerked with each hit. MacDonald took four quick steps forward and fired again, BANG. Three more giant strides and he was right beside Ben's head. BANG.

"Tough sucker," he said, holstering his gun, "but that'll do it."

The screen door slammed. I turned around and Mom was there, taking her own giant steps toward the veranda's edge.

"Get out," she yelled, arm shaking and pointing toward the road.

"He's done, Edith," MacDonald said. "I swear that this time..."

"Get out of here," she screamed.

MacDonald looked at Dad for assistance, but Dad's eyes were closed. His arms were wrapped around his body like he was trying to keep warm and he was rocking back and forth.

Corporal Stewart moved forward. "Would you like us to help you with..." he said, waving both hands toward Ben's body.

Mom looked around, stepped back and picked up the stool that I had just been sitting on. She threw it crashing down the steps. It rolled halfway to the police cruiser.

"Now Edith," Corporal MacDonald said, "there's no need for that."

"The next thing hits somebody," she said.

Both men walked backwards toward the cruiser. As they passed the stool, Constable Stewart bent down and stood it upright. They opened the car doors and checked that the flaps over their handguns were secure before sliding in. Gravel spun as they performed a perfect three-point turn and left the yard.

"Roger, you take Dad inside," Mom said.

I reached for his hand and tugged. He opened his eyes, pulled his hand away, took a breath and straightened up.

"No, I've got to finish this," he said.

"Then we'll do it together," Mom said.

He looked at her for a long time, and the stiffness seemed to drain from his shoulders. He nodded.

"Roger," Mom said, "you go inside and see what's on TV."

"Ah, but I..."

"Roger," Dad said in that stern voice I had only ever heard him use on Ben. "Go."

I went inside and sat on the stairs that led up to my room, waiting for them to return.

For the rest of that summer, the house seemed extra quiet. Mom was as gentle as I could imagine. There was no talk of getting another dog. I started running short distances on the dirt roads with Dad. He gave me pointers about the proper stride, what part of the foot to land on, and how to breathe. When he was training seriously and went over the longer distances, I took my bike and set out paper cups filled with water on certain fence posts he was going to pass.

Dad became more involved with looking after the chickens over the summer, fixing the fence so they couldn't get out. That fall he took over the butchering for the first time. He kept the axe razor-sharp, and became very accurate with his swing.

GROUND RULES

I stopped the Cadillac at the entrance to the fair-grounds and buzzed down the window. The old fellow collecting the admission looked familiar. *Dudley* popped into my head as he bent over, turning his head and squinting with the eye closest to me. He slapped the car roof and stood up.

"Without those sunglasses, I'd say you're Fred Norman's boy," he said, daring me to deny it. "Freddy Junior. Been a long time."

"Ten years," I said.

"That's what I'm saying. Got something for you." Dudley reached under the card table that his cash box was sitting on and pulled out a black garbage bag. FRED JR. was printed in red letters on masking tape. "Your Blooper uniform. They came just in time."

"Bloopers?" I asked. "I'm playing with the Alumni."

Dudley raised the bag up to the car window. "Tacky name, eh? School had a contest. I liked Alumni better myself."

He was too close, leaning in the window and drumming his fingers on the car roof. His breath smelled of snuff, and I could see the brown-stained crease on one side of his mouth. When he smiled, his top lip caught where an eye tooth was missing. I pulled the bag in and set it on the seat beside me.

"Leather buckets," Dudley said. "Very nice. Cost you a buck to get in. We usually charge out-of-towners a toonie, and Caddy drivers five, but seeing as you're Alumni, I'm letting you in at cost." He grinned.

I had a strong urge to toss the garbage bag back to old Dudley, stick the Caddy into reverse, and escape. The Bloopers. What next? Exploding softballs and clown umpires? If I hadn't just driven five straight hours, and if the nearest lounge serving decent Scotch wasn't over an hour away, I would have left right then.

Instead, I peeled off my shades and tucked them carefully into my shirt pocket. *You can never go back, Fred, it's one of Darwin's evolutionary principles.* Harvey Phillips had said that during our last weekly status meeting. He was miffed because I had declined an invitation to join him and his perky wife for an executive fondue this very night. All of the right people were going to be there, and I was the only non-partner invited. Instead, I had opted for a ball tournament in the old hometown.

I tucked a five into Dudley's shirt pocket and said, "Keep it." I buzzed up the window and accelerated, raising some dust that floated over the card table.

The invitation to the ball tournament had come in March, to the apartment I used to share with Linda. My ex wasn't talking to me by then, and had thrown all of my unopened mail into a cardboard box she left in the lobby by the security doors. I found the invitation while looking in the box for a Toastmasters plaque I wanted to hang in the study of my new condo. Mr. Ellis, my high school fastball coach, was organizing an alumni team to enter the town's annual Sports Day, on the second Saturday in June – *a chance to renew old acquaintances and have some exercise at the same time.*

My first instinct was to toss the invite and forget all about it. I had no need or desire to return to Saskatchewan's Great Southwest. My father Fred Sr. transferred out of Dolguard to the Royal Bank's Saskatoon office during my first year of university. Prior to that move, Dad's career had stagnated for over a decade in this dried-up community. A few more years and he would have remained trapped in Dolguard until retirement. This town was inescapably part of my past, but held no place in my future. Reunions didn't interest me. Exchanging rose-coloured memories of past catches or glorious home runs was a waste of billable time. A trip back wouldn't even be considered a good business decision, because the town was too far away from Saskatoon to draw any potential clientele. Besides, I wanted to attract customers with money, which wasn't something this farming community was known for.

Still, I kept the ball tournament invitation in my briefcase for over a week. One of my time management techniques is to handle paper only once before dealing with it. I picked up the invitation, reread and refiled it, twice a day for eight days. I'm not an impulsive or frivolous person, which makes me a good chartered accountant, but I have to confess that I finally decided the tournament invitation's fate by a coin toss. The single toss turned into a best of eleven before I gave up, filled out the form and sent it back. As an escape clause, I wrote along the bottom that I couldn't guarantee to stay all day.

I parked the Caddy close to the school, far enough away from the diamonds that a foul ball wouldn't hit it. I got out, carrying the garbage bag and my own small gym bag. I heard someone call my name and looked around. Up by the school entrance, our old coach Mr. Ellis was waving, motioning me over. He looked heavier than I remembered, and his hair was now more white than grey. Otherwise, he looked the same. He had been a good teacher, explaining history and geometry in a language we could all understand. I had expected him to eventually take a better job teaching in one of the cities, or to become the school district's director of education. I was prepared for his patented firm handshake but the quick hug that I got instead caught me off guard.

"It's good to see you, Junior, or do you prefer Fred now? You took so long in answering I thought you weren't coming. You almost missed out on the personalized uniforms."

"As I said, Mr. Ellis, I might not be able to stay for the whole day."

"Well, we know you're a busy man. There's a lot planned, though, including a barbecue tonight. Enjoy what you can. The others are down in the gym, putting on their uniforms. Go on down. I'm waiting for the stragglers. Barney Reynolds will be the last to show up. Not much ever changes, does it?"

I smiled and shrugged. Being stuck here, Mr. Ellis wouldn't understand how wrong he was. Only in this place did life stagnate.

On my way to the gymnasium, I looked in one of the classrooms. I was prepared for the small room, but the bare cinderblock walls and two blackboards flanking the teacher's desk, all underneath the framed picture of the Queen, gave me a chill. Out of a graduating class of eleven, I had been the only one to go on to university. Most of the boys had gone farming or migrated to the oil patch's quick money long before graduation. One girl took a hairdressing course and another took book-keeping through correspondence. Everyone else worked and went to the bar until they eventually married some-one local.

The door to the boys locker room was propped open with an old runner. A dozen men all shockingly famil-iar were inside, laughing and horsing around like kids. I gave a quick wave and hello before sitting down on the low bench. I was intent on unzipping my gym bag and examining the contents. The room was quiet.

"Junior, you old tycoon, good to see you again."

I looked up. It was Jamie Robertson, sitting across from me. For two years Jamie had played first base with me at second. We had thought we were pretty good. Jamie was extending his hand. I reached across and shook it.

"Hi, Jamie. You on first?"

"I'd better be. Too old to throw or run."

Everyone laughed. The noise started up again. I glanced around. I knew all of the faces but had no idea if the guys were married or divorced or had kids or had been to jail. Not that I cared. They talked around me.

"Scoop, are the wives coming over to watch the Classic?"

"Helen's picking Sue up at eleven. I think she hopes it'll be over by the time they get here."

"Hey Mark, little Lucy still got chicken pox?"

"Yeah, we're worried the baby'll get it."

"Hey, Junior, you married yet?" It was Dunc Robertson, Jamie's younger brother. He had always been a hellraiser and I was surprised he wasn't making license plates in some penitentiary. I shook my head.

"Too busy making money, eh? I've been by the place you work in Saskatoon, that office tower."

"Is that right?" I said, forcing a smile. "You should stop in next time."

"Yeah, maybe I will. We could have a coffee."

"Good."

"Yeah, good."

I pulled out the shirt for my uniform and held it up. It was white with green trim. *Bloopers* was crested on the front. The back said JUNIOR NORMAN and had my old number, 15. For once in our lives, we would look like a team. The school had promised every year to buy new uniforms if we won the district playoffs. Twice we were runners-up and, in grade twelve, the final playoff game went into extra innings, but we never won. Now, a decade later, we could strut around in fancy uniforms.

Barney Reynolds was the last one to straggle in,

reminding me of how appropriately he fit into this slow-moving, slow-thinking town. By the time Mr. Ellis showed up at the door, there were sixteen of us sitting in bright new uniforms. Mr. Ellis had a uniform, too, with 0 for the number and COACH instead of his name.

"It's time to go, guys," he said. "I just want to say that it's real nice you could all make it here today. It means a lot to the school and to the town...and me, too."

"Hey, coach," Dunc Robertson asked, "are we gonna say the team motto?"

Barney Reynolds piped up, "Win or lose, there's always booze."

Everyone laughed. Then, with Mr. Ellis leading, we repeated what had been a ritual before every game:

> *Win or lose, you shouldn't care,*
> *Play it hard, play it fair.*

The team filed out of the school and over to the ball diamond. I thought there must be a parade or some special presentation because the stands were full and people were lining the fences. Once we walked onto the diamond and started warming up, I heard clapping and realized that the crowd was there for us. Why this spectacle would interest anyone but the team and some of their families I couldn't imagine, but there must have been over a hundred people. I tossed the ball back and forth with Jamie to loosen up, and started to feel pretty good. Those squash games were paying off. When Mr. Ellis hit grounders to the infield, I anchored second and only booted one slow roller.

Mr. Ellis must have had some influence over the tournament draw. The Bloopers were pitted against a CPR work crew that was repairing the railroad tracks west of town. They showed up with eight players. The fellow who came over to borrow some balls so they could warm up said he hadn't been to bed yet. It looked like a common malady. They went into the stands to recruit a ninth player. They tried to get a young blonde in the third row but her father vetoed that idea, so they settled for a boy with his own glove who had been shagging foul balls.

We won the toss and I was trotting out to second base when I heard a loud roar, and a rusty black Oldsmobile tore through the right-field gate. It spun in a complete circle and headed for the infield. The umpire, who had been sweeping off home plate, stood and stared. The car shot off the grass and onto the dirt infield as the ump beat me into our dugout. The driver hit the brakes and the car skidded sideways down the first-base line, stopping at home plate.

The roar of the car's engine had been drowning out any other sounds. Now, with it idling and straddling home plate, I could hear the whoops and cheers coming from the CPR bench. One of them ran out behind home plate and signaled *safe*. Their ninth player had arrived.

The driver wasn't satisfied with his grand entrance. He sat at home plate revving his engine and spinning the tires, then hot-braked partway down the third-base line. He tore around the infield, between the base paths and the pitchers mound, ripping up more ground. The dust rose and the roar of the motor echoed. We all stayed put. He fishtailed around the infield three times before thundering out the way he had entered. The CPR crew came rushing out of their dugout, cheering and waving their arms. I heard one of them shout, "Attaboy, Rusty. That's three-zip."

The dust slowly settled on the ruts that scarred the infield. We came out of the dugout in a daze. The crowd was buzzing and I could still hear Rusty's car tires squealing in the distance. People in the stands were turned around, following the car's progress. A man wearing a straw hat in the top row was giving the play by play:

"He's going out the gate...ohh, he just missed Dudley...down past the post office, turning onto main street...car's smoking now...."

The pitch of the car's motor suddenly changed to a high whine then stopped.

"Motor's blown. Car's coasting to a stop about three blocks down."

"Hear that? Bastard blew his motor."

"Serves him right."

"What an ass. Field's ruined."

I pounded my glove. I had actually been starting to get into this ritual and now it was over because of some typical, small-town stunt. I checked my watch, calculating whether I could still make the fondue party.

Dunc Robertson moved forward. "Let's go get the bastard."

There was a two-second pause, and then the team came alive. Our entire ball team rushed off the field and piled into a half-ton truck. As I waited my turn to hop in, I saw the CPR crew standing on the edge of their dugout, watching us but not moving. When I squeezed into the back of the truck, everyone was chirping.

"Hey, we're ready. Let's lock an' load."

"Yaa-hew, wagons HOOO."

The truck took off, doing some wheel spinning of its own. I could see the gleams in the eyes around me, just as I knew there was something glinting in mine. I looked at Jamie and he was watching me. I grinned. The truck hit a bump and we all jiggled. Dunc hooted and the guys in the front of the truck hollered back. We were on a mission.

"That jerk better have a health plan."

"Don't matter, he's going down."

Our truck flew down the three blocks and stopped at an angle in front of the dead Olds. We hopped out and gathered at the side of the car.

I couldn't see the driver until I got up close. He was sprawled face up on the front seat, with his eyes shut. One of our guys threw the door open and the culprit was dragged out by his feet. The kid wasn't more than twenty, with stringy hair to his shoulders. His T-shirt had bunched up to his armpits, revealing a thin, sun-burnt chest. The terror in his face as he thumped to the ground showed that he knew he had messed with the wrong town.

"HOLD IT!" The voice belonged to Mr. Ellis. He moved to the front of the crowd and peered down at the kid.

"Can you hear me?" he asked.

The kid looked up with eyes as big as hubcaps and nodded.

"Speak up, no-mind," Dunc said.

Mr. Ellis bent lower to get a better look. "You realize that your Dukes of Hazard stunt just ruined our ball diamond?"

The kid pulled himself up by holding onto the car door. "I wrecked Too Tall's car. Any of you guys mechanical?"

I could feel the excitement of the chase draining away. Reason would prevail after all.

"You're coming with us," Mr. Ellis said.

"What about the car?" The kid pulled his T-shirt down and tucked it into his bluejeans.

"You can walk back, after you rake the diamond."

"I'm not raking no diamond. I'm sick. My buddies'll..."

"Hurry up. It's going to be a hot day."

We grabbed the kid and hauled him to the truck. We tossed him into the back just as someone murmured, "Trouble."

A yellow CPR truck was rumbling down the road toward us. It stopped right behind the half-ton. The CPR ball team piled out until all eight stood in front of their truck. None of them looked over twenty-five and their work obviously involved considerable muscle-building labour. One of them, a big husky fellow with a muscle shirt and a blue tattoo on each bicep, stepped forward. He had a knife sheath strapped to his belt

"What's shaking, Rusty?"

"These guys are jerkin' me around, Too Tall."

Rusty stood up and tried to climb out of the back of the half-ton. He was very shaky.

"Stay right there, Rusty," Mr. Ellis said. He stepped forward and looked up into Too Tall's face. "We're taking him back to the diamond. There's quite a mess to fix."

Too Tall cleared his throat and spat, lofting the phlegm onto the bumper of the half-ton. I curled my fists and realized I was still wearing my ball glove. I took it off and wedged it into my left armpit. Some of the Bloopers were moving forward and the CPR crew was fanning out behind Too Tall.

Someone pushed up beside me and I glanced to see who it was. I didn't recognize the fellow's face but the logo on his red uniform said *Rebels,* which had always been the name of Dolguard's men's fastball team. The guy nodded and said, "'Lo, Junior." I nodded back and looked behind me, noticing more red uniforms. Vehicles were stopping in the street and people were piling out. Others were streaming down the three blocks from the fairgrounds. The crowd was swelling and nobody was siding with the CPR team. If they thought they could waltz into our town and rip it up, they had some fast rethinking to do.

"Shape Rusty's in right now," Too Tall said, looking around, "could take him all day to finish."

"That's a shame," Mr. Ellis said. "Some of you guys look like you could play ball."

"Too Tall?" Rusty called, "Can I get out now?"

"You stay put," Too Tall said, and then he looked up into the sky for a few seconds. He looked around once more, taking in the growing crowd and his uneasy crew. His eyes lingered over the ruined car, then back to Rusty in the half-ton. He cleared his throat and said, "Okay, Pops, let's get that diamond fixed. We got some tools in the truck. We'll use Rusty to brush off home plate."

"Agreed," Mr. Ellis said.

Too Tall turned to go.

"And then..." Mr. Ellis continued.

Too Tall slowly turned back. "Then?"

"Then we're going to kick your butt."

The teams loaded up again and drove back to the fairgrounds. Out on the diamond, players and some of the fans were already starting to repair the damage. The CPR crew worked in pairs, spelling each other off, except for Rusty, who they kept busy raking. Every time he stopped to lean on his handle, someone prodded him into action. I supervised the area between second and the pitcher's mound. Even the umpire smoothed out around home plate. After half an hour of hard work, the field still had some soft spots but the game could begin.

We trotted out onto the field amid clapping, cheering, and tooting horns. The Rebels sat behind our dugout, offering advice and encouragement. From the beginning it was obvious that the game wouldn't be a defensive battle. The CPR boys could pound the ball, and got four runs before a Norman-Robertson double play ended the inning.

Too Tall was the CPR's pitcher, and he let out a giant grunt every time he wound up the windmill and fired the ball. It looked like a pea coming in, almost too fast to swing at. Luckily his ball control didn't match his intimidating style. We got three runs back with some timely walks and well-placed errors. I was sitting beside Barney Reynolds when our third run crossed the plate, and Barney held up his hand for a high-five. I gave it a little tap.

In the final inning, the bottom of the fifth, the CPR was ahead fourteen to twelve. Everyone on the bench had played at least two innings. I had walked, singled twice, and flied out. I had played errorless ball – unless you counted a couple that a pro might have knocked down – before being replaced in the fourth inning. I did a quick audit of the scoresheet. Fourteen – twelve was correct. We had given it a good shot, nothing to be ashamed of. Too Tall had found his range the last couple of innings, and runs were getting scarce.

A roar went up from the stands. With one out, Dunc had just leaned in and taken one for the team, right in the thigh. I winced as Dunc hobbled toward first. Mr. Ellis, coaching from his spot by third base, signalled time out and motioned for me to go in as a replacement runner.

I paused at the dugout entrance to pat Dunc on the arm, "How's it feel?"

"Hurts like hell," Dunc said. "Can he wing 'em."

I started toward first base just as Dunc said, "Do it, Freddy buddy, we need you. Let's beat these goofs."

That's right, I thought, as I lifted and stretched my legs at first, we're still in it. A break or two, and who knows?

"Go for two, get the double and we're outa here,"

their second baseman was reminding the rest of the infield, "Come on T.T., you big arm, you hummer, you."

Too Tall was tentative after drilling Dunc, and his first pitch to Slick Johnson was in the dirt. It scooted to the backstop and I was on second, standing up. Too Tall kicked the dirt, smoothed the front of the mound, and sent the second pitch straight down the pipe. Slick was ready and sent a slow, two-hopper to third. The third baseman fielded it cleanly but instead of taking the easy out at first, threw to second to initiate the double play. It surprised everyone else, and the second baseman made a nice catch to save the ball from rolling into right field. I dove back to the base and avoided the tag.

Car horns were tooting and the stands were alive with people standing and cheering. Runners on first and second, one out. Barney Reynolds was up. He had struck out both times since replacing Jamie in the third. I looked down to where Mr. Ellis was coaching at third base. Would he pull Barney and put Jamie back in? No, his signal to Barney was a wink and a thumbs-up sign. Too Tall also remembered Barney.

Grunt, Whump. Strike one.

Grunt, Whump. Strike two.

Barney stepped out of the batter's box and signalled time out. He grabbed some dirt and wiped the sweat off his hands onto his pants, leaving stains on the clean legs. He stepped back into the box, and I could see how tightly he was gripping the bat handle.

As Too Tall wound up, Slick and I chattered from the bases, "Come on, Barney boy, now you see it, buddy, only takes one. Little single, fella, pound it outa here," and the CPR boys were chanting "Come on, big arm, way up on 'em, T-T, Give em the dark one, big shooter, come on, you hummer, you." Too Tall grunted and let fly. Barney grunted and swung late, like always. The ball hit the end of the bat and went flying into right field, where Rusty had been safely stashed – until now. Everyone yelling his name gave Rusty a start, and he came running in looking for the ball as it sailed over his head. I was tagging in case it was caught and headed for third when it went past Rusty. I looked up and saw Mr. Ellis' arm spinning like a windmill, signalling me home.

I crossed home plate standing, with Slick Johnson two steps behind. The game was tied. We both turned to see where Barney had ended up. I was appalled to see that Barney was stretching the double into a triple. The throw from the cut-off man to third was wild and it looked like Barney just might make it. He didn't slide, though, and was going so fast that he ran right off the base and got caught in a rundown between third and home. The crowd was yelling, Mr. Ellis was running back and forth beside Barney hollering instructions, and I was standing behind home plate screaming, "Back, back, back to third. Sliiiiide." Again Barney fooled everyone, charging past the catcher who had chased him up the line and heading for home. Too Tall, covering home, caught the high throw from third and brought his big arm down in a swoop. Barney dove headfirst into that soft dirt, burrowing and clawing like a badger. His right arm came up under the tag.

"SAAAFFE," roared the umpire. Too Tall threw his glove and ball in the air and reached down to haul

Barney up by his collar. Too Tall swatted some dust off the front of Barney's uniform and Slick, Mr. Ellis, and I were all close enough to hear him say, "Good slide, puff-ball."

I was the first one through to give Barney a hug.

Due to the long delay in getting our first game started, we didn't have much time to savour our victory. After the handshakes, we had to move to another diamond for our next game. We walked over as a group, slapping, shoving, and congratulating each other. I walked beside Jamie.

"No errors yet today, Junior. Pretty smooth," Jamie said.

"Yeah, but I'll be stiff tomorrow."

"Me, too," Jamie said. "Coach Ellis claimed that if we won a game, we'd have to come back next year to defend."

I nodded, only half-listening, swinging my glove and enjoying the victory.

"Would you, Junior?"

"Would I what?" I slowed down and stopped.

"If this team, the Bloopers, if we played again, would you come back next year?" Jamie was smiling but I could sense the seriousness behind the question.

Earlier, I would have simply lied, whipping off some comment about how busy it is this time of year. *But hey, send me the invite. Who knows what I'll be up to by then?* Now I couldn't say it. I looked around at this collection of people I didn't know anymore, some walking ahead with their wives and kids, others explaining what they were doing and feeling that exact second Barney dove.

Fans were busy moving their cars and lawn chairs over to the other ball diamond. I felt accepted, not because of having the most billable hours or working enough over-time in a year to destroy a relationship, but by just being there, being a part of it all.

Jamie stood waiting. I could feel the heat of wind-burn on my cheeks. I tugged on the brim of my ball cap.

"Let's go get 'em," I said.

Jamie smiled and slapped me on the back. We started forward again, toward the next diamond and almost certain slaughter.

The Road Les Travelled

It was my idea to take the trip in the first place. I knew that my father would love to explore the maze that was the Hockey Hall of Fame in Toronto. I had been there twice, awed by the displays. After the first trip, I brought him back a magazine that explained all about the exhibits. The second time, I delivered a blue golf shirt with the Hall of Fame emblem on the pocket, and he immediately put it on over top of his cowboy shirt with the pearl buttons. I brought up the idea at Thanksgiving, as we all hunkered down around the turkey.

"How about taking a trip?" I asked.

"Oh, we've thought of it," Mom said, "but Dad isn't feeling so well. We wanted to take one of those two-week bus tours to Nashville. And I've always wanted to see the East Coast. You know, where Anne of Green Gables grew up? But we just don't have the energy anymore."

Dad grunted and reached for the buns. He always heaped a big mound of potatoes onto the middle of his plate, then indented the top of Potato Mountain and filled it with gravy, which ran down the side like lava from a volcano. Today, gravy was dripping off the edge of his plate onto the table. He broke the bun and tried sopping up the gravy with the top half. My sister Gail reached over with her fork and pushed back the edge of his potato mountain, making room for the gravy to pool on his plate. He handed her the bottom half of his bun, which she buttered and handed back.

"Doctor," Dad said.

"That's right," Mom said. "We've got doctor's appointments twice next week, and Dad has to get his prescription filled on Thursday."

"I wasn't thinking of next week," I said.

Dad tapped the tabletop with his index finger and said, "Pills."

Mom said, "Oh," and hopped up, going to the cabinet beside the table and opening a drawer. "Did you have the pink one already today?"

Dad looked at her blankly.

"Well, let's see. You had one brown one first thing, and you don't take another one of those until bed. The cod liver oil was at breakfast, and what do the little white ones say? Here we go."

She handed him a little white pill, which he put on top of his gravy bun.

"Didn't he take the pink one with his water?" Gail asked. "After the football game?"

"That's right, dear," Mom said. She sat down and explained across the table, "You took the pink one before we ate, so that's all you need."

Dad nodded, bit into the bun, and swallowed.

"I said I wasn't thinking about next week," I said, a little louder. "Just maybe sometime before Christmas."

"Maybe somewhere warm?" my brother-in-law George piped up.

"Dad doesn't like heat," Gail reminded her husband, using her *let me slowly explain it to you* tone that I remembered so well from our childhood.

"Christmas is a rush," Mom said, "what with cards to send, presents, baking. Where are we having it this year?"

"We went to George's parents last year," Gail said.

"That's settled then. And if Christmas is going to be here, there's no way we could go anywhere until after that."

"I was thinking," I said, "of the Hockey Hall of Fame."

There was silence for ten seconds. Not even a fork moved.

Then Dad said, "Okay." He got up from the table and walked toward the bedroom.

"Are you all right?" Mom asked.

Dad waved his hand and kept walking.

"The Hall of Fame." George spoke each word as if it was capitalized. "You've been there, haven't you, Les?"

"Twice," I said, pleased with my worldliness. I work at Sears in Regina. Both times I had been to head office in Toronto for training, I had arranged a visit to the shrine.

My travelling through work combined with extensive credit card use had allowed me to collect roughly a zillion air miles. I had enough saved for all three of us to fly from Regina to Toronto and back on a weekend. I mentioned that to Mom, so she wouldn't start worrying about the cost.

"Oh, we couldn't do that," she said.

"Sure you could," I said. "The air miles are just sitting there. We'd better use them up before the airline decides to take them away."

"It's not that, Les," Mom said. "It's your dad. He can't fly."

At that moment Dad re-entered the room. He was carrying something. He sat back down, pushed his plate forward, and opened up a magazine. It was the one I had given him after our first trip, explaining everything to be seen and done at the Hall. He looked up and cleared his throat as if to say something, but then turned his entire focus onto the magazine.

I gave Mom a puzzled look. She pointed to the left side of her chest and mouthed, "Heart."

Then I remembered. Dad's heart rate fluctuated, and he took some pills to regulate it. The doctor had advised against flying, due to the sudden changes in altitude. Mom had told me about this over the phone. "No more flying, the doctor said. I had to smile to myself. It's hard enough getting him out of the house except to see the doctor, let alone fly anywhere. No, we've never seen the inside of an airplane and now I don't expect we ever will."

I looked over at Dad, flipping through the magazine and pointing out items to Gail that he had previously checked off as interesting. There seemed to be something on every page.

Driving northeast from Dolguard three hundred and twenty kilometres to the outskirts of Regina always took my parents five hours. That was driving just below the speed limit and taking two breaks. Regina to Toronto was another twenty-five hundred kilometres. Erasing the airplane from the scenario had ballooned a three-day weekend into a two-week marathon.

"When?" Dad asked.

I looked at Mom, who was looking at Gail.

"Wish I could go," George said.

"The baby's due on November 20th, George," Gail reminded him, "and I could be early."

"The baby!" Mom said. "Good heavens, nobody's going anywhere until this baby's born."

"Why?" Dad asked, looking at Mom, "It's not going."

"But, the..."

"George, you had something to do with this kid. But Les and I, we'd be in the way."

Maybe I could put him on a Greyhound bus heading east one morning, and fly out the next night. Maybe the CPR still ran passenger cars on special request, for humanitarian reasons.

Dad closed the Hall of Fame magazine and set it down on the table. He folded his hands over top of it and looked at me. "Les, we'll take the Olds."

I coughed.

"It needs an oil change," Mom said, "and the tires aren't good. It shimmies at eighty."

"They aren't leaving tomorrow," said George. He smiled at me. "Les has got it all figured out. Otherwise he wouldn't have mentioned it. Is there pumpkin pie, Mom?"

"Check the schedule," Dad said. "See who the Leafs are playing."

"That's right," George said. "You should plan the trip around when the Leafs are at home. Maybe see two games."

"Not everyone's a farmer," I said, "with a winter schedule revolving around the curling rink's square draw. I'll have to see when I can take holidays."

Gail said, "George isn't curling this year."

"I'm not?"

"Not with the new baby in the house."

George nodded sullenly, knowing when to shut up.

"Maybe," Gail said, looking at me with eyes that said more than the words, "you should plan the trip for January."

I could see that Dad had lowered his head, and was slowly rubbing his temple. Mom saw it, too.

"No," she said. "If these fools plan to go, travelling weather's always better before Christmas."

Gail and George live near Medicine Hat. Even though it's in Alberta, it's an hour closer to my parents' home in Dolguard, Saskatchewan than I am from Regina. Gail nurses and George sort of farms. He grows specialty crops like lentils, chickpeas, and sunflowers. There are gas wells scattered all over this old CPR land that he still has the mineral rights for, so he's kept pretty busy the rest of the year cashing the royalty cheques.

He rents out his pasture to a rancher, and the only rocks he picks up are at the back of a curling sheet.

George likes to make out that he's a jock, but I always tell him that curling isn't really even a sport. It's like bowling. You don't need to get in shape to do either, you just need a pulse. Four years ago George played lead for a Medicine Hat team that qualified for the provincial tournament to determine who represented Alberta at the Brier. They lost in the quarterfinals, but give George a drink, and he starts replaying every game of that tournament. In a bar he uses beer bottles to show the position of each rock in the house, and in a restaurant he switches to the little coffee creamers. Watching curling in person is painful enough, but having someone replay it with slow motion analysis and non-dairy creamers is a cure for insomnia.

I like to tease George, but all things considered, Gail could have ended up with a lot worse. She's three years older than I am and always seemed so strong and confident, almost defiant. In her teens she stayed out late at some dance, got grounded, and then stayed out again the next chance she got. Dad had a spanking stick that he used liberally, but even that didn't dampen her free spirit.

Gail moved to Medicine Hat after graduation. She worked at a shoe store in the mall for a year. I remember being surprised when she enrolled in Nursing at Medicine Hat College. I had thought she would eventually become a poet, or an actress. Maybe she realized that she liked to help people. She sent a card for my graduation, partly to inform us all that she was engaged to a fellow from around the Hat called George.

The phone rang as we were having pumpkin pie for dessert. It was my Uncle Richard from Moose Jaw. Mom talked briefly with him on the phone by the table, and then went into the bedroom to continue. By the time she came back out, the ice cream had melted all over her pie.

"Harold," she said, "your brother wants to have a word."

Dad picked up the phone. "Rich, how's life in the Jaw? Oh, I'm feeling okay...no, not sleeping that great...tried that, didn't seem to help...listen, we're going to the Hall...the Hockey Hall of Fame...in Toronto...no, just me and Les.... Driving, taking the Olds."

Dad listened for another ten seconds and then put his palm over the receiver. "Your uncle wants to come along," he told me.

My uncle had started his career as a brakeman for the CPR. Thirty-five years later, he retired as an engineer. He was two years older than Dad but, other than his hip replacement and bypass surgery last year, was healthy. He could help drive. I nodded.

"Good idea, Rich... We're not sure yet. In the next month or so.... Right, we're checking the schedule to take in a Leafs game.... Yep, we'll let you know."

Dad listened again, and I could tell by his mouth tightening that he didn't like whatever he was hearing. "No, I'm fine...maybe later on, but things are fine right now...I will, Rich. Bye."

Then he hung up. My Dad's side of the family tree didn't waste time on long hellos or goodbyes. I attrib-uted much of this clan coldness to my grandfather, who died last year at ninety-four. At birthdays and even the biannual family reunion you would see the occasional handshake, but a quick nod was more likely than hugs and kisses. The ladies would stay in the kitchen, drinking coffee and washing dishes, talking quietly as they prepared the next meal. If the men decided to play cards around the kitchen table, then the ladies moved into the living room. The uncles were loud and gruff, always kidding each other about the slow girl who used to live next door or about one of them being a little light in the loafers, and joking about each other's needing help counting their cards.

The ladies' conversations became more interesting the softer they spoke. If they were laughing and loud, I stayed near the men. If the ladies were suddenly quiet, I moved to them, ears straining. I remember listening in on one such conversation between Grandma and Mom, as they sat side by side in the viewing room of the funeral home. They were telling about the last time Grandpa had been in the hospital.

Grandma had been alone with him in his room. The metal chair squeaked as she leaned forward to wipe the corner of his mouth. Grandpa's gnarled hand, still the size of a catcher's mitt, squeezed hers.

"How you feeling, Father?" she had asked.

He raised and lowered his salt and pepper eyebrows which, after seventy years of marriage, she knew meant "so-so."

"Doctor Schultz was by, asked if you were in pain."

She paused and cleared her throat. "Said he'd give you something stronger."

Grandpa had closed his foggy eyes. "Nahh." After a short silence, he rolled his head to one side. "Where's Richard?"

She explained that Richard and everyone else had gone to the cafeteria in the basement for a bite of supper.

"You get some rest." She patted his hand and pulled the covers up to his chin. "They'll be back soon."

He pushed the covers down again, exposing his white chest. "Mother, there's something," he wheezed, "something I been thinking about."

The thought flashed through her mind that maybe he sensed this was the end. He had only grunted a dozen words at her all week, although the nurses who looked in on him claimed he was still teasing them.

"When we lost the farm in '37, you stood by me."

She patted his arm as she remembered wondering how they would ever survive with four little mouths to feed.

"And then you just nodded that day in '39 when I came home and said I'd enlisted."

She shut her eyes. At least it had been a paycheque, and later on he had looked so handsome in his uniform.

"When the Elevator shut down in '66 and they wrote to retire me, you were the one who opened the letter."

She looked back over her shoulder for Richard or Harold, seeing only a nurse walking down the hallway. She wondered if this was the end, his last conscious thoughts. Even if it was the morphine spinning his mind, she should try to remember his exact words to pass on to the rest of the family.

"Billy drowned out fishing, remember? You answered the phone, and told me to turn down the TV, something had happened to our Bill."

She nodded, her breath caught in her throat. How hazy that funeral had been, trying not to imagine that they were burying a son. Both of Bill's boys had driven down yesterday, had come to see Grandpa one last time.

"Now I got tubes running in and out of me. I look over and there you are."

She leaned forward and felt his forehead, surprised by the coolness.

"I just finally," he rasped, "finally figured something out."

He turned his head on the pillow and looked into her eyes, waiting for her to ask. She wouldn't. She could stop time itself if only she didn't ask. He kept waiting, with his jaw set. She didn't need, didn't want to hear those awkward words said out loud. Not now. She could hear him breathing. A phone rang down the hall. Eventually, like every other time for over seventy years, she gave in.

"What's that you've finally figured out, Father?"

"I figure...you're bad luck."

After leaving the table, I checked the NHL schedule that was sitting on top of the TV. The Leafs played Chicago at home on Thursday November 16th and then St. Louis on Saturday, the 18th. The Saturday night game would be televised on Hockey Night in Canada. I knew that Dad would prefer watching the Leafs play Montreal, but that wasn't possible until February. Still, he seemed pleased when I told him the teams.

"Chicago's one of the original six," he said. "Bobby Hull, Stan Mikita, Bill White. Remember that time we heard Dennis Hull speak at the Broncos Sports Dinner in Swift Current?"

I nodded and smiled, remembering Hull's contagious laugh.

"And St. Louis," Dad said. "They were the first expansion team to make it to the Stanley Cup final. Remember Bobby Orr's goal in overtime, when he went flying through the air?"

George nodded. "I was hoping St. Louis would win at least one game because Boston was so cocky. I liked Glenn Hall in goal, and Barclay Plager's grit on defence."

"None of those guys have played for years," I said.

"It's part of the history, Les," Dad said. "That's what makes it. If you don't know or appreciate the tradition, it's just another game."

"History leads to legend," George said. He reached for our coffee cups and also gathered in the salt and pepper shakers. "Did I ever explain the McCall rink's shot that forced us into extra ends up in Edmonton?"

"Yeah, you did. You hit the headpin, didn't you? And then someone pushed the button and the bowling pins got reset?"

Dad laughed and George tossed the salt shaker at me. It would have been a good throw if they had got on the brooms a bit earlier.

Back at Sears, I asked for the ten days off. My supervisor turned down my request, because in retail the busiest time of the year is the pre-Christmas rush. We weren't on really good terms anyway. During my performance review he said that he was ninety-nine percent convinced that sales wasn't really my thing, would never be my "passion." With cutbacks and competition, all of his team needed to be onside and committed to achieving the same goals. Maybe I should re-evaluate my options. I would have liked to accommodate him, but with only my grade twelve education and the "saving for university" fund at fewer than three hundred dollars, I couldn't resign. He was now "documenting my objectives and lack of results." I figured I had until summer.

I decided to bypass him and go directly to the manager, who didn't know me nearly as well. Once I explained about driving my father to Toronto, and the reason, he agreed to give me the time off. He even said that he would send an e-mail to Head Office and see if we could use Marketing's corporate seats for the Thursday night game against Chicago.

Over the next two weeks, I talked on the phone every second night with one family member or another. Dad wanted me to give him the inside scoop on a good place in Regina to get new tires.

"Goodyear, Canadian Tire, LePages Tire Corral, Costco, wherever. It's a city, Dad."

"Yeah, but you've got the connections. You must know the deals."

"Sears sells tires," I reminded him.

"Crap," he said, "seconds. What's a clothing store know about tires?"

"Whatever," I replied.

Mom wanted to be sure that I was okay with her staying in Medicine Hat with Gail instead of driving with us to Toronto.

"That's fine, Mom, as long as you promise me that it doesn't free up George to come along."

Uncle Richard wanted to make sure that I reserved rooms in a Toronto hotel downtown right away, because there were three times as many people in the city of Toronto as in all of Saskatchewan.

"Wow, Uncle. It must be like Agribition there every day of the year."

George wanted me to pick him up one of those Hall of Fame T-shirts, and a keychain. I said I would definitely bring him back some shampoo from one of the hotels we stayed in, and a shower cap. Then Gail got on and suggested that I write down the various times during the day when Dad was supposed to take his pills.

"You write it down, Ms. Nurse, and I'll follow your directions."

Dad called back to say that the Olds now had clean oil. I reminded him to bring along his Esso credit card.

Mom informed me that George would drive them into Regina in the Olds. Then he would drive her back to Medicine Hat in my Mustang. I said to remind him that our cars took unleaded gasoline, not diesel.

I called Uncle Richard and begged him one last time to get us a train ride. "Pull some strings. You're there thirty-five years, and there's no favours to call in?"

"Unless you want to sit in a boxcar," he said, "there's nothing I can do. I wasn't there at the Last Spike and I didn't invent the hopper car, you know. Most of the time I just sat in a caboose and did paperwork. That doesn't exactly entitle me to call up the president of the CPR and request a special train for me, my brother, and Loss."

L*oss* is Uncle Richard's nickname for me. Most people think it's just a twist on Les, but he and I know what it really means. Seven years ago, we all went camping at Buffalo Pound Provincial Park for one of our biannual non-touchy-feely family reunions. One of the weekend's activities was a golf tournament. For the first time, I was allowed to play in an adult foursome. Dad, Uncle Richard and I played with Stan Heintz, who was dating my cousin Sylvia. I had been playing almost daily on Dolguard's sand greens that summer, and was hitting my irons consistently. Dad and Uncle commented on my ability to keep up, but Stan seemed miffed. Maybe he was trying to impress the potential father-in-law, but I quickly noticed two things about his golf game: number one, he always found his ball no matter where it had been hit and number two, no matter how many swings he took, he couldn't count past six.

Dad and Uncle didn't get out golfing much, and we walked the entire course. They both tuckered out on the back nine and became contenders for the Most Honest Golfer award. I was up two strokes on Stan playing the seventeenth. He could hit the ball a lot longer, but was used to playing on grass greens. The Buffalo Pound greens were sand, like the Dolguard course. I was one-putting every second green while he was always taking two. We teed off on seventeen, both hit with our irons twice on the fairway and two-putted. Dad was keeping score and I hollered over to him, "five."

Stan smiled, shook his head and said, "Catching you. Got me a four."

If this had been the first occurrence, I would have assumed Stan had miscounted, since it was getting near the end and we were all tired. If I had known him better, or he was one of the family, I would have made some joke about his counting ability, like the uncles did when playing cards. It wasn't, though, and I didn't.

As we walked to the eighteenth tee, I thought: *What does winning this particular golf game mean to me? Nothing, really. I've already proven my point that I can play with the men. It must mean a lot to Stan, though, in order for him to cheat to win the game.*

Stan's tee shot went out of bounds into the field. Miraculously, it must have hit a rock and bounced back into play because within minutes he had found it just inside the fence, on a nice clump of grass. We both got onto the green in three. Buffalo Pound's eighteenth green is small, maybe twenty-five feet in diameter, with the cup in the centre. The longest possible putt from anywhere on the green is about twelve feet. Part of the procedure on a sand green is to smooth out a path between your ball and the cup with a metal roller. Stan made a nice putt and the ball dropped in the hole.

"YES!" he roared, pumping his fist in the air. "Give

me a big par four, Harold. Puts a little pressure on the midget."

I could see the sweat on Stan's face, the desperation in his eyes. Dad and Uncle had putted out in two and were about to walk away. I tapped the ball and it came up about two feet short of the hole.

"Ohhh," Stan said, "Looks like we'll be tied. Coin toss for the win?"

Uncle Richard snorted and mumbled, "Not with your coin."

Dad had his head down, adding up the scores. I hit my next putt wide. Stan made a gagging sound and grabbed his throat, as if I had choked. I shrugged and tapped it in for a six. Stan was the winner by a stroke.

Uncle Richard came over as I was getting my ball out of the hole. On sand greens, the golf ball leaves a trail as it rolls through the sand toward the hole. Uncle studied my ball's trail, which had missed the hole by at least six inches. He looked at me hard as he grabbed the rake and started erasing our footprints and ball trails as a courtesy to the group waiting behind us.

"Harold, you and Stan go on ahead. I'll help Les finish up here."

I put the flag in the hole while he finished raking. The other two were gone around the corner before he spoke.

"What was that?"

"What was what?"

"Duffing your last few shots."

"I didn't duff, I just..."

"You hadn't missed a putt all game, let alone twice."

"Pressure, I guess," I explained. "Stan wanted it more than me."

"Listen, Loss," Uncle Richard said, holding up his index finger. "You always try your best, no matter what it is you're doing. Easing up creates bad habits. Remember that. It may be unsportsmanlike to cheat, but trying to lose isn't being very honest, either."

I've remembered that advice. Just in case I ever forget, Uncle continues calling me Loss.

On Saturday, my last day of work before the trip, I got an e-mail from my manager informing me that the tickets for the Sears corporate seats would be waiting at our hotel. He also wished me good luck on the trip, and said that if I needed any extra time off, just to call and he would personally take care of it. My internal radar detector started beeping. That sounded too nice. When he ended with "Sears has stores all across Canada, so if you run into any sort of trouble on your trip, don't hesitate to drop by one of our many locations for quality assistance," I almost gagged. He was forgetting that I had trained and worked in the trenches. There were Les clones in every store across Canada, and providing quality assistance was not our number one aim. Hitting the urinal might be.

In mid-afternoon, while helping a customer in Appliances, I got paged to the phone.

"Les, I'm glad I caught you. It's Mom."

"Mom, is everything okay?"

"Yes, fine. I just wanted to let you know that we got

to Uncle Richard's around one-thirty. It was faster than we had planned because George drove. We're just finishing our coffee, then we're going to get some new tires." She paused and lowered her voice. "Your Uncle knows a place," she said, speaking as if they were stocking up on moonshine.

"That's wonderful, Mom. See you later. I have to get back to work."

"Goodbye, dear. See you later."

I picked up pizza for supper, and Mom had brought along a sausage casserole.

"Just pop it in the oven," Mom said. "It only needs to be warmed up."

"I'll just nuke it in the microwave."

"Well, your father prefers it warmed in the oven. It browns the sausages more. There's no hurry."

M om and Dad's house in Dolguard was white and as big as a castle, with Dad unquestionably the king. Early in their marriage Mom had sprung meals on him like vegetarian lasagna, eggplant parmesan, and once even quiche, but Dad refused to allow any surprises in his kingdom. He was a ruler with meat and potatoes tastes, and had a strict routine to be followed. There was always a pot of stew bubbling on the stove Friday evening. Saturday would be roast chicken. Sunday's noon meal was always roast beef, with the potatoes browned in the roaster. We would munch on roast beef buns for Monday's lunch, with chicken soup for supper. Tuesday was hamburger and Wednesday was fish sticks.

Thursday was our mystery supper, because Dad ate out at the Lions Club that night. Mom tried exotic dishes like chicken stir-fry, perogies or tacos on Thursdays.

I said to Mom, "You're not heading to Medicine Hat tonight?"

"Oh," she said, looking at George. "I suppose Gail *is* all alone. George, will she be expecting us tonight?"

George shook his head. "I'll phone her, though, and make sure she's feeling okay. We have friends there she can call if it's an emergency."

I have a two-bedroom apartment, so Mom and Dad got my bed while I shared the second bedroom with Uncle Richard, and George slept on the couch. Uncle snored so loud I went out to the living room around three a.m., and dozed in the big armchair.

The plan was to leave around eight-thirty a.m. and spend the first night east of Winnipeg. George gave me Gail's written schedule for Dad's pills, and Mom showed me how to give him his needle. George asked me to show him how to retract the roof on my Mustang.

"It's mid-November, George," I said.

"Yeah, but if we get one of those Indian summer days while you're gone," he whined, "it'd be a shame to waste it."

"Medicine Hat *is* warmer than here," Mom added, "more like Dolguard weather, only..."

"Warmer," I finished for her.

By the time we got the Olds fully packed, had one more cup of coffee, and said our goodbyes, it was eleven.

Uncle Richard said he knew a good place just east of Regina to stop for lunch.

I drove, with Uncle Richard sitting beside me in the front. Dad was stretched out in the back with a pillow and a newspaper. Uncle Richard unfolded a roadmap.

"I'm pretty sure," I said, "we just stay on Number 1 and head east for the next three or four days."

"I like maps," Uncle said. "I check off the towns as we go by and can tell you things."

"Like what?"

"Oh, the name of the next town, how far it is, stuff like that."

I nodded. "Good information. They should think about putting stuff like that on a sign."

"Smart aleck."

"You know all these towns anyway, don't you? You were raised around here, remember?"

Uncle nodded. "Yeah, south of here. It was different then. We didn't travel as much or as far as you kids do now. Going eight miles to a dance in the next town on a Saturday night was a big deal back then."

"Now they bus kids an hour and a half into Dol-guard," Dad said from the back.

"Hey, Harold," Uncle said, "remember the night we went to Creelman in Reg's new car?"

"Yeah," Dad said, "that was some adventure."

"Our buddy Reg," Uncle explained, "was the first one of our gang to get a car. He had a '46 Chevy, and he claimed it could get up to sixty miles an hour on the straightaway."

"How fast are we going?" Dad asked.

"Cruise is set at a hundred and ten," I said. "That's kilometres per hour."

"Feels faster," Dad said.

"Anyway," Uncle continued, "we decided to test it out one night, going to this dance. There were four of us in the car. Reg and I were in the front, and your dad and Reg's younger brother Bobby were in the back, leaning over the front seat. Everybody's eyes were glued to this round speedometer. We get to this straight section and Reg puts the pedal to the metal."

"Fifty-four," Dad said from the back.

"Fifty-five," Uncle added.

"Fifty-six," Dad said, louder.

"Fifty-seven, and the car was shaking bad," reported Uncle. "Reg's gritting his teeth, his knuckles are white and the needle bounces to fifty-eight."

Uncle and Dad combine to shout, "Fifty-nine!"

Then Uncle says softly, "Fifty-eight.... Fifty-seven... Fifty-six."

Even though I've heard the story before, I laugh along with them.

"And what did Reg say?"

"Oh yeah," Uncle said. "Reg said that there was too much weight in the car. By himself he had got it up to sixty-two."

Dad said quietly behind me, "I was scared."

"How fast can the Olds go?" I asked.

The speedometer was numbered up to two hundred kilometres, which translated into one hundred and twenty miles per hour.

"George had it up to one-fifteen between the Jaw and

Regina," Uncle reported. "Trying out those new tires."

"Miles or klicks?"

"Klicks," Dad said. "It's a solid car, but I like keeping it to the speed limit."

Uncle Richard turned the radio on to a country channel, and I could hear the rustle of the newspaper behind me. I tapped the cruise control a couple of times, edging the needle up past one-fifteen.

We made it to Winnipeg in time for supper at Bonanza. We decided it was far enough on the first day, so we pulled into a Super 8. The only non-smoking room they had left had one king-sized bed in it. They moved a cot into the room as well, which Uncle Richard said he would flip me for.

"Heads, I win; tails, you lose."

"Whatever," I said, unhooking the metal latches on the cot's sides and testing the mattress for firmness.

Dad and Uncle Richard sat at the little table and told stories about football's Blue Bombers and hockey's Jets, while I flipped through the channels looking for a good movie.

"The best line I ever saw play on a regular team," Dad was saying, "was Ulf Nilsson at centre, Anders Hedberg on right, and Bobby Hull on left."

Uncle Richard nodded. "Speed, power, and brains. They had it all."

I put on my coat. "Going for a Coke. Want anything?"

They both shook their heads.

"Too much caffeine," Uncle Richard said. "Would there be hot milk down there?"

I shrugged and Dad said, "I'll just turn in."

I sat down in the lobby and read the *Winnipeg Free Press* for over an hour. When I went back to the room, they were both asleep. I lay awake on the cot for a long time, trying to find a comfortable bump and listening to their breathing. With my head under the pillow and by pressing the sides down against my ears, Uncle's snoring was only a dull rumble.

The next morning was my first experience with getting Dad ready for the day all by myself. He was at a loss as well, being used to Mom knowing what to do, and in what order.

"Okay," I said when I came out of the shower, "who's next, or do you guys only bath on Saturday nights?"

"Did you run my tub?" Dad asked.

"I was just going to," I said. "How hot do you like it?"

"Medium," Dad said.

He just sat there on the bed. Through asking specific questions that he answered with a shrug, nod or "no," I was able to determine that he always had his pills and a glass of water *before* the bath. Once he finished bathing, but before drying off, was when he had the needle.

Besides emulating Grandpa's lack of emotional expression, Dad had also learned the art of being served through years of observing him and Grandma in action. If Grandpa wasn't sitting at the kitchen table playing cards, he was usually lying on the couch in the living room. Directly across from his couch stood the television set. The walnut cabinet was three feet high, four feet wide and thirty inches deep, more furniture than entertainment unit. The top overflowed with picture frames showing graduations, weddings, grandchildren, and family clusters. Potted plants rotated on and off, as well, depending on the season. Two of Grandma's favourite ceramic ornaments, a sleeping dwarf and a brown collie, were positioned on the floor at the front corners of the cabinet.

A large television aerial swaying fifteen feet above the roof, clamped on a pole strapped to the side of the house, allowed the TV to pick up CBC and CTV. The twenty-four-inch screen hissed mostly snow as the round dial was clicked from 2 to 13, and back to 2. The television always stayed off until Grandpa Carson gave the command. Whenever he wanted the television on, he would yell, *"Mother!"* and Grandma would hurry in from the kitchen. She stood to the side, turned on the TV and waited thirty seconds for it to warm up. When the picture appeared, she made sure it was on the channel Grandpa wanted before hustling back to the kitchen. The living room could be full of people, any one of them capable of pulling the knob, but Grandpa always yelled, "Mother." If at some point he wanted to switch channels, "Mother" echoed through the house, and in she came. If he fell asleep on the couch, the television stayed on until Grandma came into the room and turned it off.

One Thanksgiving when I was twelve and we were all watching this, Mom had what she called an epiphany. She decided that the perfect Christmas gift from the family would be a channel changer. She said that she realized there were only two channels to choose from, but it could also be used to turn the television on and off. It would save Grandma a lot of steps every day. Mom had Uncle Richard investigate, because he lived in a city and would know where to look and who to ask. Uncle Richard reported back that since it was an older-style TV, an additional small box was needed that hooked into the back of the television. The remote control gadget "talked" to the box, which in turn activated the TV.

I was nearly as excited about Grandma and Grandpa Carson's present as my own that Christmas. Grandpa unwrapped the paper and opened the cardboard box. I could tell that he didn't know what it was. He set it on the coffee table while Grandma said, "How nice," and handed him the next present to open.

Once the gift pile under the tree had been depleted, Dad handed Uncle Richard the package. He hooked up the box to the back of the TV, moved some pictures from the top of the television and set the box on the front corner. Then he put the batteries into the remote control and handed it to Grandpa.

"Here," he said. "Try it. This button turns the TV on or off, and these two buttons change the channels. This is the volume."

Grandpa pushed a button and the TV clicked on. In thirty seconds he flipped from CBC to CTV, and back again. He smiled and shook his head at the wonder of it. The family all clapped.

Grandma said, "There you go, Father," and headed back to the kitchen.

At Easter, everyone was back. After supper, the men went into the living room to sit down while the women cleared the table. I couldn't see the channel changer box on top of the TV, so I walked right up to the set and saw that the box was still there, surrounded and covered by pictures and Easter cards. Grandpa stretched out on the couch and picked up the remote control.

"Mother!" he hollered.

Grandma scurried in and over to the television cabinet. She moved the pictures and cards away from the front of the box. Grandpa then pointed the remote control at the TV and clicked. Grandma moved the pictures and cards back in place before returning to the kitchen.

Grandpa saw everyone looking at him and said, "Quite the thing."

Uncle Richard got dressed while Dad had his bath. Uncle watched *Canada AM* with me for fifteen minutes and then went down for breakfast. He came back to the room with some milk and Dad ate dried cereal at the little table. Uncle and I picked him out some clean clothes and Dad finished dressing. I grabbed a coffee to go as I checked out, and we were on the road a little before ten o'clock.

Things went pretty smooth for the first hour or so. Then as we crossed the Manitoba border into Ontario, Dad shouted from the back, "Hat!"

"What about your hat?" Uncle asked.

"It's gone," Dad said. He sat up and Uncle leaned back over the seat, checking the floor and under the blanket.

"Left at the hotel," Dad said.

"We've gone too far to turn back," I said. "Do you have your wallet?"

"Uhh... yep."

"Your coat?"

"Wearing it."

"Okay," I said. "Not to worry. We'll get it on the way back."

"It's my favourite," Dad said. "Wanted to watch the game in it."

"Listen," I said, "when we stop tonight I'll phone the Winnipeg Super 8 and make sure they keep it for us at the front desk."

Uncle Richard asked where we had reservations in Toronto.

"The Royal York. Why?"

"You know, Loss, they could send it COD," he said.

"It's a hat," I said.

"It's his Leafs hat," Uncle corrected.

Dad sighed. "Always check the room just before you leave," he said. "Last thing Mom does is look under the bed."

"Your hat was under the bed?"

"As an example. You never know."

"Dad, I had the suitcases. My arms were full."

"Shouldn't try taking everything in one trip," he said. "No shame in going back a second time. You made sure you had a coffee."

I clicked the cruise control up to one-twenty.

I tried to strike up a few conversations after that, but Dad pretended not to hear me. We stopped for a snack in Kenora, and I phoned the Winnipeg motel. The number was on the bill. They had already found the hat.

"It looks special," the girl on the phone said, "with all those pins on it."

"It sure is," I said.

She said they would be happy to send it COD to the Royal York, but she was disappointed that we weren't staying in one of their ten Super 8s scattered throughout the Toronto area.

"We wanted something close to the Hockey Hall of Fame," I said.

"Oh, are you those guys travelling there from Saskatchewan?" she asked.

"We are," I said, surprised that she would know that.

"I read about you guys."

I substituted "heard" for "read" in my mind, assuming that she had talked to Uncle Richard when he went down for breakfast.

"We'll send the hat free of charge. Good luck to you all."

I automatically said "Thanks" and she rattled off "Have a great day" before hanging up. It took a few seconds to register what she had said. They were paying? That was what I called customer service.

I went back to the table in the restaurant and sat down.

"The hat'll be at the Royal York in Toronto when we check in," I said.

Dad smiled and looked at Uncle. "Good thinking, Rich."

I pushed them hard and refused to stop again until we made it to Thunder Bay. Dad was cheerful in the back, nibbling on some rice cakes that Mom had packed, but Uncle Richard was stiffening up and getting grumpy. We found a Super 8 along the highway and had the same sleeping arrangements.

I had planned to make Sault Ste. Marie the next day, but both men were slow and cranky in the morning. After doing Dad's ritual and finally getting them into the car, I drove down to the lakefront where we watched the big ships being loaded with grain.

"I always wondered about those grain cars rolling by," Dad said. "Rolling across the prairie, getting onto a boat, crossing the ocean and ending up as somebody's bread half a world away."

"You never told me that," I said.

"It'll be freeze-up soon," Uncle said. "Then the ships will have to wait until spring."

I didn't want to think about what spring would or would not bring. We ate lunch in downtown Thunder Bay, and then hit the road. I asked Uncle to find a radio station for the news at the top of the hour. He found Thunder Bay's CBC station, 570. The major news story was about some American tourist down East who had been charged with spanking his own daughter in a parking lot.

"Discipline," Uncle Richard said. "Respect. It's what's missing in kids today." He paused to consider his own statement, then added over his shoulder, "Remember that time we were caught smoking under the school steps?"

Dad grunted so Uncle continued, "We were hauled into the principal's office, both of us. Old man..."

"Edwards," Dad finished. He stretched his arm over the front seat and Uncle whapped his hand twice with the map.

"That strap hurt," Uncle said, "How many whacks? A dozen?"

"Three," Dad growled.

"Felt like more," Uncle said. "but you'd know. Edwards had you in there almost every week."

"Hand got pretty hard," Dad said. "Then we'd go home..."

"And Mom would have heard somehow," Uncle continued, "and she'd say, 'Wait until your Pa gets home.'"

"That razor strap," Dad said.

"And he didn't discriminate," Uncle said. "He would hit anybody."

I had never heard the "strap at school" story before, but I had seen Grandpa's razor strap hanging on a nail behind their kitchen door. Sometimes after Dad had taken me over his knee at home, he would say how lucky I was because his one-by-two spanking stick was only eighteen inches long and didn't hurt nearly as much as Grandpa's razor strap had.

"That was my only time smoking at school," Uncle said. "Edwards taught me a lesson. Now they can't even raise their voice, let alone touch a kid."

When I'm working in the store and hear some parent holler, and then the kid ducks and puts up a hand to cover their head, I feel queasy. I usually head for a coffee break about that time.

We made it as far as Wawa by Tuesday evening. Wawa

didn't have a Super 8, so we stayed at the Travelodge. Uncle Richard had brought in the road map, and was studying it.

"You know," he said after supper, "at this rate we'll probably get to Sudbury tomorrow, and then it's still a long drive in to Toronto on Thursday. We have to check into the Royal York, get Harold's hat, pick up the hockey tickets and go to the rink."

"I want to be there early," Dad said. "For warm-ups."

"It's going to be tight," I said, "especially when we never get moving until noon."

Uncle Richard bent over the map. "From Sudbury, it looks like less than four hundred klicks into Toronto. No problem."

I called Medicine Hat from our room in Wawa to check in with Mom and also to see if I was an uncle yet. George answered the phone.

"Les, you sly dog. How are the celebrities?"

"Celebrities?"

"Don't give me that. There's been stories in the papers all week."

"George, what are you talking about?"

"You know all about it. The first headline said...let's see here, we cut them all out. Oh yeah, 'Sears Employee on Pilgrimage.' The one today says 'Sears Helps Final Wish Come True.'"

"And it's about us?" I asked.

"Sort of. Mainly how Sears gave you time off to take your sick dad to the Hall of Fame in Toronto, and how they're offering help at all their stores along the route, and giving you tickets to their corporate box for Thursday's game."

"But nobody's talked to us," I said.

"I guess no one knew where you were," George explained. "We've had a couple of calls from reporters wondering how they could reach you."

"Well, don't tell them," I said.

"Your Mom mentioned that you were staying at the Royal York in Toronto."

"Wonderful," I said. "Listen, let me explain this to Dad and Uncle Richard. Then I'll call back and everyone can talk."

I hung up the phone. Just hearing my side of the conversation had grabbed their attention. Uncle had already muted the TV and Dad was sitting up on the bed.

"It looks like my employer is after some publicity," I said. Then I explained to them what was happening.

"There was something in the paper about us?" Dad asked.

I nodded.

"Front page or Sports section?"

I said I didn't know.

"Depends," Uncle said, "on which paper it was in."

"It would have only been in the *Leader-Post*," I said. "George said they had cut out the articles."

Then that woman's voice from the Super 8 echoed in my head, saying over the phone, "I've read about you", and I remembered that the only paper in the lobby had been the *Winnipeg Free Press*.

"Does any of that matter?" Uncle Richard asked.

"It means it'll be more public than I was prepared for," I said.

"As long as they don't get in our way," Dad said.

I called back to Medicine Hat, and this time Gail answered.

"So you haven't popped yet?" I asked.

"Nope, and I'm feeling fine. You guys could be back before the baby arrives. Sounds like you've been busy, though."

"It's all a misunderstanding that I'll straighten out once we get to Toronto. Put Mom on and I'll pass the phone to Dad."

They talked for less than five minutes. Dad's voice was low. I imagined Mom asking if he was feeling all right, and if he was getting enough to eat, and if he had missed any pills. He answered in short, tired sentences.

Dad lowered the receiver and asked me, "Anything for your mother?"

I nodded and took the phone.

"Hi, Mom. We'll be in Sudbury tomorrow night, and then we'll get into Toronto in good time the next day. We'll call you from the Royal York on Thursday night."

"Okay, dear. And if any more of those reporters call?"

"Tell them we're on schedule."

"On schedule, I'll say that. It *is* kind of exciting, don't you think?"

I looked over at Dad and Uncle Richard, lying side-by-side in their underwear, watching a fishing show. We had been together for more than seventy-two hours straight now, and there was no end in sight.

"Good night, Mom," I said.

The next morning, Dad was the first one awake. He took his pill and needle, but refused the bath.

"Let's get this show on the road," he said.

Uncle went to the motel office to get us each a coffee to go, and Dad tooted the horn as I took one last look around the room, and then checked under the bed.

Uncle was studying the map, talking to himself and adding up the kilometres, as we cruised through Sault Ste. Marie and headed for Sudbury.

"Unc," I asked, "what are you looking forward to the most?"

"Seeing the game," he said. "Being in Maple Leaf Gardens. I listened to Foster Hewitt on the radio and I've watched *Hockey Night in Canada* on TV for so many years it feels like I already know the place."

Uncle Richard had played junior hockey with the Moose Jaw Canucks, who at the time were affiliated with the Chicago Blackhawks. Dad had told me about the time they were all back home listening to the game being broadcast on the radio and the announcer had called Uncle Richard "the player most likely to put the puck in the net." He was gritty and, if he had been a bit bigger or there had been more than six teams in the NHL back then, would have made it to the "Show."

Uncle went on to play with Moose Jaw's best senior team, the PlaMors. Their name was pronounced like it was really spelled "Play Mores," and they were in the Western Senior Hockey League. Once they were playing the Saskatoon Quakers and Uncle Richard went into the corner with a Saskatoon player, both fighting for the puck. Uncle came out with the puck and a piece of his opponent's ear. In his later years, playing old-timer hockey at the Civic Centre, the opposition still gave him a wide berth.

Uncle now looked out the side window at the lake we were driving beside, and said, "I've dreamed of playing on that ice a million times."

I glanced at him. "When was the last time you dreamed that?"

He looked back at me. "Last night."

Uncle shifted and said over his shoulder, "Harold, what are you looking forward to the most?"

"The Hall of Fame," Dad said, "no doubt. History, trophies, memories, that old equipment. All together."

"Did you know there's a complete replica of the Montreal Canadien's dressing room?" I asked.

"Booo," Dad said.

"Hold on," I said. " It's so real that you can imagine you're right there, getting ready for the game. There's monitors up above showing other players in the room taping their sticks, getting dressed, tightening their skates. Then the coach comes onto the screen, gives a pep talk and says it's time. You go out this door to the roar of the crowd, and it feels like you're right in the middle of the game."

"I'll like that," Uncle said.

"There's always old film being shown in these side rooms," I said. "Playoff highlights, interviews, and team profiles."

"Gonna watch them all," Dad said.

"There's some neat high-tech stuff, too," I said. "You can put on a blocker and mitt, and hold a goalie stick, and pretend to stop the pucks that two Leaf forwards shoot at you. Kind of virtual reality."

"Hunh?" Dad asked.

"It's not real. You see it happening on a TV screen but it's not really taking place. It's done with computers."

"We'll leave that to you," Uncle said.

"Oh, and you can shoot the puck at a screen, for accuracy and speed."

"Show your dad the statistics section," Uncle said, "and he'll be happy for years."

"Something Dad'll be good at," I said, "is playing that interactive game where a group of people answer hockey trivia questions. The results are shown up on a screen as you play."

"I may never leave," Dad said, and coughed.

As we approached Sudbury in mid-afternoon, Uncle said, "You know, we could probably make Parry Sound, or even Barrie."

"How long?" I asked.

"Two or three hours."

"How are you feeling back there, Dad?"

"Full steam," he said, and took a breath, "ahead."

"You know," I said, "tomorrow's a full day. How about we stop here and get a good rest?"

"You tired?" Uncle asked. "Want me to drive?"

"No, I'm okay," I said, nodding toward the back.

"Ahh," Uncle said. "According to this map, the most logical place to stop would be Sudbury. Let's find a motel."

"Maybe we should grab a bite to eat first," I said, not happy with Dad's colour. He was shaking when we got to the restaurant, and I wondered if we should even go in. He needed food, though. Once he had something in his stomach and his white pill, he said he felt better.

Uncle looked through the *Toronto Sun* for any mention of us, but didn't find anything. He seemed disappointed.

"Maybe it's blown over," he said.

"We'll see tomorrow," I said. "Hope it isn't a slow news day."

The beauty of a Super 8 is that you can check into any location on the continent, and your room looks the same. That's also the curse. I woke up Thursday morning thinking we were still in Winnipeg. It wasn't until I showered that I realized we were almost there.

D riving into Toronto in early afternoon, Uncle Richard had the city map open and was directing me to the Royal York.

"How many lanes does this highway have?" he asked as cars passed us on both sides.

"Imagine this at rush hour," I said.

"Sky Dome?" Dad asked.

"Yep, right there. And it looks like the roof's closed today."

"Just further along on your left, gentlemen," I said, "is your destination, the Royal York."

"Looks like a castle," Uncle said, "or a palace."

"Wow," Dad said.

"There, up ahead," Uncle shouted, pointing, "that's the exit. You need to get over one lane – no, other way – one more – there."

I looked in the mirror and could see Dad's head at the back window, eyes glued to the Sky Dome until it dipped out of sight.

"We swing under the highway and work our way back toward the lakefront," Uncle said.

We eventually pulled into a loading zone at the side of the Royal York. A bellboy signalled us from the sidewalk and Uncle rolled down his window.

"No stopping," the bellboy said, "unless you're a bus."

"We have reservations," said Uncle, and then looking at me, "don't we?"

I nodded.

"Pull around the front, and someone will park it for you," the bellboy said.

"La de da," Dad said.

I edged back out into the traffic and we slowly made our way down the block. After a few honks of encouragement from the cars around us, I stopped at the front of the building. My door opened and a voice said, "Will you be staying with us, sir?"

I nodded and a braided jacket with epaulettes on the shoulders appeared. "You can leave the keys in the car, sir, and we'll take it from here."

Dad, Uncle Richard, and I stood on the sidewalk at the bottom of the stairs going into the hotel and looked up.

"It's a castle," Dad said.

"More like a presidential palace," Uncle said. "A castle's cold and windy. This looks quite comfortable."

Inside the hotel lobby, the elegance continued. I managed to get Dad safely resting on a plush couch. Uncle had stopped to watch people going up and down a big spiral staircase. I walked up to the counter to register. I gave my name to the cheerful guy behind the check-in counter, whose silver oblong badge said he was *Charles.*

When Charles came back he was smiling more, and he said, "Ah, Mr. Carson, we've been expecting you. How was the trip?"

"Fine, Charles," I said, feeling exposed.

"Your room number is 2401. Here's the key, plus an extra. Naturally, the bar is stocked and unlocked. Your bags will be delivered. Did you have a car?"

I nodded, suspicious that he was speaking in the past tense.

"The keys will be delivered with your bags, along with the parking pass."

"What credit cards do you take?"

"The room is taken care of, sir. Enjoy your stay, and give our regards to your father."

I was slowly backing away when he snapped his fingers. "One moment, sir, you also have a package."

He slid open a drawer below the counter and produced an envelope with a Sears logo. I opened it as I walked back to the couch. Inside were two passes to their corporate seats, as well as a letter from Mr. Rupert Savoy, vice president of Sears Marketing. He welcomed us to Toronto, wished us good health as we visited, and reminded us of how much the company had helped make the trip possible. Mr. Savoy had included copies of the letter in case we wanted to pass them along to the media.

"We'll need another ticket," I said to Uncle as he joined us at the couch.

"Scalpers," Dad said. "After the puck's dropped, you'll get a seat for half-price."

"I didn't drive four days to catch half a game," Uncle said, "not to mention the warm-up."

"You two are taking the Sears seats," I said. "I'll get something close by."

"It's your company," Dad argued.

I shook my head.

"That's Loss for you," Uncle explained, "always thinking of others. Well, his *loss* is our gain."

"Mr. Carson?"

I looked up to see Charles standing beside me.

"Excuse me, sir," he said, "but I forgot there's another package here for you. It came in yesterday."

He handed me a small box with the Super 8 logo on it, which I tossed to Dad.

"Hat!" Dad said.

Room 2401 turned out to be a suite. It had a foyer with French doors opening onto a hallway. Turning right led to two bedrooms and a bathroom, straight ahead was the living room and balcony, and left gave access to the kitchen and wet bar.

"Each bedroom has its own TV set," Uncle said after his brief tour, "and another one in the living room. We could all be watching something different at the same time."

"Bet they're all cable, too," Dad said.

"Did you see the bathroom?" I asked. "That's a Jacuzzi tub. Great for relaxing."

Dad looked blank.

"You know, hot water, jet streams, bubbles...never mind."

"There's even a bar," Uncle yelled from the kitchen. "Can you imagine if..."

"Check below," I hollered back, "in those cupboards."

"Son of a...," Uncle said, lower. "Bottles of it...Scotch, rum, vodka. There's even a little fridge full of beer, and Clamato juice, and sliced lemons."

"What?" Dad said, "No bartender?"

"Dad asked if there's a bartender back there."

Uncle Richard laughed. "Not even a midget that I can find. That's it, we're outta here."

On the coffee table in front of the couch was a large fruit bowl wrapped in blue cellophane. The card read:

For the Carsons. Enjoy!
From your Sears Family

"That's some company you work for," Dad said.

Uncle had come into the living room munching peanuts.

"There's chips, chocolate bars, beer nuts, pretzels, everything," he said.

"You just help yourself?" Dad asked. "How do you know it's for us?"

"It's our room," Uncle said, tossing Dad a peanut. "Does that flashing light mean anything?"

He was pointing at the phone on the desk.

"Somebody left us a message," I said, picking up the handset.

"Probably mother," Dad said. "Woman can't live without me."

I pushed the button and followed the instructions.

"Mr. Carson, it's the *Toronto Star* calling. Please call Drew Thompson when you get in: 547-6891, extension 53. We'd like to do an interview for tomorrow's edition. It will go out on the wire and the Western papers will pick it up from there. Please call Drew, 547-6891, extension 53, before you go to the game."

I wrote down the name and number. "Some guy from the Toronto Star wants to do an interview," I said.

"You talk," Dad said. "I'm going to lie down."

Uncle said, "I'm going down to the lobby to look around."

"Okay," I said. "I'll call this guy, and you get some rest, Dad. Uncle, don't go too far, especially underground. You can walk for miles down there and it's easy to get turned around."

"I'm from the city, too, remember?"

"That's Moose Jaw, Uncle. There's more people working in this Hotel than in all of downtown Moose Jaw. It's four, so just be back within an hour. We'll need to get ready to go."

Once Uncle left, Dad checked out both bedrooms and chose the one closest to the bathroom. I pulled the curtains while he took his pill and got ready for his needle.

Once Dad was settled on top of his king-sized bed, I went back to the living room and dialed the reporter's number.

"Star."

"Drew Thompson, please."

"You've got her."

"I must have the wrong number. My message was from a man."

"Who's this?"

"I'm Les Carson, calling from the Royal York. I had a message to call..."

"Mr. Carson, you do have the right number. Larry, our administrative assistant, makes all our appointments. It frees us up to do what we do best."

"Okay, Miss Thompson, how do you want to start?"

"Let's start by you calling me Drew, and I'll call you Les."

"Fair enough, Drew. What would you like to know?"

"What possessed you to drive three days to visit Toronto?"

"It was four days, and I had some spare time."

"Come on, Les. I've driven that road. No one makes that trip if they don't have to."

"What possessed you to make it?" I asked.

"I had to. I'm originally from Weyburn; took Journalism at the U of R. I got this job through a school interview, and then couldn't afford to fly. Besides, I had my futon to haul out."

"Everywhere you go," I said, "you meet someone from Saskatchewan."

"That's why I took the story, because someone purposely driving that road for three or four days with relatives along intrigued me."

"Well, it's not as intriguing as it may seem. Dad wanted to see the Hockey Hall of Fame, and, because of his heart, he can't fly."

"Where does Sears fit into all of this?"

"I work for them in Regina."

"And it's just you and your dad?"

"And my Uncle Richard, from Moose Jaw."

She asked questions about our background and plans for the next few days. When I mentioned the hockey game, she asked, "Where are your seats?"

I told her about the two corporate Sears tickets, and how I was going to pick up another one from a scalper.

"I can get you in," she said, "with my Press Pass. I could get a photo, then we can sit in the press box and continue our interview."

That sounded good to me. She explained where the Press entrance was and we agreed to meet there.

"I'll be wearing my Saskatchewan Roughriders hat," I said.

"I could have guessed," Drew said. "What time do you want to meet?"

"We'll be there around six," I said.

"Game doesn't start until eight."

"Okay, six-thirty then."

There was a long pause at the other end.

"Dad doesn't walk very fast, and they'll want to study every inch of the place, and then there's the warm-up, and they'll want a hotdog, and..."

"Six-thirty it is. We'll have time to do a couple of interviews *before* the game starts."

I phoned down to the bell captain to arrange for a taxi to pick us up at six. He said there was a taxicab queue outside the front door, so there was no need to phone ahead.

"Good enough," I said, and hung up.

"Smart thinking to reserve, son," Dad said, "we're lucky you're here. Your Uncle and I would have just gone down and hung around the front doors."

"No problem, Dad," I said.

Maple Leaf Gardens was a twenty-minute cab ride. I could have walked there myself in fifteen minutes, but the crowded streets filled with vehicles and pedestrians made driving a slow business. It was just the right pace for Dad.

"Hey, look at that one, Rich! Green hair, and logging chains for a belt. Was that a boy or girl? Everywhere you turn, you can spot a Negro. I haven't seen an Indian, but there's lots of Pakis."

Uncle Richard continued reminding us of the number of people in Toronto.

"Why, in just in this area alone," he said, "assuming only two people per car, and the people on the sidewalk moving at three abreast and taking up three feet width-wise, that makes in this block alone, at this very moment, more people than in all of Dolguard. Think about that, you two."

"You from out of town?" the cabbie asked.

I fired back, "What was your first clue?"

"Relax, man," the cabbie said. "It's normal for the generation. Where you from?"

"Out west," I said.

"Rich, hey, Rich, look!" Dad said, pointing out the window. "Are they holding hands? Right there, crossing in front of us. Which one's the girl?"

"Keep your back to the wall when we get in a crowd," Uncle advised.

The cabbie tooted at the car in front of us as soon as the light turned green and then said, "Hey, did you hear about that Sears guy from out your way, coming in to see the Leafs?"

"No," I said. "There's our stop up ahead. How much do we owe you?"

"Can't stop here. Gotta pull around the block. Need a receipt? No? Twenty'll cover it, including gratuities."

We were waiting to pull over when the cabbie said, "Did you hear they're thinking of building a new one?"

"New what?" Uncle asked.

"Rink," the cabbie said.

Uncle snorted. "What would they do with this?"

"Tear her down."

"Condemned?" Dad asked.

"Nope," the cabbie said. "Just there's too much money to be made from those corporate boxes to just ignore it."

"Never happen," Dad said, "at least in my lifetime."

"Hope you're right, buddy," said the cabbie. "Enjoy the game."

We were early, but a crowd was already milling around the front entrance. People wearing the white and red Blackhawk sweaters mingled with every style of Maple Leaf jersey I had ever seen, and a few I hadn't. Dad pointed out a husky man wearing a sixties-style jersey with the name Horton on the back.

"Hey, Tim Horton!"

"Shhhussshh!" I hissed. "Tim Horton's dead, Dad. It's just a fan."

"Maybe his son, wearing his dad's sweater," Dad argued. "Never know until you ask."

"Back when Horton played," Uncle Richard piped up, "they didn't put names on the sweater."

"You're right, Rich," Dad said. "Good point."

I thought that the point I had made about Horton being dead was pretty valid too, but I didn't pursue it. I handed them their tickets.

"Go inside and find a place for Dad to sit down close by the entrance," I said. "I have to meet this reporter and go in using a Press Pass. Then I'll come and get you to your seats."

"Don't worry about us," Dad said, nodding and smiling at people as they brushed past.

"Uncle," I pleaded, "no wandering around, okay? Just get inside these doors and wait. We have plenty of time."

Uncle Richard nodded and took Dad's elbow. I watched as they went through the front doors and held out their tickets to the blue-uniformed man standing at the turnstile.

I touched my Roughrider hat to make sure it was snug on my head and hustled around the corner. The door I was supposed to meet the reporter at was half a block down. A Yellow cab pulled up to the curb and four men got out, all carrying small suitcases. I heard boos as they made their way through the small crowd toward the door. I heard someone whistling "Three Blind Mice" and realized that this must be the referee and two linesmen arriving for the game. The fourth would be the spare official, ready to fill in if any of the others got sick or injured.

I was watching them go through the door, which was held open by a white-haired man in a blue uniform, when I heard someone behind me say, "Les? Les Carson?"

I turned around and saw a short woman. She had dark red hair, bright blue eyes, and was wearing a Weyburn Red Wings jacket. A big leather pouch hung from one shoulder and a camera case was slung over the other.

"Drew Peterson?"

She nodded. "My real name's Nancy, but at University I started using Drew for my byline. It sounded more journalistic. Then when I moved out here, nobody knew me as Nancy, so it was just easier to be called Drew."

"What do your parents call you?"

"They don't." She handed me a badge. "Here, clip this onto your coat, and carry the camera in for me. Act like you own it. They've been cracking down on people sneaking in."

"Hey, I'm no criminal. I can find my own ticket."

"Relax, Les. Chances are we won't even get stopped. Sheesh, I'd forgotten about that *pride* thing you farmers cultivate. It's about the only crop that grows consistently out west, isn't it?"

"I'm not a farmer," I said as we breezed through the door with a nod to the doorman.

"Number seventeen," I said, pointing at her sleeve with my chin. "What year did you play with the Wings?"

"Boyfriend, last year of high school. Got traded to Estevan. I had to choose: him or the jacket."

"And?"

"I'm wearing the jacket."

We stopped at a hallway intersection. I pointed in what I thought was the direction of the front entrance. "My dad and uncle are waiting for us to join them."

"Is he in a wheelchair?"

"Who?"

"Your father. Can he walk or do we need to take the elevator?"

"He can walk," I explained, "but not for very long, or very far, without resting. An elevator would be great."

The crowd was getting thicker as we neared the entrance.

"What do they look like?" Drew asked.

I shrugged.

"Well then, what are they wearing?"

"Oh, Dad's wearing a white Leafs hat with a bunch of pins stuck all over it. Uncle Richard's bald on top, and he's wearing this black winter jacket with Co-op stitched in the front. They should be sitting down some-place."

We found them burying a hotdog in ketchup.

"Your dad started feeling woozy," Uncle said, "and then we both realized we hadn't eaten since noon. Is she the newspaper guy?"

I nodded. "Uncle Richard and Dad, this is Drew Peterson. She's been writing the articles."

"Weyburn, eh?" Dad said, nodding at the jacket. "They're doing good this year."

"Always do," Drew replied, holding out her hand. "It's a pleasure to meet you."

Uncle Richard gave a little bow, dipping the front of

his jacket into his hotdog. "Pleasure's ours," he said, wiping off the ketchup.

"You know your way around here?" Dad asked.

When Drew nodded, he held up his ticket stub. "How do we get to here? I gotta sit."

Drew took us down a hallway. The trip was slow. Dad couldn't walk very fast, even leaning on my arm. The walls were filled with pictures of former Leaf stars, and each one had to be examined and commented on. We eventually came to an elevator.

"Press C," said Drew.

"C for Corporate seats," Uncle whispered to me as the doors closed. "Everything's so logical in these big cities. Has to be, with so many people."

The doors opened again and Drew said, "Here's the Concourse level. Turn left when you get out. Your seats are right around the corner."

There were hardly any people on this level. The archway leading out to the seats was like a giant magnet, pulling Dad faster and faster with every step he took forward. Uncle Richard was speeding ahead but slowed down so they could go through the archway together. They both stopped on the landing and simultaneously let out a small moan.

"Ohh, the ice is so white," Uncle said.

"Look at all the seats," Dad said. "The Blues, the Reds. You never see them all at once on TV. Remember that time Garth Ermel came to a game? He sat way up in the Greys."

"Here are your seats," Drew said. "Right on the aisle."

"Extra big," Uncle said, "with cup holders built right in."

"Look," Dad said, "someone left their program from last game."

"They're for tonight's game," Drew said, "complimentary. All the seats along here have them. See?" She pointed up and down the row. "You don't even have to get up for refreshments, if you don't want to. A waitress comes out and takes your orders."

Dad shook his head. "Not during the game?"

"I believe so," Drew answered. "And don't be surprised if the seats in the bottom half look almost empty when the game starts. Many of those people don't get to their seats until the first period's almost over."

"Where will you guys be sitting?" Uncle asked.

Drew pointed directly across the ice, and then way up. "They don't waste any good locations on the media," she chuckled. "I usually watch the television monitor."

"City people," Dad said, shaking his head again. "Come to a real live game and either miss the first period or watch it on a TV." He sat down in his seat and flipped open the program.

Uncle said, "Maybe I'll grab us a brew before I get too comfortable. Canadian?"

"Coffee," Dad mumbled, already deep into the first article.

"Nothing for me," I said. "I don't want to topple off our perch up there."

"Let's go get a spot, then," Drew said. "You can fill me in on the trip details."

We were still an hour early and the long booth filled with chairs, telephones, and televisions was nearly empty. The players came onto the ice and went through their warm-ups as I answered Drew's questions about our trip. I watched Dad and Uncle leaning forward in their seats, taking in every movement, every action down below them. Even after the players left the ice surface, their heads followed the Zamboni back and forth as it flooded the ice, watching as intently as they had studied the stretching and shooting.

The hockey game itself seemed to lack intensity. Drew reminded me that even though this game was a rare event for us, it was just one more Thursday night in an eighty-game schedule for the players. It was their job, and on this night at least, they mainly went through the motions. The action picked up halfway through the third period, after Chicago scored to cut Toronto's lead to a single goal, 3-2. The crowd roared as a Blackhawk shot rang off the post, and I saw Uncle Richard stand as the Leafs rushed back the other way. Someone must have hollered at him to sit down, because he looked behind him as he slowly sank back into his seat. With less than a minute left to play, Chicago pulled their goalie for an extra forward and Toronto scored into the empty net. By the time the final buzzer sounded, the building was half-empty.

"It's a different atmosphere on Saturday night," Drew assured me as we made our way back down. "Players from both teams remember watching *Hockey Night in Canada* as kids, and know that they're being seen from coast to coast. It adds some zip."

Dad and Uncle Richard were still in their seats.

"Can we go and wait by the dressing rooms?" Uncle asked.

Dad's face looked grey, and his head hung down. I waited for him to say something, but he kept quiet.

"We've had enough for tonight," I said. "Tomorrow's a big day at the Hall, and then there's another game on Saturday."

"Besides," Drew added, "I wanted to ask you two a few questions about tonight's game, for tomorrow's paper."

"I think people should get here on time," Dad said.

"And not leave until it's over," Uncle added.

"At these ticket prices," Dad continued, "you'd expect them to want to see the whole game."

"It's the traffic," Uncle said. "With this many people..."

"What did you think of the game?" I asked.

"Oh, it was okay," Dad said.

Uncle nodded. "A bit scramblier than I'd have thought, but they can all turn it on when they have to."

"Just watching the warm-ups," Dad said, "you could tell that every one of them, even the guys who didn't end up playing, could shoot like a cannon."

"Watching them skate around," Uncle said, "flipping the puck up with their sticks, it was just like our kids do."

"They are kids," Drew said, "just playing a game."

"I thought the game lacked intensity," I said.

"You, Loss?" Uncle asked. "You're questioning their desire to win? Think the Blackhawks threw the game, maybe?"

I shook my head. "For the money they make, I thought it was pretty tame."

Dad hadn't joined in. I bent down to look closer and saw that his eyes were closed.

"Dad?"

His eyes fluttered open. "Hunh?"

"We're heading back to the hotel," I said. "It's time for your pills."

Drew shared a cab back with us, insisting that the newspaper pick up the tab. As the taxi pulled up to the Royal York, she asked what time we would be going to the Hall of Fame.

"Around 10:30," I said.

"Until when?"

"Until it closes," Dad said.

"I may meet up with you there," she said, "if that's all right. Now I have to go and file your story."

I waved as the taxi pulled away, and she answered with a thumbs-up.

"Nice girl," Uncle Richard said, and Dad chuckled.

"She's a reporter," I said, "just doing her job."

We ordered pizza from room service. By the time it arrived, Dad was snoring. Uncle and I managed to finish off his share.

Pepperoni never did agree with my stomach, and I tossed all night. I was running down a bumpy road, trying to catch up to my dad, who kept getting farther and farther away. When I woke up, Uncle Richard was shaking my arm.

"Wh...where, where's he going?" I mumbled.

"Who?" Uncle asked.

I blinked and rubbed my eyes. "Oh, nothing. What time is it?"

"After nine. Rise and shine my boy. It's another fabulous, grey day in the city."

"Dad?"

"He's having his bath in that big tub. We ordered in eggs benedict for breakfast. We're living like kings!"

"Only until Sunday," I said, throwing off the covers. "I'm back at work again Thursday."

"Newspaper was delivered with the breakfast," Uncle said. *"Globe and Mail,* though. We'll have to look for Drew's paper – the *Star,* right? – on our way to the Hall."

"Why? Oh, the article."

"And she took our picture, too," Uncle said. "Maybe we'll get recognized and have to sign autographs."

I was enjoying my eggs when there was a knock at the door. Uncle Richard opened it and a bellhop walked in, pushing a wheelchair. It had "Royal York" printed in big letters across the backrest.

"Compliments of the hotel," he said.

Uncle reached into his pocket and dug out a loonie, something I'm sure he had only seen done on television.

The bellhop held up his hand. "It's all been taken care of, sir," he said. "There's a note explaining that along with the newspaper." Then he backed out, shutting the door behind him.

Uncle reached down into the chair and picked up the *Toronto Star* off the seat.

"There's a note here," he said, "from Drew. It says:

Les, I don't want to intrude, but thought you may not know that the Hotel has complimentary wheelchairs. Should make it easier to get around, and help your dad last the long day at the Hall. The article's on page S1 — photo got bumped by the picture of the stock car accident. Hi, Richard! Maybe catch you guys later. Covering a university basketball tourney today. Cheers, Drew."

Uncle handed me the note while he opened the newspaper to section S.

"Nope." Dad was standing in the hallway just outside the bathroom, pointing at the wheelchair.

"It's for your own good," I said. "I should have thought of it earlier."

"I'm no cripple," Dad said.

"You can walk when you want, and sit when you get tired," I said. "Best of both worlds. I'll push it."

"I was studying the maps downstairs," Uncle Richard piped up, "and you can walk from here to the Hall, all underground. Never have to go outside. It's only about four blocks, as the crow flies."

"I'll walk," Dad said.

I sighed. "I'll take the wheelchair, just in case. We can put our coats and stuff on it."

"Like a shopping cart," Uncle said.

I nodded and Dad grunted.

The trip over was painfully slow. After the third bench-break, I convinced Dad to sit in the wheelchair "just until we get to the Hall." Uncle Richard studied each map we came to, explaining what building or tower we were at the bottom of, and directing us which way to turn. We only had to backtrack once before seeing the Hall of Fame entrance. There was a lineup at the admission window, so I pushed the wheelchair to the back of the queue. When I stopped, Dad stayed sitting.

Uncle pointed to our right. "Look, a gift shop. Should we get something now?"

I shook my head. "That's the exit," I explained. "Everyone leaving passes through the store, and usually buys something."

"Clever marketing," Uncle said.

"Robbers," Dad replied.

"And you haven't even seen the prices yet," I said.

After we had paid to get in, the ticket guy said, "Thank you for visiting us."

As we walked through toward the first exhibits, Uncle leaned over the wheelchair and whispered, "I think he recognized us."

Dad nodded knowingly just as the ticket guy said to the people right behind us, "Thank you for visiting the Hall of Fame."

Our view opened up and we could see the first big, bright room with rows of exhibits and displays.

"Ohhhh," Uncle Richard sighed.

I was looking ahead, walking right behind the wheelchair. When it suddenly stopped, one of the handles dug into my stomach.

"Ouch," I said.

Dad was leaning forward and his head slowly swiveled from side to side, like the turret on one of those big Panzer tanks from World War Two. He spotted his target and rolled forward. He was starting with the player inductees. There were rows of panels with individual information and statistics about each player, as well as audio and sometimes even video. Dad was thorough, reading every piece of information and listening to all options of the voice and video recordings. He would get up from the wheelchair to examine the photographs up close. After finishing with an exhibit he opened up his Hall of Fame magazine and checked off that specific display.

Uncle Richard moved faster, but slowed the whole process down by continually coming back and explaining what was up ahead to Dad. The wheelchair was easy to roll on the cement floor, so Dad could slowly move ahead by himself. I went into one of the side theatres to watch the old films, and after each segment, got up to check on his progress. At the pace he was going, I figured we wouldn't be out of there until the new millenium.

By the time Dad made his way to the area where the Hockey Trivia game was played, Uncle Richard had already won twice and was waiting to challenge him.

"Wheel right up, old-timer," he said. "Let me show you a thing or two about hockey trivia."

There were ten stations arranged in a circle where the players stood, facing inward. Each person selected a different NHL team name for identification. The question was displayed on an overhead screen in the middle and the contestants entered their answers on a keypad in front of them. Everyone who answered the question correctly got a point and the first one to ten points was the winner. The standings were displayed on the screen, showing the team names and their point totals. I played the first game and chose Islanders as my team name. I ended up eighth. The BlackHawks, – probably Uncle Richard – were third. The Red Wings won and I only had to glance at the smirk on Dad's face to know which team he had chosen. We played again and this time I was sixth. The Hawks were first and the Red Wings second. Dad disputed one of the answers and wanted to lodge a protest with someone in charge, but Uncle said, "Come on, quit whining and let's play the rubber match."

"Is anyone else hungry?" I asked.

They both nodded but neither made a move to leave the game. I left them hunched over their keypads and went back to the entrance. The ticket seller gave me a pass so I could get back in without having to pay again, and then I went out into the underground maze. I thought it might take a while to find a food court or something, but directly across from the Hall was a store that sold sandwiches and drinks.

I was walking back toward the Hall entrance beside the lineup of people waiting to get in, with my arms full of submarine sandwiches and chocolate milks, when I heard, "Leeess! Hey, Les!" I looked behind me down the hallway and didn't see anyone I recognized. People in the queue were looking around, too. "Leeess!" Was there another Les in the crowd? A man wearing a green Saskatchewan Roughriders jacket in front of me pointed up over my shoulder. I turned and saw Drew, waving and walking down some stairs that I assumed led from the street.

"I was wondering how I'd find you," Drew said. She was carrying that big black satchel and had a camera around her neck.

"How was the basketball?" I asked.

"Fine," she said, looking around. "How are things going here? Crowded?"

I shook my head. "It's a big place, and *most* people are moving through pretty quick."

She caught the inflection and my meaning, and grinned. "Some people aren't lucky enough to be world travellers," she said, "who get to visit places like this more than once."

I nodded. "I hate thinking about it," I said, "so usually don't, but this is definitely Dad's only chance to see this stuff."

"Here," she said, "let me help you carry some of that food."

When we got to the ticket taker, I showed him my pass. He nodded absently and then smiled. "Hi, Drew."

"Hey, Ron. How's business?"

"It's been real good. I think your piece about those guys coming all the way from Alberta...."

"Saskatchewan," I said.

"Whatever. I think it's got some locals wondering what they've been missing. Lineups all week."

"Ron," said Drew, pointing to me, "this is Les Carson, one of the fellows I wrote about."

Ron seemed to notice me for the first time, and stuck out his hand. "Nice to meet you," he said.

"Likewise," I said. "Here, Drew, let me pay your way in."

They both laughed.

"Drew doesn't pay," Ron said. "Get moving. You're holding up the line."

"One of the perks," Drew said softly as we went though. "This is a great place to do some quick research, so I come here a lot."

Dad and Uncle Richard were still playing the trivia game, although there was a small lineup behind them waiting their turns to try. Detroit and Chicago were tied, but for second place. The Edmonton Oilers were in first, and stayed there as the last two questions were answered.

"Uncle," I said loudly, "Dad, let's eat."

They both looked grumpy, surveying the other players as they moved toward us.

"So who's the Oiler?" Uncle asked.

Dad nodded toward a long-haired teenager wearing a Montreal Canadiens sweater and walking away from us.

I coughed and asked innocently, "Beaten by a Habs fan?"

"Fluke," Dad said.

"Just happened to get asked the ten questions he knew," Uncle added.

The Hab sweater was out of sight now. I didn't mention that the long-haired teenager also happened to be a girl.

"Drew!" Uncle said. "How goes it today?"

"Excellent." Drew answered. "It's Friday, snow is in the air, and we're at the Hall. What more could you want?"

Uncle laughed, but I heard Dad mumble, "A new heart."

Drew knew the Hall inside out, and while we were

munching on our subs, she told us about her favourite spots. Uncle wrote them down on a napkin, while Dad compared them against his check marks in the magazine.

"I could see you two," Drew said, "as colour commentators. You've got to check out the TSN trailer. It shows what goes into broadcasting a hockey game, how they decide what camera angles to use and all that."

"Radio," Dad said.

In his best Foster Hewitt imitation, Uncle Richard intoned, "Good evening, hockey fans from coast to coast in Canada, and around the world on short-wave."

"Oh, that's good," said Drew to a beaming Uncle. "You'll have to try out the Gondola. There are four booths, each with a recording of a famous goal. There's Paul Henderson's against the Russians, and also Mario Lemieux from Gretzky against the Czechs. You hear the announcer and see the action, and then the video's replayed, with you calling the play-by-play. It's harder than it sounds."

We had talked about that specific exhibit in the car on the trip out, but now Uncle acted like it was the first he had heard of it, and it was one of the Seven Wonders of the World. "Wow. That sounds amazing. Where was that again?"

I rolled my eyes. "I expect we'll find it sooner or later," I said. "We're combing through this place like it's a crime scene."

"Lighten up, Loss," said Uncle.

"Loss?" asked Drew.

"Oh, for Pete's sake," I said, "let's get moving."

Having Drew there made the time go by a bit quicker. While Dad and Uncle pored through the posted statistics for each inductee, we tried out the games like goaltending and shot accuracy. The Gondola was entertaining, with Uncle speaking so fast and with such excitement that you couldn't understand a word he was saying. When it was my turn, I caught myself watching the play and forgetting to speak, so I had to skip some description to get to the ending on time. Dad was better, but spoke too slowly as the play developed. Since he wouldn't skip ahead, he ended up explaining the action after the fact. Drew was good with the details, but I thought her voice became too high-pitched whenever the goal was scored. Naturally, Uncle thought she walked on water.

By four o'clock, Dad was beat. I could see it in the way his shoulders were drooping. When he thought no one was looking, he would close his eyes.

"Time to go," I said.

"No way," Dad answered, tensing up.

"We haven't hit the Habs dressing room yet," Uncle said, "and then there's the room with all the trophies, and then the..."

"Souvenirs," Dad added.

"We'll come back again tomorrow," I said. "It's not going anywhere."

There was a five-second pause while they thought through this option.

"We do have all day," Uncle conceded. "Game doesn't start until..."

"Seven," Dad said.

"We'll get back here around ten," I said, "and be done by mid-afternoon."

"Still gives us time for a nap and a snack before the game," Uncle said. "Sounds good to me. I could use another day here, and I am getting overloaded."

Dad nodded.

"Wait then," Drew said. "Let me get a couple of pictures of you looking at the displays before we go. In case I can use them in a follow-up article."

"Where do you want us?" Uncle asked.

"How about around that Trivia game?" Drew asked.

"As long as they don't start playing another game," I said.

"Wimp," Dad said.

I got in the picture, too, standing on Dad's left with Uncle on the right. Then Drew took a handful of us each individually looking at the displays. On our way out, we went through the gift store and looked at some of the merchandise. Uncle picked up a keychain with the Hall of Fame emblem attached.

"For the Olds," he said. "Something for the old girl to remember the trip by."

Drew smiled and I said, "Fine, but that's all. Let's leave the rest of the shopping for tomorrow."

"Sheesh," Uncle said, "I don't remember bringing the wife along."

"You're already married?" Drew sighed. "Just my luck."

We all laughed at that.

Drew walked back to the Royal York through the Underground with us and then left, after saying she would see us again on Saturday.

Back in our hotel room, Dad wheeled straight to the bathroom. Uncle poured two white rum and Cokes and opened me a Budweiser while I listened to our phone messages. Mom had called, wondering how we were doing, and so had some guy from Sears Marketing, asking if we had enjoyed using the complimentary tickets.

We sat in the living room watching television. After ten minutes, Uncle got up to open the balcony doors a crack, and I went to check on Dad. The wheelchair was outside the bathroom door, but the room was empty. He was curled up on his bed, breathing deeply. I covered him with the white terry cloth bathrobe and went back to the living room.

"Dig into that second drink," I told Uncle Richard, "Dad's out. I'll grab a menu and see what we can order for supper."

"Okay," Uncle replied, eyes still glued to the TV. "Then maybe we can call up one of these movies they're advertising."

I ordered barbecued ribs and Uncle Richard insisted on baby calf liver. Room Service said it would be forty-five minutes. I gave Mom a call while we were waiting.

"Hello, Les," she said. "How was the day at the Hall of Fame?"

"Outstanding," I said. "Dad's exhausted and sleeping. It was a pretty full day."

"How's he holding up?"

"Pretty good," I said. "He's not complaining."

"Is he taking his pills?"

"Yep, and he's being pretty independent about it, too.

Maybe not having you around to do everything for him is a good thing."

"That makes me feel better," Mom said.

"I didn't mean it that way," I said. "It's just…"

"I know what you mean," Mom said. "Sometimes, well, it's just easier to do it."

I nodded, remembering the few times I had crossed him. He could make the entire family's life miserable for weeks at a time, and hold a grudge for months.

"How's Gail feeling?" I asked.

"She's fine. We had some excitement last night. She was craving East Indian food, so George ordered in from the Bombay Club. She went to bed early and then sat up around midnight, complaining of cramps. George got all excited, rushing around and getting ready to go. Then she burped, said 'too much curry,' lay back down and went to sleep. Poor George, he looked so disappointed, standing there with her suitcase in one hand and coat in the other."

"Do they know whether it's a boy or girl yet?"

"I'm not sure," Mom said. "At the last ultrasound, Gail still couldn't decide if she wanted to know or not. So she asked the nurse to write it down on a piece of paper and fold it up. When she got home, she put the paper into the little wedding ring box she keeps in her jewellery case. I've seen her holding the box, but I don't think she's read the paper yet."

"How about George?"

"Everyone knows he can't keep a secret, so telling him wasn't an option."

I chuckled, remembering playing poker with him. Mom was right.

"What are you doing tomorrow?" she asked.

"Oh, we didn't finish at the Hall, so we're going back for a few hours. Then it's the game."

"Okay, don't let him get worn down. We'll be watching on TV, in case they show the crowd. Where are you sitting?"

My mind blanked out for an instant, and then I couldn't catch my breath.

"Les? Are you still there?"

"Unnh, yeah. Someone's at the door. Gotta go."

I hung up and leaned forward, head in my hands. We didn't have any tickets for the Saturday night game. I had been so busy thinking of getting here, and picking up the Sears tickets for Thursday's game, and visiting the Hall, that I hadn't planned anything for Saturday.

"Les," Uncle Richard said, "you're white as a ghost. Everything okay at home?"

"They're fine," I moaned. "We're screwed."

Uncle put his drink down. "What is it?"

"We don't have any tickets for tomorrow night's game."

"What? Of course we do. We've been planning this for..."

I shook my head. "Didn't get any."

Uncle snorted. "You're kidding."

I shook my head again, looking at him so he would know I wasn't fooling.

"Loss," he said, "if this is a joke..."

"Wish it was."

He exhaled loudly. "Okay, let's think. There's the ticket office...."

"Always sold out for Saturday."

"What about the Sears seats?"

"They gave me the Thursday tickets because Saturday was already committed for some salesman award."

"Scalpers?"

"If we've got a couple of hundred dollars a ticket."

Uncle shrugged. "Nothing else is costing us anything, so it's an option. What about Drew?"

"I expect the Press Box will be packed, since it's Saturday and televised."

"She'll have connections. Maybe she can scrounge up a ticket, call in a favour."

"I think you watch too much TV," I said. "I'd hate to bother her, even if I knew how to get hold of her."

Uncle leaned forward and tugged his thick wallet out of his pants pocket. He unfolded it and shuffled through the bills. "Her cell number," he said, pulling out a business card.

"I didn't get one of those," I said.

"You snooze, you lose."

"Since you're on such good terms," I said, "maybe you should give her a call."

"If I had been the one to mess up," he said, "then I would."

"Okay," I sighed, "give me the card."

The answering machine picked up. It didn't give her name, but said, "You have reached 781-4867. Leave a message." It sounded like her voice, and the number matched the one on the card, so I said, "Drew, this is Les Carson. We have a problem. No tickets for tomorrow night's game. Don't ask how, but I forgot. Can you help? We're willing to pay scalpers, but wanted to check with you first. Call me if you have any contacts that we could buy a ticket from. Thanks." I left the Royal York's phone number and our room, in case she had forgotten.

"I wonder where she is?" Uncle asked.

I shrugged. "Maybe out with her girlfriend."

He looked at me sharply.

"Just kidding," I said.

Dad woke up just after we had finished eating. He came rolling into the front room in the wheelchair. Our kitchen had a microwave, so I warmed up some garlic toast we hadn't eaten, and he ate some coleslaw. There was milk in the fridge, and he had his pills with a cup of that. We hadn't discussed the topic, but neither Uncle nor I mentioned the ticket mix-up with him. I figured that two of us worrying about it was enough, and Uncle seemed more interested in finishing the bottle of white rum than tattling.

"We were thinking of watching a movie," I said. "Any requests?"

"Magnificent Seven," Dad said.

"That's a little old," I said. "It may not be on, especially pay-per-view. Any other choice?"

"Any Western with Dean Martin's good," he said. *"Rio Bravo?"*

"Okay, let me look." I flipped through the *TV Guide.* "How about a Western with Clint Eastwood? Do you like him?"

"Sure," he said, *"Rawhide."*

"This is a little newer," I said, "It's called *The Unforgiven.* It's got Gene Hackman in it, too."

Dad nodded and Uncle Richard said, "Lots of action in that. When's it start?" He held up his glass. "Time for a top-up?"

Drew didn't return our call that night. By morning I started to worry that perhaps I had left the message on the wrong phone. Who wouldn't leave their name on their recording? "Hello, you've reached the number you dialed" seemed like a useless message to me. She was probably thinking anyone who drove across three provinces to go to a hockey game without reserving any tickets was as useless as ankle guards, too.

I phoned the ticket office at Maple Leaf Gardens from my room. The person on the other end chuckled when I asked for tickets to that night's game. I left my name and where we were staying, in case something came up at the last minute. I tried Drew's number again, but hung up when the recording came on.

Dad was sitting by the outside door in his wheelchair, rocking back and forth, while Uncle was still in the shower. "Let's go!" he hollered as Uncle stepped out of the bathroom in his white terry cloth robe.

"Shhhuusshhh," Uncle hissed. "Pour me some juice while you're waiting."

Dad had his tattered Hall of Fame magazine out, reviewing the places he still wanted to see. "Two-thirds done," he said as we rode the elevator down to the underground maze.

I didn't want to spoil Dad's day at the Hall by having him worrying about the game tickets, so I didn't say anything. Uncle Richard must have had the same thought, because he also kept quiet.

The fellow at the admissions counter remembered me. "Hey, Drew's friend," he said, "How's it going?"

"Great," I said, stalling until Dad and Uncle had moved on. "Say, you wouldn't know where a guy could pick up some tickets to tonight's game, would you?"

He thought for a second, and then shook his head. "Maybe someone out front of the Gardens. Get there early and maybe you can find some regular guy just trying to dump his tickets. Don't sound desperate. Scalpers show no mercy. They'll ask for your first-born."

"Thanks for the advice, man," I said, and hustled off to catch up to the men.

The first highlight of the day was the Canadiens' dressing room. We sat through the whole procedure twice: the players getting ready for the game, the coach's talk, the walk out onto the ice surface. It was so real that it didn't take much to imagine that you were really there.

The second highlight was the room with all the trophies. I asked a guy behind us to take a picture of the three of us around the Stanley Cup. Dad stood up for it, pushing the wheelchair out of the shot. Uncle Richard had his picture taken with every major trophy, even the Lady Byng, the one trophy he said he had never wanted to win.

The third and most unexpected highlight was just before the entrance into the gift shop. There was a line-up waiting to go up to a long wooden table. Sitting behind the table, signing autographs, were two older men. I got closer and read a sign to the left of the table, identifying them as Gump Worsley, the Montreal

Canadiens' legendary goaltender, and Johnny Bucyk, star left winger with the Boston Bruins. Both Dad and Uncle Richard recognized them without the sign's help. They stayed back, as if moving closer would reveal that it wasn't really the two Hall of Famers, but impersonators acting as them for the show. Bucyk waved his hand in the air as he talked to someone at the table, and I saw the glint of the big Stanley Cup ring on his finger. I moved closer, surprised at how small both men looked; and old. They would both be around sixty, I realized, but had also led hard lives. Gump had stopped pucks in the era before goalie masks, and Bucyk had been an average-sized man playing a hard-nosed winger, long before the invention of the armour worn now.

"Get in line," I said. "Talk to them."

"They can sign my book," Dad said.

Uncle pulled out a ten-dollar bill. "The best ten bucks I'll ever never spend," he said.

When they eventually got up to the table, there were glossy pictures of Worsley and Bucyk already autographed that could be purchased, so Uncle did that. Both men added "To Richard" just above their names, using black felt pen. They were friendly, and not at all in a hurry. They seemed to enjoy reminiscing almost as much as Dad and Uncle. The lineup was getting longer and longer, and still they talked. Jean Beliveau, Gordie Howe, and Bobby Orr were all evaluated. Tim Horton was the strongest defenceman Bucyk had ever played against, and the hardest shot the Gumper had faced belonged to Bobby Hull.

"We'd better move along," I finally said, nodding toward all the faces watching us in the lineup.

"Oh yeah," Uncle said.

Dad shrugged.

They all shook hands, and Dad rolled away in a daze.

"Nobody's gonna believe this," Uncle Richard said.

"I took a couple of pictures of you talking and shaking hands," I said.

"That's my boy," Dad said.

They were so pleased with themselves that I almost got them through the gift shop without buying anything.

An hour and two hundred dollars later, we were back in our hotel room. I helped Dad to lie down for a rest, and noticed that the message light was flashing.

"Les, this is Drew. Got your message. Listen, normally I'd get you all into the Press Box, but there's no way on a Saturday. I'm even relegated to standing room only. I've been calling all over since last night, and we may have caught a break. I'm waiting for a return call, but a friend said that his in-laws have offered him their two tickets for tonight as an anniversary present. His wife would rather go to *The Phantom of the Opera*. I said I'd get tickets for that, and we could swap. He's just checking that it won't cause a family crisis. It would be a bit tricky to lie about because the seats are right behind the Leafs bench, so they get seen on television. I'll call you back when I hear."

Uncle Richard was watching me as I hung up the phone. I held my right hand out flat and wobbled it back and forth. "Touch and go," I said, "but she's got a lead."

"She'll come through," he said.

"Looks like only two tickets," I said, "so you guys can go."

Uncle shook his head. "It's Father and Son night. There won't be another chance."

"He'd rather go with you."

"Are you kidding me?" Uncle asked. "You're giving him the time of his life."

"The seats are right behind the Leafs bench," I said.

Uncle smiled. "That would be something you don't see every day," he said.

"I can go another time," I said. "I'm here at least once a year through work. Or if I really wanted to go tonight, I'd get a scalper ticket."

"This *could* be our last chance," Uncle conceded.

"It's settled, then," I said. "I'm going to order up some food, and make sure Dad's got the right pills, and then you're set."

Half an hour later there was a knock on the door.

"It's probably the food," I said, going to open the door.

It was a bellhop, with an envelope in his hand. "For Les Carson," he said.

I said that I was he, signed for it, and tipped him two dollars. Inside were two hockey tickets and a note, which said *You owe me two theatre tickets. What's on for tomorrow? — D.*

The universe seemed to be unfolding as it should, until I woke up Dad.

"You'd better eat something," I said. "The game's in less than two hours."

"Not going," he said.

"What?"

"Bushed," he said.

"But the game, Leafs and the Blues."

"Seen one," he said. "Gotta rest."

"You'd better eat," I said, "and have a pill. Then you'll feel better."

He shook his head. "You guys go. I'm okay here."

"But your ticket..."

"You guys go early," he said, "sell mine."

I didn't tell him that we only had two tickets anyway. I went back out to the living room, where Uncle Richard was taste-testing the bottle of dark rum.

"He's not going," I said. "Too tired."

"You're sure?" Uncle asked.

I nodded. "He's got that look," I said.

"It's settled then," Uncle said. "It's just you and me, Loss, out on the town."

I sat down. I looked out the balcony at the lights of Toronto twinkling in the late afternoon haze. Dad's tattered Hall of Fame book lay on the coffee table, beside the bag of souvenirs he had bought at the store.

"I'm not going either," I said.

Uncle Richard chuckled. "Right," he said, "and I'm starting on left wing."

"I'm serious. He shouldn't be alone." I started ticking points off on the fingers of my right hand. "He needs his pills, he hasn't eaten, he looks pale...."

"You're beginning to sound like your mother," Uncle said.

I paused to consider that for a moment. "Thank you," I said.

Then Uncle Richard wasn't going, either. I finally convinced him that *someone* had to go, or Drew would be disappointed.

"Tell you what," I said, "I'll call her and explain what's going on. Maybe she can meet you between periods or something, and you can pay her for the tickets."

Uncle nodded and dug her business card out of his wallet again. I dialed and ended up talking to her answering machine again. "Hi Drew. Les again. We got the tickets and owe you big time. Slight change of plans. Dad's beat, so he and I are staying here. Uncle Richard's going by himself, so if you get a chance, he'd love to buy you a hotdog." I flinched as Uncle punched my shoulder. "Thanks again. Uh, hope you get this message, and we'll see you soon. Bye."

When the food arrived, I checked in on Dad but he was sleeping again. I woke him up to have his pill, and talked him into at least eating some bread. Then he felt good enough for the mushroom soup and the tapioca pudding.

"Late," he said. "Better go."

"On our way," I answered. "I'll put the chicken fingers over by the microwave in case you get hungry."

He nodded, waved me away and then when I was at the doorway, called, "Les?"

I stopped, wondering what was on his mind.

"Remote," he said.

I found the remote control on the side table. I turned on the TV, found a channel that the game would be on and handed the remote to him. He grunted his thanks as I left.

Uncle was standing outside the bedroom door with his coat on. "You didn't tell him," he said.

I shrugged. "Saves an argument. You sure you know the way?"

Uncle looked hurt. "Listen, I've been guiding you guys around pretty successfully from the moment we left Regina, so I think I can find the front of the hotel, get into a cab and say 'Maple Leaf Gardens.' "

I smiled and pulled my brand new Hall of Fame money clip out of my front jeans pocket. "Here, take some cash for the tickets. If you do run into Drew, make sure she takes it."

Uncle shook his head. "I'm paying," he said, and scurried out the door.

I cracked open a beer and sat in the living room, flipping through Dad's Hall of Fame magazine. I was surprised to see that he had rated each display on a scale of 1 to 10, and in some cases commented on what he had or had not liked. I went back to the front and started over, reading the articles and his notes in the margins. As I worked my way through the magazine, his thoroughness and consistency impressed me. He hadn't skipped any pages, and had even updated a few of the displays that had changed since the magazine had been printed. There was a blank page at the end of the magazine, and that's where the Worsley and Bucyk signatures were scrawled. They had both dated and put "HHOF" below their names. Dad had given this page a 9. His comment was "Rushed."

By the time I made it through to the end of the magazine, it was almost time for the game to start. I set my empty beer bottle on the table and started down the hallway to check on Dad.

"Who's there?" he shouted.

"It's me, Dad," I said, coming around the corner.

"What the...? You're late!"

"I'm not going. Uncle Richard's long gone."

"What?"

"I'm staying with you."

"No need."

"Wanted to."

He thought about that for a few seconds, and then nodded toward the TV. "Game's starting."

"Do you mind?" I asked, pointing beside him on the bed.

"Suit yourself," he said, shuffling over a bit.

I hadn't told him that our seats were right behind the Leafs bench. I was anxious to see what his reaction would be when he recognized Uncle Richard. The first time the camera panned the bench was during "O Canada," and all the players were standing up blocking the view. The second time, it was a close-up of the coaches huddled together discussing strategy, and you couldn't see clearly behind them. The third time, St. Louis had received a penalty and the Leafs were sending out their power play. The camera zoomed in on the coach moving behind the bench, hollering at the players he wanted out next. Over the coach's left shoulder, nose pressed up to the glass, was Uncle Richard's face. Dad sat forward to take a closer look.

"That looked like..."

"It was."

"Behind the bench?"

I nodded.

"Bugger," Dad chortled. "He'll be telling the coach what to do by the time she's over."

"I expect he's already doing that," I said.

From then on, we both watched intently. Even on the wide shots of the whole ice surface, we concentrated on looking at the bench area, trying to catch a glimpse of Uncle.

"There," Dad would shout, pointing, or I would say, "He's clapping."

At the start of the second period, Uncle was talking to a woman sitting beside him.

"That's Drew," I shouted. She said something and pointed directly at the camera. Uncle held up a sign that read "Don Cherry for Mayor of Moose Jaw."

Dad hooted. "That'll get 'em going back home," he said.

I had never seen Dad so happy. Every few minutes he would snort in amazement, or say, "That's something," or just shake his head. That surprised me because I had expected him to be more envious of Uncle Richard, but he was obviously pleased. The game got to be 4 to 1 for St. Louis, and both teams just seemed to be putting in time. The producers started looking for some other angle on the excitement. After a whistle there was a brief tussle in front of the Blues' net and the camera showed Uncle doing his *stir the pot* dance.

"Now he's just showing off," Dad said.

The seat beside Uncle Richard was empty again in the third. Twice we saw him holding up his sign, but the camera didn't focus in enough to read it. Then with two minutes left and the score 4-2 for the Blues, there was a whistle. They zoomed in on the Leafs bench, trying to catch the coach signalling his goalie to the bench in favour of an extra attacker. Right above the coach's head a sign waved that said THANKS, LES!!

The announcer said, "Well, at least there's one thankful fan here tonight."

The colour commentator said, "He's either a Blues fan or just thankful that this game is almost over."

"Wrong!" Dad said. I felt his hand patting the bed and thought he was looking for the remote control, which was in my lap. I picked it up with my left hand to pass over to him, but by then he had found my right hand and covered it with his left. I didn't know what to do. We hadn't held hands since.... I couldn't remember ever having held his hand before, although as a toddler I must have, as we walked along somewhere together.

"Thanks from me, too," he said, patting my hand while still looking at the television.

"For what?"

"For bothering."

"It was no bother," I said.

"Taking two old farts on the road," he said, "is no picnic."

"I'd do it again," I said, meaning it.

"Don't put any money on it," he said, squeezing my hand.

I looked over at him. "Dad?"

He turned and looked past me. I didn't say anything until he eventually focused on my face.

"Thank *you.*" The break in my voice surprised me, as did the wet drop running down the side of my nose.

He didn't say anything, but in my eyes his face seemed to shift. The years dropped from around his eyes and the wrinkles disappeared from his forehead. His cheeks filled out, and he once again looked like that trusty giant from my early memories. My throat was tight and I knew that I couldn't speak. Water had pooled at the end of my nose and dripped onto the bedspread.

Dad gave my hand an extra squeeze and then let go. He turned back to the television set, tapped his watch with a finger and said in a gruff voice, "Pills."

I sniffed and nodded.

Months later, at the funeral, Uncle Richard gave the eulogy. I felt okay as he went through the obituary part of Dad's life, where he was born, who he had married, who was left behind. I even noticed Gail smile and glance at George when Uncle mentioned the newest addition, Nathan Harold. It made me a bit sad to think that I would be moving further away from my first nephew, but the Marketing job at Sears' Toronto office had been too good to turn down. My supervisor had been adamant that I take it.

Then Uncle Richard said, "The lesson that my brother taught me that will always stay with me doesn't come from our childhood, our wild teen years, any sporting escapades, or our famous regular reunions. A few months ago, we took a trip to Toronto with my nephew, Les. I remember coming back to the hotel after Saturday night's hockey game and going up to our room. It was dark, but I could hear a television set on. I

went down the hallway to the bedrooms and there was
Harold, sound asleep on the big king-sized bed. Sawing
logs beside him was Les. I looked around for the remote
control to turn the TV down. I had to turn on a lamp
and finally found it lying between them on the bed. I
expected there had been a struggle over it, because both
of them had a hand partly covering the remote." People
in the pews chuckled. "When I went to pull it away
from them, though, I noticed that neither hand was really gripping the remote. The little finger on each of their
hands was hooked together, like we used to do when we
made a pinkie promise, and the remote just happened to
be sheltered underneath that. I pulled it out and their
hands stayed where they were, fingers twined together."
Uncle stopped and took a drink from the water glass,
cleared his throat and continued, "He was a man of surprises, our Harold Carson. I felt like I was intruding, so
haven't mentioned it to anyone until now. But discover-
ing that side to my brother helped when I sat with him
at the end. I was finally able to tell him what he meant
to me. That one-sided conversation I'll keep between
him and me, but I'm thankful that I was able to say it."

When Uncle came down the steps from the altar, I
stood and met him by the casket. I hugged him, and he
hugged me back. I was about to let go when I felt other
arms and there was Gail encircling us both, and then
Mom, and George, and Aunt Edith, and Cousin Sylvia.
I could see that others were standing and I'm sure the
minister was annoyed with the service being delayed,
because later on he only sang three verses of the final
hymn, "Amazing Grace." It didn't matter.

PHOTO: DONNA KANE

ABOUT THE AUTHOR

Chris Fisher is the author of two previous short fiction collections, *Sun Angel* and *Voices in the Wilderness*. *Sun Angel* was a winner in the first-ever Saskatchewan Book Awards. Chris's stories were featured in an edition of *Coming Attractions,* Oberon Press's influential anthology of new writers. His stories have appeared in anthologies and in literary and other periodicals.

Chris Fisher grew up in a half-dozen small southern Saskatchewan communities, and after a stint in Regina, moved back to another one, Lumsden. He plays and coaches both hockey and baseball, and works for the City of Regina.